The Expressman And The Detective

Allan Pinkerton

THE

EXPRESSMAN

AND

THE DETECTIVE.

By ALLAN PINKERTON.

FIFTEENTH THOUSAND.

CHICAGO:
W. B. KEEN, COOKE & CO.,
113 AND 115 STATE STREET.
1875.

The Lakeside Press.

Printing Statement:

Due to the very old age and scarcity of this book,
many of the pages may be hard to read due to the
blurring of the original text, possible missing pages,
missing text, dark backgrounds and other issues
beyond our control.

Because this is such an important and rare work, we
believe it is best to reproduce this book regardless of
its original condition.

Thank you for your understanding.

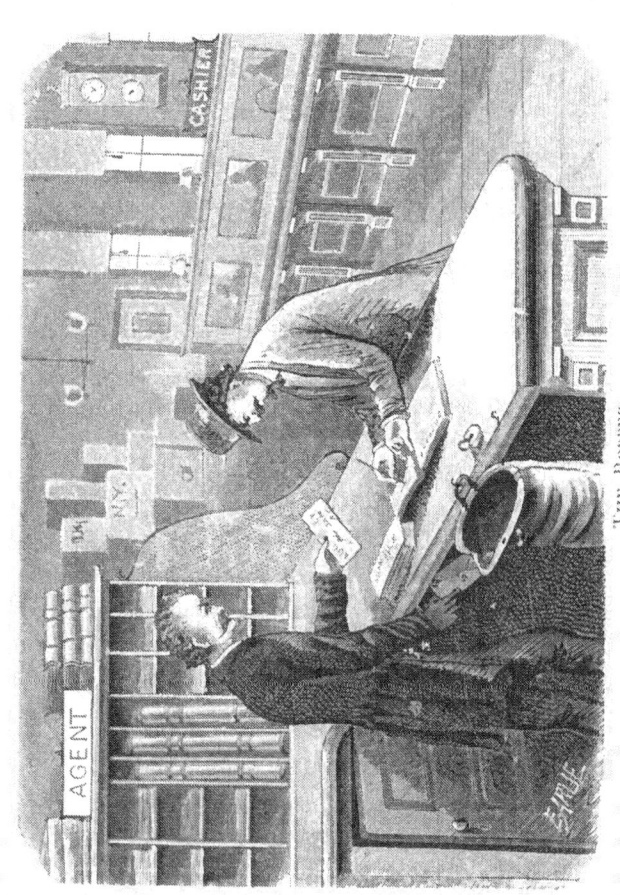

THE ROBBER.

PREFACE.

DURING the greater portion of a very busy life, I have been actively engaged in the profession of a Detective, and hence have been brought in contact with many men, and have been an interested participant in many exciting occurrences.

The narration of some of the most interesting of these events, happening in connection with my professional labors, is the realization of a pleasure I have long anticipated, and is the fulfilment of promises repeatedly made to numerous friends in by gone days.

"THE EXPRESSMAN AND THE DETECTIVE,"

and the other works announced by my publishers, are all *true stories*, transcribed from the Records in my offices. If there be any incidental embellishment, it is so slight that the actors in these scenes from the drama of life would never themselves detect it; and if the incidents seem to the reader at all marvelous or improbable, I can but remind him, in the words of the old adage, that "Truth is stranger than fiction."

ALLAN PINKERTON.

CHICAGO, October, 1874.

PUBLISHERS' NOTICE.

The present Volume is the first of a series of Mr. Allan Pinkerton's thrilling and beautifully written

DETECTIVE STORIES,

all true to life—founded upon incidents in the experience of the great chief of all detectives.

At intervals the following will appear:

"CLAUDE MELNOTTE AS A DETECTIVE."
"THE TWO SISTERS AND THE AVENGER."
"THE FRENCHMAN AND THE BILLS OF EXCHANGE."
"THE MURDERER AND THE FORTUNE TELLER."
"THE MODEL TOWN AND ITS DETECTIVE."

That these Volumes will meet with a cordial reception we have no doubt.

W. B. KEEN, COOKE & CO.

ILLUSTRATIONS.

THE EXPRESSMAN

— AND —

THE DETECTIVE.

CHAPTER I.

MONTGOMERY, Alabama, is beautifully situated
on the Alabama river, near the centre of the State.
Its situation at the head of navigation, on the Alabama
river, its connection by rail with important points, and
the rich agricultural country with which it is surrounded,
make it a great commercial centre, and the second city in
the State as regards wealth and population. It is the
capital, and consequently learned men and great poli-
ticians flock to it, giving it a society of the highest rank,
and making it the social centre of the State.

From 1858 to 1860, the time of which I treat in the
present work, the South was in a most prosperous condition. "Cotton was king," and millions of dollars were
poured into the country for its purchase, and a fair share
of this money found its way to Montgomery.

When the Alabama planters had gathered their crops

of cotton, tobacco, rice, etc., they sent them to Montgomery to be sold, and placed the proceeds on deposit in
its banks. During their busy season, while overseeing
the labor of their slaves, they were almost entirely
debarred from the society of any but their own families;
but when the crops were gathered they went with their
families to Montgomery, where they gave themselves up
to enjoyment, spending their money in a most lavish
manner.

There were several good hotels in the city and they
were always filled to overflowing with the wealth and
beauty of the South.

The Adams Express Company had a monopoly of the
express business of the South, and had established its
agencies at all points with which there was communication by rail, steam or stage. They handled all the money
sent to the South for the purchase of produce, or remitted
to the North in payment of merchandise. Moreover, as
they did all the express business for the banks, besides
moving an immense amount of freight, it is evident that
their business was enormous.

At all points of importance, where there were diverging
routes of communication, the company had established
principal agencies, at which all through freight and the
money pouches were delivered by the messengers. The
agents at these points were selected with the greatest
care, and were always considered men above reproach.
Montgomery being a great centre of trade was made the
western terminus of one of the express routes, Atlanta
being the eastern. The messengers who had charge of
the express matter between these two points were each

provided with a safe and with a pouch. The latter was to contain only such packages as were to go over the whole route, consisting of money or other valuables. The messenger was not furnished with a key to the pouch, but it was handed to him locked by the agent at one end of the route to be delivered in the same condition to the agent at the other end.

The safe was intended for way packages, and of it the messenger of course had a key. The pouch was carried in the safe, each being protected by a lock of peculiar construction.

The Montgomery office in 1858, and for some years previous, had been in charge of Nathan Maroney, and he had made himself one of the most popular agents in the company's employ.

He was married, and with his wife and one daughter, had pleasant quarters at the Exchange Hotel, one of the best houses in the city. He possessed all the qualifications which make a popular man. He had a genial, hearty manner, which endeared him to the open, hospitable inhabitants of Montgomery, so that he was "hail fellow, well met," with most of its populace. He possessed great executive ability and hence managed the affairs of his office in a very satisfactory manner. The promptness with which he discharged his duties had won for him the well-merited esteem of the officers of the company, and he was in a fair way of attaining a still higher position. His greatest weakness—if it may be so called—was a love for fast horses, which often threw him into the company of betting men.

On the morning of the twenty-sixth of April, 1858, the

messenger from Atlanta arrived in Montgomery, placed his safe in the office as usual, and when Maroney came in, turned over to him the through pouch.

Maroney unlocked the pouch and compared it with the way-bill, when he discovered a package of four thousand seven hundred and fifty dollars for a party in Montgomery which was not down on the way-bill. About a week after this occurrence, advice was received that a package containing ten thousand dollars in bills of the Planters' and Mechanics' Bank of Charleston, S. C., had been sent to Columbus, Ga., via the Adams Express, but the person to whom it was directed had not received it. Inquiries were at once instituted, when it was discovered that it had been missent, and forwarded to Atlanta, instead of Macon. At Atlanta it was recollected that this package, together with one for Montgomery, for four thousand seven hundred and fifty dollars, had been received on Sunday, the twenty-fifth of April, and had been sent on to Montgomery, whence the Columbus package could be forwarded the next day. Here all trace of the missing package was lost. Maroney stated positively that he had not received it, and the messenger was equally positive that the pouch had been delivered to Maroney in the same order in which he received it from the Atlanta agent.

The officers of the company were completely at a loss. It was discovered beyond a doubt that the package had been sent from Atlanta. The messenger who received it bore an excellent character, and the company could not believe him guilty of the theft. The lock of the pouch was examined and found in perfect order, so that it evidently had not been tampered with. The messenger was positive that he had not left the safe open when he went out of the car, and there was no sign of the lock's having been forced.

The more the case was investigated, the more directly did suspicion point to Maroney, but as his integrity had always been unquestioned, no one now was willing to admit the possibility of his guilt. However, as no decided action in the matter could be taken, it was determined to say nothing, but to have the movements of Maroney and other suspected parties closely watched.

For this purpose various detectives were employed; one a local detective of Montgomery, named McGibony; others from New Orleans, Philadelphia, Mobile, and New York. After a long investigation these parties had to give up the case as hopeless, all concluding that Maroney was an innocent man. Among the detectives, however, was one from New York, Robert Boyer, by name, an old and favorite officer of Mr. Matsell when he was chief of the New York police. He had made a long and tedious examination and finding nothing definite as to what had become of the money, had turned his attention to discovering the antecedents of Maroney, but found nothing positively suspicious in his life previous to his entering the employ of the company. He discovered that Maroney was the son of a physician, and that he was born in the town of Rome, Ga.

Here I would remark that the number of titled men one meets in the South is astonishing. Every man, if he is not a doctor, a lawyer, or a clergyman, has some military title—nothing lower than captain being admissible.

Of these self-imposed titles they are very jealous, and woe be to the man who neglects to address them in the proper form. Captain is the general title, and is applied indiscriminately to the captain of a steamer, or to the deck hand on his vessel.

Maroney remained in Rome until he became a young man, when he emigrated to Texas. On the breaking out of the Mexican war he joined a company of Texan Rangers, and distinguished himself in a number of battles. At the close of the war he settled in Montgomery, in the year 1851, or 1852, and was employed by Hampton & Co., owners of a line of stages, to act as their agent. On leaving this position, he was made treasurer of Johnson & May's circus, remaining with the company until it was disbanded in consequence of the pecuniary difficulties of the proprietors — caused, it was alleged, through Maroney's embezzlement of the funds, though this allegation proved false, and he remained for many years on terms of intimacy with one of the partners, a resident of Montgomery. When the company disbanded he obtained a situation as conductor on a railroad in Tennessee, and was afterwards made Assistant Superintendent, which position he resigned to take the agency of the Adams Express Company, in Montgomery. His whole life seemed spotless up to the time of the mysterious disappearance of the ten thousand dollars.

In the fall of the year, Maroney obtained leave of absence, and made a trip to the North, visiting the principal cities of the East, and also of the Northwest. He was followed on this trip, but nothing was discovered, with the single exception that his associates were not always such as were desirable in an employé, to whose keeping very heavy interests were from time to time necessarily committed. He was lost sight of at Richmond, Va., for a few days, and was supposed by the man who was following him, to have passed the time in Charleston.

The company now gave up all hope of recovering the money; but as Maroney's habits were expensive, and they had lost, somewhat, their confidence in him, they determined to remove him and place some less objectionable person in his place.

Maroney's passion for fine horses has already been alluded to. It was stated about this time that he owned several fast horses; among others, "Yankee Mary," a horse for which he was said to have paid two thousand five hundred dollars; but as he had brought seven thousand five hundred dollars with him when he entered the employ of the company, this could not be considered a suspicious circumstance.

It having been determined to remove Maroney, the Vice-President of the company wrote to the Superintendent of the Southern Division of the steps he wished taken. The Superintendent of the Southern Division visited Montgomery on the twentieth of January, 1859, but was anticipated in the matter of carrying out his instructions, by Maroney's tendering his resignation. The resignation was accepted, but the superintendent requested him to continue in charge of the office until his successor should arrive.

This he consented to do.

CHAPTER II.

PREVIOUS to Maroney's trip to the North, Mr.
Boyer held a consultation with the Vice-President
and General Superintendent of the company. He freely
admitted his inability to fathom the mystery surrounding
the loss of the money, and thought the officers of the
company did Maroney a great injustice in supposing him
guilty of the theft. He said he knew of only one man
who could bring out the robbery, and he was living in
Chicago.

Pinkerton was the name of the man he referred to.
He had established an agency in Chicago, and was doing
a large business. He (Boyer) had every confidence in
his integrity and ability, which was more than he could
say of the majority of detectives, and recommended the
Vice-President to have him come down and look into the
case.

This ended the case for most of the detectives. One
by one they had gone away, and nothing had been devel-
oped by them. The Vice-President, still anxious to see
if anything could be done, wrote a long and full statement of the robbery and sent it to me, with the request
that I would give my opinion on it.

I was much surprised when I received the letter, as I
had not the slightest idea who the Vice-President was,

and knew very little about the Adams Express, as, at that time, they had no office in the West.

I, however, sat down and read it over very carefully, and, on finishing it, determined to make a point in the case if I possibly could. I reviewed the whole of the Vice-President's letter, debating every circumstance connected with the robbery, and finally ended my consideration of the subject with the firm conviction that the robbery had been committed either by the agent, Maroney, or by the messenger, and I was rather inclined to give the blame to Maroney.

The letter was a very long one, but one of which I have always been proud. Having formed my opinion, I wrote to the Vice-President, explained to him the ground on which I based my conclusions, and recommended that they keep Maroney in their employ, and have a strict watch maintained over his actions.

After sending my letter, could do nothing until the Vice-President replied, which I expected he would do in a few days; but I heard nothing more of the affair for a long time, and had almost entirely forgotten it, when I received a telegraphic dispatch from him, sent from Montgomery, and worded about as follows :

"ALLAN PINKERTON: Can you send me a man — half horse and half alligator? I have got 'bit' once more! When can you send him ? "

The dispatch came late Saturday night, and I retired to my private office to think the matter over. The dispatch gave me no information from which I could draw any conclusions. No mention was made of how the rob-

2

bery was committed, or of the amount stolen.   I had not received any further information of the ten thousand dollar robbery.   How had they settled that?   It was hard to decide what kind of a man to send!   I wanted to send the very best, and would gladly go myself, but did not know whether the robbery was important enough to demand my personal attention.

I did not know what kind of men the officers of the company were, or whether they would be willing to reward a person properly for his exertions in their behalf.

At that time I had no office in New York, and knew nothing of the ramifications of the company.   Besides, I did not know how I would be received in the South.   I had held my anti-slavery principles too long to give them up.   They had been bred in my bones, and it was impossible to eradicate them.   I was always stubborn, and in any circumstances would never abandon principles I had once adopted.

Slavery was in full blossom, and an anti-slavery man could do nothing in the South.   As I had always been a man somewhat after the John Brown stamp, aiding slaves to escape, or keeping them employed, and running them into Canada when in danger, I did not think it would do for me to make a trip to Montgomery.

I did not know what steps had already been taken in the case, or whether the loss was a heavy one.   From the Vice-President's saying he wanted a man " half horse, half alligator," I supposed he wanted a man who could at least affiliate readily with the inhabitants of the South.

But what class was he to mix with?   Did he want a man to mix with the rough element, or to pass among gentlemen? I could select from my force any class of man he could wish. But what *did he wish?*

I was unaware of who had recommended me to the Vice-President, as at that time I had not been informed that my old friend Boyer had spoken so well of me. What answer should I make to the dispatch? It must be answered immediately!

These thoughts followed each other in rapid succession as I held the dispatch before me.

I finally settled on Porter as the proper man to send, and immediately telegraphed the Vice-President, informing him that Porter would start for Montgomery by the first train. I then sent for Porter and gave him what few instructions I could. I told him the little I knew of the case, and that I should have to rely greatly on his tact and discretion.

Up to that time I had never done any business for the Adams Express, and as their business was well worth having, I was determined to win.

He was to go to Montgomery and get thoroughly acquainted with the town and its surroundings; and as my suspicions had become aroused as to the integrity of the agent, Maroney, he was to form his acquaintance, and frequent the saloons and livery stables of the town, the Vice-President's letter having made me aware of Maroney's inclination for fast horses. He was to keep his own counsel, and, above all things, not let it become known that he was from the North, but to hail from Richmond, Va., thus securing for himself a good footing with the inhabitants. He was also to dress in the Southern style; to supply me with full reports describing the town and its surroundings, the manners and customs of its people, all he saw or heard about Maroney, the messengers and other employés of the company; whether Maroney was married, and, if so, any suspicious circumstances in regard to his wife as well as himself — in fact, to keep me fully informed of all that occurred. I should have to rely on his discretion until his reports were received; but then I could direct him how to act. I also instructed him to obey all orders from the Vice-President, and to be as obliging as possible.

Having given him his instructions, I started him off on the first train, giving him a letter of introduction to the Vice-President. On Porter's arriving in Montgomery he sent me particulars of the case, from which I learned that while Maroney was temporarily filling the position of agent, among other packages sent to the Montgomery office, on the twenty-seventh of January, 1859, were four containing, in the aggregate, forty thousand dollars, of which one, of two thousand five hundred dollars, was to be sent to Charleston, S. C., and the other three, of thirty thousand, five thousand, and two thousand five hundred respectively, were intended for Augusta. These were receipted for by Maroney, and placed in the vault to be sent off the next day. On the twenty-eighth the pouch was given to the messenger, Mr. Chase, and by him taken to Atlanta. When the pouch was opened, it was found that none of these packages were in it, although they were entered on the way-bill which accompanied the pouch, and were duly checked off. The poor messenger was thunder-struck, and for a time acted like an idiot, plunging his hand into the vacant pouch over and over

again, and staring vacantly at the way-bill. The Assistant Superintendent of the Southern Division was in the
Atlanta office when the loss was discovered, and at once
telegraphed to Maroney for an explanation. Receiving
no reply before the train started for Montgomery, he got
aboard and went directly there. On his arrival he went
to the office and saw Maroney, who said he knew nothing
at all of the matter. He had delivered the packages to
the messenger, had his receipt for them, and of course
could not be expected to keep track of them when out
of his possession.

Before Mr. Hall, the route agent, left Atlanta he had
examined the pouch carefully, but could find no marks
of its having been tampered with. He had immediately
telegraphed to another officer of the company, who was
at Augusta, and advised him of what had happened.
The evening after the discovery of the loss the pouch
was brought back by the messenger from Atlanta, who
delivered it to Maroney.

Maroney took out the packages, compared them with
the way-bill, and, finding them all right, he threw down
the pouch and placed the packages in the vault.

In a few moments he came out, and going over to where
Mr. Hall was standing, near where he had laid down the
pouch, he picked it up and proceeded to examine it. He
suddenly exclaimed, "Why, it's cut!" and handed it over
to Mr. Hall. Mr. Hall, on examination, found two cuts
at right angles to each other, made in the side of the
pouch and under the pocket which is fastened on the
outside, to contain the way-bill.

On Sunday the General Superintendent arrived in

Montgomery, when a strict investigation was made, but nothing definite was discovered, and the affair seemed surrounded by an impenetrable veil of mystery. It was, however, discovered that on the day the missing packages were claimed to have been sent away, there were several rather unusual incidents in the conduct of Maroney.

After consultation with Mr. Hall and others, the General Superintendent determined that the affair should not be allowed to rest, as was the ten thousand dollar robbery, and had Maroney arrested, charged with stealing the forty thousand dollars.

The robbery of so large an amount caused great excitement in Montgomery. The legislature was in session, and the city was crowded with senators, representatives and visitors. Everywhere, on the streets, in the saloons, in private families, and at the hotels, the great robbery of the Express Company was the universal topic of conversation. Maroney had become such a favorite that nearly all the citizens sympathized with him, and in unmeasured terms censured the company for having him arrested. They claimed that it was another instance of the persecution of a poor man by a powerful corporation, to cover the carelessness of those high in authority, and thus turn the blame on some innocent person.

Maroney was taken before Justice Holtzclaw, and gave the bail which was required — forty thousand dollars — for his appearance for examination a few days later; prominent citizens of the town actually vieing with one another for an opportunity to sign his bail-bond.

At the examination the Company presented such a weak case that the bail was reduced to four thousand dollars, and Maroney was bound over in that amount to appear for trial at the next session of the circuit court, to be held in June. The evidence was such that there was little prospect of his conviction on the charge unless the company could procure additional evidence by the time the trial was to come off.

It was the desire of the company to make such inquiries, and generally pursue such a course as would demonstrate the guilt or the possible innocence of the accused. It was absolutely necessary for their own preservation to show that depredations upon them could not be committed with impunity. They offered a reward of ten thousand dollars for the recovery of the money, promptly made good the loss of the parties who had entrusted the several amounts to their charge, and looked around to select such persons to assist them as would be most likely to secure success. The amount was large enough to warrant the expenditure of a considerable sum in its recovery, and the beneficial influence following the conviction of the guilty party would be ample return for any outlay securing that object. The General Superintendent therefore telegraphed to me, as before related, requesting me to send a man to work up the case.

CHAPTER III.

MR. PORTER had a very rough journey to Montgomery, and was delayed some days on the road. It was in the depth of winter, and in the North the roads were blockaded with snow, while in the South there was constant rain. The rivers were flooded, carrying away the bridges and washing out the embankments of the railroads, very much impeding travel.

On his arrival in Montgomery he saw the General Superintendent and presented his letter. He received from him the particulars of the forty thousand dollar robbery, and immediately reported them to me.

The General Superintendent directed him to watch — "shadow" as we call it — the movements of Maroney, find out who were his companions, and what saloons he frequented.

Porter executed his duties faithfully, and reported to me that Montgomery was decidedly a fast town; that the Exchange Hotel, where Maroney boarded, was kept by Mr. Floyd, former proprietor of the Briggs House, Chicago, and, although not the leading house of the town, was very much liked, as it was well conducted.

From the meagre reports I had received I found I had to cope with no ordinary man, but one who was very popular, while I was a poor nameless individual, with a profession which most people were inclined to look down upon with contempt. I however did not flinch from the undertaking, but wrote to Porter to do all he could, and at the same time wrote to the General Superintendent, suggesting the propriety of sending another man, who should keep in the background and "spot" Maroney and his wife, or their friends, so that if any one of them should leave town he could follow him, leaving Porter in Montgomery, to keep track of the parties there.

There were, of course, a number of suspicious characters in a town of the size of Montgomery, and it was necessary to keep watch of many of them.

Maroney frequented a saloon kept by a man whom I will call Patterson. Patterson's saloon was the fashionable drinking resort of Montgomery, and was frequented by all the fast men in town. Although outwardly a very quiet, respectable place, inwardly, as Porter found, it was far from reputable. Up stairs were private rooms, in which gentlemen met to have a quiet game of poker; while down stairs could be found the greenhorn, just "roped in," and being swindled, at *three card monte.* There were, also, rooms where the "young bloods" of the town — as well as the old — could meet ladies of easy virtue. It was frequented by fast men from New Orleans, Mobile, and other places, who were continually arriving and departing.

I advised the General Superintendent that it would be best to have Porter get in with the "bloods" of the town, make himself acquainted with any ladies Maroney or his wife might be familiar with, and adopt generally the character of a fast man.

As soon as the General Superintendent received my

letter he telegraphed to me to send the second man, and also requested me to meet him, at a certain date, in New York.

I now glanced over my force to see who was the best person to select for a "shadow." Porter had been promoted by me to be a sort of "roper."

Most people may suppose that nearly any one can perform the duties of a "shadow," and that it is the easiest thing in the world to follow up a man; but such is not the case. A "shadow" has a most difficult position to maintain. It will not do to follow a person on the opposite side of the street, or close behind him, and when he stops to speak to a friend stop also; or if a person goes into a saloon, or store, pop in after him, stand staring till he goes out, and then follow him again. Of course such a "shadow" would be detected in fifteen minutes. Such are not the actions of the real "shadow," or, at least, of the "shadow" furnished by my establishment.

I had just the man for the place, in Mr. Roch, who could follow a person for any length of time, and never be discovered.

Having settled on Roch as the proper man for the position, I summoned him to my private office. Roch was a German. He was about forty-five years old, of spare appearance and rather sallow or tanned complexion. His nose was long, thin and peaked, eyes clear but heavy looking, and hair dark. He was slightly bald, and though he stooped a little, was five feet ten inches in height. He had been in my employ for many years, and I knew him thoroughly, and could trust him.

I informed him of the duties he was to perform, and

gave him minute instructions how he was to act. He was to keep out of sight as much as possible in Montgomery. Porter would manage to see him on his arrival, unknown to any one there, and would point out to him Maroney and his wife, and the messenger, Chase, who boarded at the Exchange; also Patterson, the saloon keeper, and all suspected parties. He was not to make himself known to Floyd, of the Exchange, or to McGibony, the local detective. I had also given Porter similar instructions. I suggested to him the propriety of lodging at some low boarding house where liquor was sold.

He was to keep me fully posted by letter of the movements of all suspected parties, and if any of them left town to follow them and immediately inform me by telegraph who they were and where they were going, so that I could fill his place in Montgomery.

Having given him his instructions, I selected for his disguise a German dress. This I readily procured from my extensive wardrobe, which I keep well supplied by frequent attendance at sales of old articles.

When he had rigged himself up in his long German coat, his German cap with the peak behind, and a most approved pair of emigrant boots, he presented himself to me with his long German pipe in his mouth, and I must say I was much pleased with his disguise, in which his own mother would not have recognized him. He was as fine a specimen of a Dutchman as could be found.

Having thoroughly impressed on his mind the importance of the case and my determination to win the esteem of the company by ferreting out the thief, if possible, I started him for Montgomery, where he arrived in due time.

At the date agreed upon I went to New York to meet the General Superintendent. I had never met the gentlemen of the company and I was a little puzzled how to act with them.

I met the Vice-President at the express office, in such a manner that none of the employés were the wiser as to my profession or business, and he made an appointment to meet me at the Astor House in the afternoon. At the Astor House he introduced me to the President, the General Superintendent of the company, and we immediately proceeded to business.

They gave me all the particulars of the case they could, though they were not much fuller than those I had already received from Porter's reports. They reviewed the life of Maroney, as already related, up to the time he became their agent, stating that he was married, although his marriage seemed somewhat " mixed."

As far as they could find out, Mrs. Maroney was a widow, with one daughter, Flora Irvin, who was about seven or eight years old. Mrs. Maroney was from a very respectable family, now living in Philadelphia or its environs. She was reported to have run away from home with a roué, whose acquaintance she had formed, but who soon deserted her. Afterwards she led the life of a fast woman at Charleston, New Orleans, Augusta, Ga., and Mobile, at which latter place she met Maroney, and was supposed to have been married to him.

After Maroney was appointed agent in Montgomery he

brought her with him, took a suite of rooms at the Exchange, and introduced her as his wife.

On account of these circumstances the General Superintendent did not wish to meet her, and, when in Montgomery, always took rooms at another hotel.

The Vice-President said he had nearly come to the conclusion that Maroney was not guilty of the ten thousand dollar robbery; but when my letter reached him, with my comments on the robbery, he became convinced that *he was* the guilty party.

He was strengthened in this opinion by the actions of Maroney while on his Northern tour, and by the fact that immediately on his return the fast mare " Yankee Mary " made her appearance in Montgomery and that Maroney backed her heavily. It was not known that he was her owner, it being generally reported that Patterson and other fast men were her proprietors.

This was all the Vice-President and General Superintendent had been able to discover while South, and they were aware that I had very little ground on which to work.

I listened to all they had to say on the subject and took full memoranda of the facts. I then stated that although Maroney had evidently planned and carried out the robbery with such consummate ability that he had not left the slightest clue by which he could be detected, still, if they would only give me plenty of time, I would bring the robbery home to him.

I maintained, as a cardinal principle, that it is impossible for the human mind to retain a secret. All history proves that no one can hug a secret to his breast and live.

Everyone must have a vent for his feelings. It is impossible to keep them always penned up.

This is especially noticeable in persons who have committed criminal acts. They always find it necessary to select some one in whom they can confide and to whom they can unburden themselves.

We often find that persons who have committed grave offenses will fly to the moors, or to the prairies, or to the vast solitudes of almost impenetrable forests, and there give vent to their feelings. I instanced the case of Eugene Aram, who took up his abode on the bleak and solitary moor, and, removed from the society of his fellowmen, tried to maintain his secret by devoting himself to astronomical observations and musings with nature, but who, nevertheless, felt compelled to relieve his overburdened mind by muttering to himself details of the murder while taking his long and dreary walks on the moor.

If Maroney had committed the robbery and no one knew it but himself, I would demonstrate the truth of my theory by proving that he would eventually seek some one in whom he thought he could confide and to whom he would entrust the secret.

My plan was to supply him with a confidant. It would take time to execute such a plan, but if they would have patience all would be well. I would go to Montgomery and become familiar with the town. I was unknown there and should remain so, only taking a letter to their legal advisers, Watts, Judd & Jackson, whom I supposed would cheerfully give me all the information in their power. I also informed them that it would be necessary to detail more detectives to work up the case.

I found the officers of the company genial, pleasant men, possessed of great executive ability and untiring energy, and felt that my duties would be doubly agreeable by being in the interests of such men.

They ended the interview by authorizing me to employ what men I thought proper; stating that they had full confidence in me, and that they thought I would be enabled to unearth the guilty parties ere long. They further authorized me to use my own judgment in all things; but expected me to keep them fully informed of what was going on.

I started for Montgomery the same day, but was as unfortunate in meeting with delay as were my detectives. The rivers were filled with floating ice and I was ice-bound in the Potomac for over thirty hours. I was obliged to go back to Alexandria, where I took the train and proceeded, via West Point and Atlanta, to Montgomery. On the journey I amused myself reading Martin Chuzzlewit, which I took good care to throw away on the road, as its cuts at slavery made it unpopular in the South. At the various stations planters got aboard, sometimes conveying their slaves from point to point, sometimes travelling with their families to neighboring cities. I did not converse with them, as I was not sure of my ability to refrain from divulging my abolition sentiments. On my arrival in Montgomery I took up my quarters at the Exchange and impressed upon Mr. Floyd the necessity of keeping my presence a secret. He had no idea that I was after Maroney, but supposed I was merely on a visit to the South.

I took no notice of Maroney, but managed to see Porter

and Roch privately.   They informed me that they had discovered little or nothing. Maroney kept everything to himself. He and his wife went out occasionally. He frequented Patterson's, sometimes going into the card rooms, drove out with a fast horse, and passed many hours in his counsel's office. This was all Porter knew.

Roch was to do nothing but "spot" the suspected parties and follow any one of them who might leave town. He was to be a Dutchman, and he acted the character to perfection. He could be seen sitting outside of his boarding-house with his pipe in his mouth, and he apparently did nothing but puff, puff, puff all day long. There was a saloon in town where lager was sold and he could, occasionally, be found here sipping his lager; but although apparently a stupid, phlegmatic man, taking no notice of what was going on around him, he drank in, with his lager, every word that was said.

I found that Mrs. Maroney was a very smart woman, indeed, and that it would be necessary to keep a strict watch over her. I therefore informed the Vice-President that I would send down another detective especially to shadow her, as she might leave at any moment for the North and take the forty thousand dollars with her.

I had no objections to her taking the money to the North. On the contrary, I preferred she should do so, as I would much rather carry on the fight on Northern soil than in the South.

I found Messrs. Watts, Judd & Jackson, the company's lawyers, were excellent men, clear-headed and accommodating. They gladly furnished me with what little information they possessed.

CHAPTER IV.

BEFORE I left Montgomery on my return to the North, I became acquainted with the local detective, McGibony, without letting him know who I was. In accordance with a plan which I always carry out, of watching the actions of those around me, I kept my eye on him, and found that he was quite "thick" with Maroney. He boarded at the Exchange, drank with Maroney in saloons, and even passed with him into the card-room at Patterson's.

At this time McGibony had in his charge a distinguished prisoner, being no less a personage than the old planter whom Johnson H. Hooper so graphically described as "Simon Suggs;" by which name I will continue to call him.

Suggs had been arrested for the commission of a series of misdemeanors, but, as he was a great favorite, he was allowed the freedom of the city, and was joyfully welcomed at the hotels and saloons.

Simon was about fifty-six years old, the dryest kind of a wit, and extremely fond of his bitters. He lived about forty miles out from Montgomery, on the Coosa river, but about a week prior to the time I saw him, had come to Montgomery to see his friends. Simon's morality was not of the highest order, and the first place he visited was Patterson's saloon. Here he met a few congenial

3

spirits, took several drinks with them, and then, being "flush,"— a very unusual thing for him — he proceeded to " buck the tiger." Like too many others, he bucked too long, and soon found himself penniless. Not to be outdone, however, he rushed out and borrowed one hundred dollars from a friend, promising to return it the first thing in the morning. With this money he returned to the unequal contest, but before long was again strapped.

In the morning, as he was walking along the street, in a very penitential mood, he was accosted by his friend, who demanded of him the one hundred dollars he had borrowed. Simon put on a very important air, and in a tone of confidence which he was far from feeling, assured him he should have the money before he left town.

As Simon strolled along, puzzling his brain as to how he could raise the necessary funds to pay off his friend, he saw the tall, ungainly form of a backwoods planter shuffling down the street towards him.

The planter was dressed in a suit of butternut, which had become very much shrunken, from exposure to all kinds of weather. His coat sleeves did not reach far below his elbows, and there was a considerable space between the bottom of his breeches and the top of his shoes. He was as "thin as a rail," and if he stood upright would have been very tall, but he was bent nearly double. He had a slouched hat on, which partly concealed his long, lantern-jawed visage, while his shaggy, uncombed hair fell to his shoulders, and gave one a feeling that it contained many an inhabitant, like that which caused Burns to write those famous lines containing the passage :

> " Oh, wad some power the giftie gie us,
> To see *oursels* as *ithers* see us ! "

As he came down the street he stopped occasionally and gawked around.

Simon was always ready for fun, and determined to see what the planter was up to. Accordingly, as they met, Simon said, " Good mornin' ! "

" Good mornin' ! " replied the gawky.

" Have yer lost summat ? " asked Simon.

" Wal, no, stranger, but I wants to git some money changed, and I 'll be durned if I can diskiver a bank in this yar village."

" Bin sellin' niggers, eh ? "

" You 're out thar," replied the planter. " I 've bin sellin' cotton."

" I 'm jist the man to help yer ! I 'm gwine to my bank. Gin me yer money, and come along with me and I 'll change it for yer ! "

The gawky was much pleased at Simon's kind attention, and remarking that " he reckoned he was the squarest man he had met," he turned over his money — some four hundred dollars — to Simon, and they started off together to get it changed.

On the road Simon stepped into a saloon with the planter, called up all the inmates to take a drink, and telling the planter he would be back with the money in a few minutes, started off.

Fifteen minutes passed away. The planter took several drinks, and began to think his friend was a long time in getting the money changed, but supposed he must be detained at the bank. At the end of half an hour he began to grow decidedly uneasy, but still Simon did not come. At the expiration of an hour he was furious, and if Simon had fallen into his hands at that time, he would have doubtless been made mince meat of unceremoniously.

Simon, on leaving the saloon, had gone to his friend and, out of the poor planter's funds, had paid him the hundred dollars he owed him, and, with the three hundred dollars in his pocket, started for Patterson's.

He proceeded to " buck the tiger," and soon lost nearly all of it. To see if his luck would not change, he gave up the game, and started at " roulette." Here he steadily won, and soon had over seven hundred dollars in his possession. He was now all excitement, and jumped with many a " whoop-la " around the table, to the great amusement of the spectators. He was about to give up play, but they urged him on, saying he had a run of luck, and should not give up till he broke the bank. Thus encouraged, he played for heavy stakes, and was soon completely " cleaned out," and left Patterson's without a cent.

He went to a friend and borrowed twenty-five dollars to help him out of town. He was considered good for a small short loan ; and going to his hotel, he paid his bill, and mounting his dilapidated steed, started for his home, forty miles distant, at as great a speed as he could get out of his poor "Rosinante." In the South, men, women and children, always make short journeys on horseback. Simon travelled for two hours, when he reached the Coosa river, about fifteen miles from Montgomery. At this point lived a wealthy widow, with whom he was well acquainted, and here he determined to pass the night.

He was joyfully welcomed by the widow, who ordered one of her negroes to put up his horse and conducted him into the house. She had a good supper prepared, Simon ate a hearty meal, spent a few delightful hours in the widow's company, and was then shown to his room. He was soon in the arms of Morpheus, and arose in the morning as gay as a lark. Throwing open the casement, he let in the fresh morning breeze and took in at a glance the rich Southern landscape. Immediately below him, and sloping in well kept terraces to the banks of the Coosa, was a trim garden, filled with flowers, among which, in fine bloom, were numerous varieties of the rose. The sluggish waters of the Coosa flowed without a ripple between its well wooded banks, the trees on opposite sides often interlocking their branches. Beyond the river was a wilderness of forest; the slaves were going to their labor in the cotton fields, singing and chatting gaily like a party of children. It was indeed a beautiful scene, and who could more thoroughly appreciate the beautiful than Simon? Hurriedly dressing himself, he went to the breakfast room, where he found waiting for him the buxom widow, dressed in a loose morning robe, admirably adapted to display the charms of her figure.

After a delicious repast of coffee and fruit the widow proposed that as it was such a lovely morning they take a boat-ride on the river. Simon willingly acquiesced, and the widow, after ordering a well filled lunch-basket to be placed in the boat, not forgetting a "little brown jug" for Simon, took his arm, and tripping gaily down to the river, embarked. Simon pulled strongly at the oars until a bend of the river hid them from view of the plantation, when, taking in the oars, he seated himself by the widow, and placing an oar at the stern to steer with, they glided down the river. Simon was married, but was a firm believer in the theory advanced by Moore, that

—"when far from the lips we love,
We've but to make love to the lips we are near."

The persimmons hung in tempting bunches within easy reach overhead, and Simon would pull them down and shower them into the widow's lap. Occasionally he would steal his arm around her waist, when she, with a coy laugh, would pronounce him an "impudent fellow." Occasionally he would raise the little brown jug and take a hearty pull; finally he stole a few kisses, the widow dropped her head resignedly on his shoulder, and so they floated down the current, loving "not wisely, but too well." On and on they floated, entirely oblivious of time, when they were suddenly startled by a wild halloo. The widow started up with a scream, and Simon grasped the oars as soon as possible. Just in front of them, seated on his horse, and with his revolver ready cocked in his hand, sat the deputy sheriff of Montgomery. "Simon Suggs," said he, "jist you git out of that thar boat and come along with me; I've got a warrant for your arrest!"

"Oh! hav yer?" said Simon, "that's all right; I'll jist take this yar lady hum, git my critter, and come in to Montgomery."

"No," said the inexorable deputy, "that won't do, jist you git out of that thar boat and come with me."

The widow now interposed, and in plaintive tone said,

"But, sir, what am I to do? It will never do for me to return without Mr. Suggs; what will my niggers think of it? You, Mr. Deputy, can get into the boat with us and go to my house; while you are eating dinner I will send one of my niggers to fetch your horse."

The deputy was finally persuaded to take this course, and securing his horse, he got into the boat.

It will now be necessary to relate how the deputy happened to appear at such an inopportune moment for Simon. The planter, after awaiting the return of Simon for over two hours, was informed by the saloon keeper to whom he appealed, that he had entrusted his money to Simon Suggs, and that his chances of ever seeing it again were poor indeed. On discovering this he swore out a warrant against Simon and placed it in the hands of the sheriff to execute.

The Sheriff found that Simon had left town, and immediately his deputy, mounted on a fast horse, started in pursuit. The deputy passed Simon at the widow's, and went directly to his house. He found Mrs. Suggs at home, and demanded of her the whereabouts of Simon. Mrs. Suggs said she did not pretend to keep track of him; that he was a lazy, shiftless fellow, who never supported his family; that about a week previously he had left home, and she had not set her eyes on him since.

The deputy informed her that Simon had committed a grave offense, and that he had a warrant for his arrest.

Mrs. Suggs ended the interview by saying she always thought Simon would come to a bad end, and slammed the door in the deputy's face.

The Deputy Sheriff passed the night at a friend's, and

the next morning retraced his steps, making inquiries along the road at the different plantations, endeavoring to get some trace of Simon. When he reached the widow's he was told by a slave that "Massa Simon" and the "Missus" had shortly before gone down the river for a boat ride, and taking a short cut through the fields he headed them off.

The return journey was against the current, and Simon was pulling away at the oars, the perspiration starting in large drops from his forehead and running down into his eyes, or streaking his cheeks, while the deputy was gaily entertaining the widow, who was about equally divided in her attentions. As they proceeded Simon would say, "A very deep place here;" "bar here;" "push her off a little from that snag," etc., and the deputy would occasionally supply the widow with persimmons. While in the deepest part of the stream the widow discovered a splendid bunch of persimmons hanging from a bough which reached to the centre of the river. She declared she *must* have them. Simon rested on his oars, while the gallant deputy got on the seat, and by raising himself on his tip toes, just managed to reach the bough, a good strong one, and, grasping it with both hands, he proceeded to bend it down so as to reach the fruit. At this inopportune moment Simon gave way to his oars, and left the poor deputy hanging in the air.

"Hold on! hold on!" yelled the deputy; "don't you know you are interfering with an officer of the law?"

"My advice ter you is to hold on yourself," was all the consolation he got from Simon, while the widow was convulsed with laughter.

At this inopportune moment Simon gave way to his oars, and left the poor deputy hanging in the air.—Page 49.

Leaving the deputy to extricate himself from his awkward position as best he could, Simon rowed rapidly to the house, sent a negro to bring the deputy's horse, and after eating an enormous lunch, mounted and started for home.

The deputy hung to the limb and yelled for assistance, but no one came, and he found he could hold on no longer. He could not swim, and he felt that in dropping from the limb he would certainly meet a watery grave. All his life he had had a horror of water, and now to be drowned in the hated liquid was too hard. He made desperate efforts to climb up, on the limb, but could not do it. His arms were so strained that he thought they would be pulled from their sockets. He had strung many a negro up by the thumbs to thrash him, but he little thought he should have been strung up himself. His strength rapidly failed him, and he found he could maintain his hold no longer. Closing his eyes, he strove to pray, but could not. Finding the effort useless, he let go his hold, while a cold shudder ran through his body — what a moment of supreme agony! — and dropped into the river. Over such harrowing scenes it were better to throw a veil of silence, but I must go on. He dropped into the river, and as the water was only knee deep, he waded to the bank.

His combined emotions overcame him, and on reaching the bank he threw himself down under the shade of some trees and, completely exhausted, sunk into a deep sleep. How long he slept he could not tell, but on awaking he sprang up and hurried to the place where he had left his horse. Finding it gone, he walked into Montgomery and reported to the Sheriff, not daring to face the widow after the ridiculous tableau in which he had been the principal performer.

The Sheriff procured the services of McGibony, and the next day went with him to Simon's home, and arrested him without difficulty.

In the North, Simon would have been kept a close prisoner; but the fun-loving inhabitants of Montgomery looked on the whole transaction as a very good joke, and Simon was decidedly " in clover," having liberty to go where he wished, and being maintained at the county's expense.

I judged from the circumstances that McGibony was not to be trusted, and concluded that authorities who could execute the law so leniently, would be poor custodians for a prisoner of Maroney's stamp.

On my return trip to Chicago I stopped over at Rome, Ga., where Maroney's father lived. I discovered that the doctor lived well, although he was a man of small means. I took a general survey of the town, and then went directly to Chicago.

CHAPTER V.

ON arriving in Chicago I selected Mr. Green to "shadow" Mrs. Maroney. Giving him the same full instructions I had given the other operatives, I despatched him for Montgomery. He arrived there none too soon.

Mrs. Maroney had grown rather commanding in her manners, and was very arrogant with the servants in the house. She also found great fault with the proprietor, Mr. Floyd, for not having some necessary repairs in her room attended to.

One of the lady boarders, the wife of a senator, treated her with marked coolness; and these various circumstances so worked on her high-strung temperament that she was thrown into an uncontrollable fit of passion, during which she broke the windows in her room.

The landlord insisted on her paying for them, but she indignantly refused to do so. On his pressing the matter, she determined to leave the house and make a trip to the North.

Porter had become quite intimate with the slave-servants in the Exchange, and easily managed to get from them considerable information, without attracting any special attention.

One of the servants, named Tom, was the bootblack of the hotel. He had a young negro under him as a sort of an apprentice. The duties of the apprentice, though apparently slight, were in reality arduous, as he had to supply all the spittle required to moisten the blacking; and for this purpose placed himself under a course of diet that rendered him as juicy as possible.

Early in the morning Tom and his assistant would pass from door to door. Stopping wherever they saw a pair of boots, they would at once proceed to business. The helper would seize a boot and give a tremendous " hawk," which would cause the sleeping inmate of the room to start up in his bed and rub his eyes. He would then apply the blacking and hand the boot to Tom, who stood ready to artistically apply the polishing brush. During the whole of this latter operation the little negro would dance a breakdown, while Tom, seated on the chair brought for his accommodation, would whistle or sing an accompaniament. By this time the inmate of the room would have sprung from his bed, and rushed to the door, with the intention of breaking their heads — not shins — but, on opening the door, the scene presented would be so ludicrous that his anger would be smothered in laughter, and Tom generally received a quarter, as he started for the next door.

Sleep was completely vanquished by the time they had made their rounds, and the greatest sluggard who ever reiterated "God bless the man who first invented sleep," would find himself drawn from his downy pillow at break of day, with never a murmur.

Tom was naturally of an enquiring turn of mind, and as he passed from door to door saw and heard a good deal. Porter, by giving him an occasional fee, had made

Tom his fast friend, and he would often regale him with bits of scandal about different boarders in the house.

On the evening of the same day that Mrs. Maroney had given way to her temper, as Porter was passing through the hall of the hotel, he heard peals of laughter emanating from the room used by Tom as his blacking headquarters. Going in, he found Tom, perfectly convulsed with laughter, rolling around amongst the blacking brushes and old shoes, while the little negro, with his mouth wide open and eyes starting almost out of his head, looked at him in utter astonishment.

"Why! what's the matter, Tom?" inquired Porter.

It was some time before Tom could answer, but he finally burst out with :

"Oh! golly, Massa Porter, you ought to see de fun. Missus 'Roney done gone and smashed all de glass in de winder. I tell you she made tings hot. Massa Floyd say she must pay for de glass, and she tole him she's not gwine to stop in dis yer house a moment longer. Yah! yah! yah! Den Massa 'Roney come, and he fly right off de handle, and tole Massa Floyd he had *consulted* his wife. Massa Floyd tole dem dey could go somewhere else fur all he care. Massa 'Roney tole de missus to pack up and go to de North, de fust ting in de morning. So Missus 'Roney is gwine to go North. Wonder what she'll do thar, wid no niggers to confusticate? Yah! yah! yah!"

Porter drew from the darkey full particulars of the affair, and also that he had seen Maroney pass a large sum of money over to his wife.

Giving Tom a quarter, Porter hurried off after Green,

and got him ready to start the first thing in the morning. Bright and early on the twelfth of March, Porter arose, and, *quite accidentally*, ran across Tom, who had just come down with Mrs. Maroney's shoes.

"She is gwine, sure," said Tom! "she tole me to hurry up wid dese shoes. Her and Massa 'Roney am habin a big confab, but dey talk so low, dis nigger can't hear a word dey say."

Porter hurried Green to the train, and came back in time to see Maroney get into a carriage, with his wife and her daughter Flora, and drive off toward the station. Maroney secured for them a comfortable seat in the ladies' car, and, bidding them good-bye, returned to the hotel.

Of course Green was on the same train, but, as I had instructed him, not in the same car. He took a seat in the rear end of the car immediately in front of the ladies' car, whence he could keep a sharp lookout on all that went on.

Mrs. Maroney went directly to West Point, and from there to Charleston, where she put up at the best hotel, registering "Mrs. Maroney and daughter."

The next day, leaving Flora in the hotel, she made a few calls, and at two P. M. embarked on the steamer for New York, Green doing the same. They arrived at New York on the eighteenth and were met at the wharf by a gentleman named Moore, who conducted Mrs. Maroney and Flora to his residence. Green discovered afterwards that the gentleman was a partner in one of the heaviest wholesale clothing-houses in the city.

He knew nothing further about Mr. or Mrs. Maroney than that Maroney had treated him with a good deal of consideration at one time when he was in Montgomery selling goods, and he had then requested Maroney and his wife to stop at his house if they ever came to New York. Accordingly Maroney telegraphed to him when his wife left Montgomery, informing him how and when she would reach New York, and he was at the wharf to meet her.

Mrs. Maroney and Flora were cordially welcomed by Mr. Moore and remained at his house for some weeks. They were very hospitably entertained and seemed to devote their whole time to social pleasures. Green shadowed them closely and found that nothing of any importance was going on.

Porter remained in Montgomery, keeping in the good graces of Maroney and his friends, not that Maroney easily took any one into his confidence; on the contrary, although he was social with every one, he kept his affairs closely to himself.

Porter never forced himself on Maroney's company, but merely dropped in, apparently by accident, at Patterson's and other saloons frequented by Maroney, and by holding himself rather aloof, managed to draw Maroney towards him.

Maroney used to walk out of town towards the plantations, and Porter, by making himself acquainted with the planters and overseers of the surrounding country, discovered that Maroney's walks were caused by a young lady, the daughter of a wealthy planter; but no new developments were made in regard to the robbery.

I instructed Porter to "get in" with any slaves who might be employed as waiters at Patterson's, and worm from

them all the information possible in regard to the habitués
of the place.

There were several men with whom Maroney used to
have private meetings at the saloon, and Porter learned
from one of the negroes what took place at them. Maroney would take an occasional hand at euchre, but never
played for large stakes. There was little doubt but that
he had a share in the gambling bank. He frequented
the stable where "Yankee Mary" was kept, and often
himself drove her out. From the way the parties at
Patterson's talked, the negro was positive that she belonged
to Maroney.

He received several letters from his wife, which Green
saw her post, and Porter found he received in due time.
So far all my plans had worked well. The regular reports
I received from my detectives showed that they were
doing their duty and watching carefully all that occurred.
Porter, about this time, learned that Maroney intended to
make a business trip through Tennessee, and that he
would, in all probability, go to Augusta, Ga., and New
Orleans.

Everything tended to show that he was about to leave
Montgomery, and I put Roch, my Dutchman, on the alert.
I wrote out full instructions and sent them to Roch;
ordered him to keep a strict watch on Maroney, as he
might be going away to change the money, and told him
to telegraph me immediately if anything happened. It
was my intention to buy any money he might get changed,
as the bankers in Montgomery stated that they would be
able to identify some of the stolen bills. I warned Roch
against coming in contact with Maroney on his journey,

as I surmised that he was going away to see if he would be followed. This was certainly his intention.

For some time I had feared that Maroney had some idea of Porter's reasons for stopping in Montgomery, and felt that if he had, he would be completely disabused of it by discovering that Porter did not follow him. He was an uncommonly shrewd man and had formed a pretty good opinion of detectives and of his ability to outwit them.

He had seen the best detectives from New York, New Orleans and other places completely baffled. He expected to be followed by a gentlemanly appearing man, who would drink and smoke occasionally, wear a heavy gold watch chain, and have plenty of money to spend; but the idea of being followed by a poor old Dutchman never entered his head.

I charged Roch not to pay any attention to Maroney or to appear to do so until he started to leave Montgomery, and concluded by saying that I felt I could trust him to do all in his power for the agency and for my honor.

Maroney made his preparations for departure, all his movements being closely watched by Porter.

4

CHAPTER VI.

ON the fifth of April Maroney, having completed his preparations, started by the first train for Atlanta, *via* West Point. The day was a very warm one, but Maroney was accompanied to the station by a great number of friends. With many a hearty shake of the hand they bade him farewell, some of them accompanying him to the first, and some even to the second station beyond Montgomery. No one could have started on a journey under more favorable auspices.

Before the train started a German might have been seen slowly wending his way to the depot. He had no slaves to follow, or wait upon him. No one knew him, and the poor fellow had not a friend to bid him good-bye. He went to the ticket office, and in broken English said: " I vants a teeket for Vest Point ; " and stood puffing at his pipe until the clerk gave him his ticket, for which he paid, and took his seat in a car called, in the South, the "nigger car." He had a rather large satchel, and it must be confessed he was decidedly dirty, as he had been toiling along a dusty road, under the hot Southern sun.

In about ten minutes after, Maroney arrived, with his numerous friends, stepped on board, and the train slowly drew out of the station.

The German had taken a reversed seat in the rear of his car, and, apparently indifferent to the lively conversation of the negroes around him, slowly smoked his pipe. Maroney took a seat in the ladies' car, talked with his friends, among whom were several ladies, and then had a merry romp with a child. In about three-quarters of an hour he rose, and, walking to the front of the car, scrutinized the faces of all the passengers carefully. Our Dutchman gazed carelessly at him through the window of the car in which he sat. Maroney passed through the "nigger car," not thinking it worth while to take notice of its inmates, and looking on the poor immigrant as no better than a negro. Then he went into the express car, shook hands with the messenger, chatted with him a moment, and passed on to the baggage car. At the first station he stepped off, met several friends, and was well received by all. The conductor collected no fare from him, as he had been a conductor at one time, and that chalked his hat "O. K."

He left the train at every station, looked keenly around with an eye that showed plainly that he was fighting for liberty itself, and then returning, passed through it, carefully examining the faces of the passengers. By the time they reached West Point he had regained his old firmness — at least the German thought so.

If any one had watched, they might have seen the German go to the ticket office in West Point and, in broken language, inquire for a ticket to Atlanta. Having procured his ticket, he went immediately to the second-class car and continued his journey with Maroney.

At West Point Maroney met several friends, who all sympathized with him. After drinking with them he went to the train and into the express car, although it is strict rule of the company that no one but the messenger shall be allowed in it. The rule is often broken, especially in the South, where the polite messengers dislike to ask a gentleman to leave their car. The German took in all that was going on, but who cared for him? poor, stupid dolt! Maroney remained in the express car a short time, and then again passed through the train, but discovered nothing to cause him the slightest uneasiness.

On arriving at Atlanta he proceeded to the Atlanta House, and was given a room. The German arrived at the hotel soon after him, and throwing down his satchel, asked, in his broken English, for a room. The clerk scarcely deigning to notice him, sent him to the poorest room the house afforded.

Roch, finding that no train left until morning, amused himself with another smoke, at the same time noticing that Maroney was well received by the clerk, whom he knew, and by all the conductors and gentlemen who frequented the hotel. His journey had been almost an entire ovation, and he had become almost completely self-possessed.

At eleven he retired for the night. Roch, after waiting for some time, walked noiselessly down the hall to Maroney's room, and listened at the door. Finding all quiet, he walked down to the office, got the key to his room, and went to bed.

He got up early in the morning and, with Maroney, took an early breakfast. He kept a close watch on him, and learned from the conversation of some of Maroney's friends, to whom he had divulged his plans, where he was going, and by what route he intended to pursue his journey. He said that he should be gone some five weeks, but would return to Montgomery in time to prepare for his trial.

Some of his friends alluded to his arrest for the robbery. He smiled, and said they would soon find that he was not the guilty party; and moreover, that the Express Company would find that it would cost them a good deal before they got through with him, as, after his acquittal, he would certainly sue them for heavy damages. He knew the wealth of the company, and that they would "leave no stone unturned" to ruin him, but he had no fears as to the result, when the facts were laid before a jury of his countrymen.

He had many acquaintances at Atlanta, and gave himself up to enjoyment. Roch wrote to me that if he had started out with the expectation of being followed, he had no such fears now. In the evening Maroney complained to the clerk about his room, and Roch became uneasy when he found he had moved to another part of the house. He feared that Maroney might leave town by some private conveyance, and so kept a close watch on his movements. He staid up until a late hour, but finding that Maroney was safe in bed, finally retired. At a very early hour in the morning he was stirring and patiently waited for Maroney to get up. Maroney soon came down, apparently in the best of spirits, and ordered his trunk, a very large one, to be taken to the depot. Roch was seized with a desire to go through this trunk, and determined to do so if he possibly could. He had not seen it at Montgomery as it came down with the other baggage, and one of Maroney's friends had had it checked and handed the check to him when on the train. His desire was useless, as he was not destined to see the inside of the trunk, at least not for the present. He wrote to me of Maroney's having the trunk, and said I might rely on his examining it if he possibly could.

Maroney took the train for Chattanooga, still paying no fare. Roch bought a second class ticket and they were soon under way. When about one hour out from Atlanta Maroney passed through the train eyeing all the well-dressed men on board, of whom there were a great many, but paying no attention to the inmates of the "nigger car." He saw no cause for uneasiness, and soon became the happiest man on board. He passed through the cars several times before the train reached Chattanooga, and his spirits seemed to rise after each inspection. When they arrived at Chattanooga, Maroney put up at the Crutchfield House, and being very tired did not go out that evening. He seemed well acquainted with the clerk and some of the guests, drank several times with his friends, and went to his room quite early. Roch wrote to me from the Crutchfield House, where he had also put up, giving me a detailed account of all that had happened, and in a postscript said "Maroney has not the slightest idea that he is being followed, and all is serene." In the morning Maroney sauntered around the city, apparently with no particular object in view, but dropping into some of the stores to visit his friends. Finally he went into a lawyer's office where he remained some time. Roch took up a position where he could watch the office without being observed. At last Maroney came out of the office with a gentleman, went into a saloon

with him, where they drank together, and then returned
to the hotel to dinner. After dinner he smoked until
about two o'clock, and then walked out and started up
the main street of the town, towards the suburbs. The
day was intensely warm, and there were few people stirring in the streets. When Maroney reached the suburbs
he stopped and looked suspiciously around. He took no
notice of the German, who was walking along wrapped
up in his pipe, his only consolation. Being satisfied that
no one was following him, he turned around the corner
and suddenly disappeared.

When Roch got to the corner he could not see Maroney
in any direction. There were blocks of fine houses on
both sides of the street, and he was certain Maroney was
in one of them. But which one? That he could not
tell. He did not like to leave the neighborhood, but it
would not do to stay. There were few persons on the
street, and if he lingered around the corner he would
surely be noticed and suspected. He walked very slowly
around the square, but discovering nothing, and fearing
that he might alarm the quiet neighborhood, he went
back to the hotel. He was now at the end of his rope.
He was certain Maroney was in one of the houses, and
feared that he was getting the money changed. He might
have brought it with him, concealed it on his person, and
taken it with him to the house he was now in. Terribly
disappointed, he sat down and wrote to me for instructions, thinking that my letter in reply would most likely
reach him in Chattanooga. At dusk he went out to the
suburbs, but did not find a trace of Maroney. Returning
to the hotel, he found that no train left till morning, and

weary and worn he went to his room, and in a most
despondent mood, soon retired.   Early in the morning
he came down but there was no sign of Maroney   He
determined to peep into his room, and fortunately managed to do so without being discovered, finding his trunk
and a bundle of soiled linen still there.   Somewhat
reassured, he took his breakfast and went down to see
the train off.   The train started, but Maroney not putting
in an appearance, Roch began to feel that he must have
been outwitted.   As he retraced his steps to the hotel he
was astonished to see Maroney on his way to the same
place.   Roch having once more got his eye on him,
determined, if possible, to find out where he had passed
the previous night.   He thought the matter over, and
concluded that for many reasons it would be best to
change his boarding place.   The people at the hotel did
not think much of a poor German, and might conclude
he could not pay his bill, and as he did not wish to guar-
antee payment, he went to his room, brought down his
satchel, and going to the office, paid his bill.   He had
seen a German boarding-house down the street, so taking
his satchel in his hand, he went in and enquired if they
had a room to spare.   He found they had, and on glancing around discovered that the change in many respects
was for the better, as from the boarding-house he had a
clear view of all that occurred in front of the hotel.

He did not see Maroney again until evening, when he
came out, looking fresh and bright, having evidently
refreshed himself by a bath and a shave.

Maroney went into a saloon, talked to several parties,
strolled leisurely around, returned to the hotel, passed the

evening till ten o'clock with a party of gentlemen, and then retired.

Roch rose early, and found that the landlord, who, like most of his countrymen, possessed the good habit of being an early riser, had breakfast ready. After breakfast he took a seat on the verandah, and watched Maroney as he loitered around. At two in the afternoon Maroney sauntered out, and started in the direction of the suburbs.

Roch concluded he was going to the place where he had lost him the day before, and now he had the coveted opportunity of finding his hiding place.

Walking slowly after him, smoking his pipe and gaping around, until he reached a cross-street, a block from where Maroney had disappeared before, he turned down this street, walked rapidly until he reached the next street running parallel to the one Maroney was on, and turning up it he ran to the corner above, where he got behind the fence, as if urged by a pressing necessity. From his position he could see down the street without being seen.

In a moment Maroney reached the corner, a block from him. Looking around, as before, he pulled his hat over his eyes, and, walking rapidly part way down the block, he entered a comfortable looking frame-building. It was painted a creamy white, and its windows were protected by the greenest of green blinds.

CHAPTER VII.

ROCH walked around for some time, and then returned to his boarding-house. Finding no one but the landlord and the bar-keeper in the saloon, he bought a bottle of wine, and asked them to join him in drinking it. They gladly consented, and he entered into a conversation with them, in which he pretended to give them a history of his life, and his plans for the future.

He complimented the city very highly, saying that he was so much pleased with it that he had determined to buy some property there. He then informed them that he had been looking at some houses, and wished to get the landlord's opinion of them. He — the landlord — had been in the city for many years, and must be well acquainted with the value of property.

Roch now called for another bottle of wine, and proceeded to describe some of the houses at which he had been looking. He described several, but one in particular, he said, had taken his fancy; and he then described the house Maroney had entered, saying further that he thought there were several ladies there.

The landlord looked at his bar-keeper and winked, and then giving Roch a poke in the ribs, said, with a hearty laugh: "Oh! you have found them out, have you?" Then, with another poke: "You're a sly fellow, you are," and burst into a roar of laughter, in which he was heartily joined by the bar-keeper.

Roch pretended not to comprehend what they meant, and turned the conversation to other subjects. He felt very happy when he discovered the character — or rather want of character — of the house, as he now knew the business Maroney was engaged in.

Maroney did not make his appearance up to the time the train left, so Roch retired.

Early in the morning he arose, ate his breakfast, and was surprised to see Maroney, who must have returned in the night, just coming out of the hotel. Seeing Maroney's trunk just being placed on the baggage wagon, he hastily paid his bill at the boarding-house, and managed to reach the station some time in advance of Maroney.

In about half an hour Maroney came up and bought a first-class ticket for Nashville. Roch bought a second-class ticket to the same place, and took up his old position in the "nigger car."

Nothing of importance happened between Chattanooga and Nashville.

At Nashville Maroney put up at the City Hotel, while Roch obtained lodgings at a German saloon just around the corner.

Maroney met plenty of friends, who received him warmly. He amused himself by going to the livery stables, looking at the horses, and driving around the city. He met a gentleman and passed a good deal of time with him, but had no business transactions with him; merely using him as a companion to help kill time. The weather was all that could be desired, and Maroney was "gay as a lark."

The second day after his arrival in Nashville, he went

into a jeweler's, and remained over three-quarters of an hour; came out, and at the end of three hours again went in, this time stopping over an hour. When he came out Roch discovered that he had a parcel in his hand, and concluded that he had made a purchase. He at once reported the incident to me.

The third day, at train time, the trunk was again brought down. Roch went to the depot, wondering what could be the meaning of this move, as the train about to start would take them back to Chattanooga.

His suspense was soon put at rest, by Maroney's coming down and buying a ticket to Chattanooga. Roch followed suit, and they were soon on their backward track.

Maroney passed through the cars, scrutinizing the passengers, neglecting those in the "nigger car," as heretofore, which was the only incident of the trip to Chattanooga.

Here he again put up at the Crutchfield House, while Roch went back to his German boarding-house. He made some excuses to account for his sudden return, but they were unnecessary, for, so long as he paid his bill regularly, the landlord was perfectly satisfied.

The next morning Maroney visited a livery stable owned by a man named Cook, who was a great favorite. He was said to have a horse which could out-trot anything in the city. Cook and Maroney drove out several times with this horse, and Maroney examined him critically. He was a good judge of horseflesh, and when he was excited would fairly carry a person away with his vivid description of the delights of "tooling" along behind a fast horse.

Roch could not certainly tell whether Maroney had

bought the horse or not, but judged he had, as he heard Cook tell Maroney that he should expect to see him on his return to Chattanooga.

After leaving Cook, Maroney sauntered out to see his fair, but frail friends. Roch left him there and returned to have a good time with his countrymen. He had ordered up a bottle of wine, and the landlord and he were just about to have a game of euchre when he accidentally glanced up at the hotel.

It was fortunate he did so, as whom should he see going in at the main entrance but Maroney. He hastily excused himself from the game and walked out. He had gone hardly a block from his boarding-house before Maroney came down and got into a carriage. He had gone at once to his room, ordered his trunk down, paid his bill and was now being hurried to the depot.

Roch followed as fast as he could. Maroney had allowed himself barely enough time to check his trunk and step upon the train as it moved off, so that Roch had to start without his satchel and without buying a ticket. He did not think much of the loss of his baggage, that little loss being more than compensated by the joy he felt at not having lost his man.

He had not the slightest idea where Maroney was going, but took up his old position in the " nigger car" and watched closely. When the conductor came around to Maroney, Roch noticed two things: first, that Maroney bought a through ticket to Memphis; and second, that the conductor did not know him. Wherever he had gone before, he had met friends, but now he had left them all behind.

Roch followed Maroney's lead and bought a second class ticket to Memphis.

Maroney, though utterly unconscious of the fact, was as much in the power of Roch as was Sindbad the Sailor in the power of the little old man who clung to his neck with a grasp that could not be loosened. Although, literally, Roch did not touch him, figuratively he held him with a grasp of iron, and all Maroney's efforts to shake him off would have proved waste of time and strength.

A storm was impending when they left Chattanooga and it had now burst upon them in a perfect fury. Night had set in, but flash after flash of lightning lit up the sky. One moment, objects were rendered distinctly visible as they dashed by, the next they were lost in gloom. The sparks from the locomotive were quenched in the falling torrent and the roar of the train was silenced by the loud peals of thunder.

It was a wild night, but Roch got on the platform to make sure of Maroney. There were no sleeping-cars at the time and he had no trouble in getting a good view of him. Maroney was stretched out on his seat fast asleep. He watched him for some time, and then concluding that there was little danger of his attempting to leave the car on such a night, he went back to his seat in the "nigger car."

Ever since he had left Montgomery, Maroney had been executing a series of strategic movements, and now that he had undoubtedly thrown his pursuers, if there were any, off his track, why should he not ease his overwrought mind by sleep, that sweetest of all consolers?

The next morning they arrived in Memphis. The

storm had passed away, but had left mementoes in the fresh and balmy air and in the muddy streets. Maroney stopped at the Gayosa House. Roch found it an easy matter to move his baggage, and walked off with his hands in his pockets, wondering where he could get a clean shirt. He put up at a saloon where he could keep an eye on Maroney, and having bought some new shirts and a second-hand satchel, he felt once more that he was a respectable man.

From Memphis Roch wrote to me, informing me "that all was well; that Maroney seemed perfectly at ease and confident that if any one had followed him, he had, by his retrograde movement, thrown him entirely off the scent." He had not the slightest idea what would be Maroney's next move, but was certain he could keep track of him.

Maroney appeared familiar with Memphis, but had no friends there, and amused himself loitering around, occasionally going into a saloon. The second day of his stay Roch observed him write and post a letter. Then he visited the livery stables, admired some of the fine horses and afterwards strolled down to the wharf, where the steamer " John Walsh " was being loaded with cotton and tobacco. He went on board and looked over the Walsh, saw the clerk and entered into conversation with him. Roch heard the clerk say that the steamer would leave in about two hours, and concluded that Maroney was going down the river on her.

Maroney returned to the Gayosa House and paid his bill, which caused Roch to hurry to his boarding-house pay his bill, and with his newly acquired treasure, the old satchel, hasten to the river and take a steerage passage to New Orleans on the John Walsh. He was a little afraid that Maroney might begin to notice him and found it necessary to use the utmost caution. Before embarking on the Walsh he laid in a stock of "bolognas," a few pounds of the rankest "Sweitzer kase" and an abundance of "pretzels."

Coming down to the boat some time before Maroney, he filled his pipe and took a seat where he could watch all that went on. After some time Maroney drove up in a carriage, had his trunk carried up to his state-room, and, lighting his cigar, took a seat and watched the movements of the crew who were employed in taking on the cargo. It was a busy scene: the negroes toiled along under the burning sun, lightening their labors with a merry boatman's song. Their burdens were heavy, but their hearts were light.

Maroney, instead of looking down on them with the contempt he did, should have longed for their content and happiness. The meanest of them possessed what he never could possess — "a contented mind."

In less than half an hour the steamer's bell was rung, friends hurriedly bade each other good-bye, the gang-planks were hauled in, and the John Walsh was soon snorting down the river. The decks and cabins of the Walsh were crowded with passengers; ladies handsomely dressed, planters going to New Orleans on business or pleasure; tourists making a trip down the Mississippi for the first time, and being charmed with the variety of the scenes around them: all was life, gaiety and animation.

Although Maroney would have generally mingled with the passengers, "the gayest of the gay," he now kept entirely aloof from them. He was oppressed by the "weight of his secret," and sought "by solitary musings" to ease his mind. He read a little, glanced at the scenery along the river, landed and walked around at the different places where the steamer stopped, but kept entirely to himself.

5

CHAPTER VIII.

NOTHING occurred worthy of note until they arrived at Natchez, but here Roch was much amazed to see Maroney's trunk being put on the wharf-boat. He knew it was the custom of the managers of the wharf-boats to allow baggage to be left on the wharf, and to collect a small sum for storage; so he took his satchel and placed it near Maroney's trunk.

He left the boat just in time to see Maroney take the only carriage that happened to be at the river when the steamer arrived, and drive rapidly up the hill. He knew that he could get plenty of carriages in a few minutes, but by that time where would Maroney be? His only sure method was to follow him at once, and trust to finding a conveyance on the hill. He followed as fast as he could, and just as he got to the top of the hill was fortunate enough to meet a negro driving an express wagon. He immediately struck a bargain with him to drive him around town for a dollar an hour.

Roch, in his excitement had dropped his German accent, and spoke uncommonly good English for an immigrant; but the negro, being a very good talker himself, did not remark it. By Roch's direction the driver followed on straight up the street in the same direction Maroney had taken.

Maroney got out of the carriage and went into a store.

It would not do for Roch to wait on the express wagon for Maroney's reappearance. He, therefore, instructed his driver to await his return, and stepped into a store, from which, while he was examining some goods, he could also keep an eye on Maroney's carriage.

What Maroney was doing in the store, was a problem which Roch would have liked to solve.

In about fifteen minutes Maroney came out, and appearing familiar with the town, directed his driver where to take him. He was driven to a comfortable looking house; the negro driver saying something to him, and motioning toward it. Maroney answered, and the hackman drove away, while Maroney went into the house.

Roch was now at a loss what steps to take. The hack driver had not been paid, and in all probability would return for Maroney. If he watched the house, he might be discovered from behind the blinds; so he determined to keep his eye on the hack driver. The hackman drove leisurely down to a saloon, fastened his horses, and went in. Roch opened conversation with his driver, and found that he was a slave, but that he had got permission from his master to hire himself out, for which privilege he paid one hundred dollars a month. After working for some time he had been enabled to purchase the horse and wagon he drove, and as he was making money, hoped in a few years to have enough to purchase his own freedom. Roch concluded he could gain from him some information as to Maroney's driver, so he carelessly asked him if the hack driver was also hired out.

"Yes, sah, him ib my cousin," said Sambo.

Roch supposed the negro must have had his *quasi*

freedom, from seeing him go into a saloon, as the planters never allow their slaves to go into drinking-places; not because they think it immoral, but because the slaves would most likely become unfit for work.

Roch asked the negro if he knew where they kept good brandy.

"Golly, ib you want good licker, dis yer sloon is de place to find it!"

"Drive up, and we will sample some of it," ordered Roch.

Sambo willingly obeyed, and they went into the saloon. Roch again assumed his German accent.   The two negroes at once recognized each other, and Roch, in his broken way, said:

"Vel, poys, vat vill you haf?"

The niggers grinned from ear to ear, and replied:

"De same ab you, boss."

"Barkeeper, you haf any lager got?   Nein?   Och, mine Got, dis ish von h—l of a blace!   Notting put prandy und vhisky!   I pelieves I vill go by Yarmany the steamer next.   Vell, give us dree prandys!   Trink hearty, poys.   Mine frient," continued he, turning to the hackman, "your peesness ish goot?   No?"

"Yes, sah! I always dribes de gemmen what comes on de steamer. Ya, ha! Dey nearly all goes to de same place. Dis mornin' a gemmen come on de steamer, an' say, 'Here, you nigga, dribe me as fas' as you can to Mudder Bink's.' I'se yer man, says I; an' golly, didn't I make dose hosses trabel! I was gwine like de debil when he stop me, an' went to de store. Den I took him to Madam's, and he say, 'Here, Sambo, you jus' go down

"Yah, yah, yah," roared both the darkies. "you don't know Mudder Binks! why she keeps the finest gals in all de riber."—Page 69.

town, an' come fur me in two hours;' an' I's gwine back, an' if dis yer nigga don't get a fiver for his trouble, den dis court don't know itself!'"

"Mudder Beenk's?" exclaimed Roch. "Who vas das?"

"Yah, yah, yah," roared both the darkies. "You don' know Mudder Binks! Why, she keeps de finest gals on all de ribber."

Roch was happy when he heard this, as he was now positive that Maroney was not taking any action to cover up the robbery; so he settled with the expressman, and returned to the wharf-boat to look after Maroney's trunk. He saw that the trunk was still where it had been left, and on going on board of the steamer, found that most of the passengers had taken advantage of their long stay, and were visiting in the town. Roch took a seat on the wharf-boat, near the office. He puffed away at his pipe for some time, staring vacantly around, when he heard a carriage rattling down the hill. In a moment it stopped, and looking up Roch saw Maroney almost leaning over him and conversing with a gentleman in the office.

"Are you the agent of Jones's Express?" he asked.

"Yes," replied the gentleman.

"I thought your office was up the hill. Have you received a package for ————?" (Roch did not catch the name.)

The gentleman looked over his book, and said:

"No, nothing; but it may have been detained in the New Orleans office."

This was the substance of the conversation.

Maroney went into the office and remained some five

minutes, then came out, and seemed debating some subject in his mind.

The first bell of the Walsh was rung. He hurriedly ordered his trunk on board, and embarked, closely followed by Roch, "mit his satchel." They proceeded quietly on their journey until they reached New Orleans, where Maroney secured a hack and was driven to the City Hotel. He passed the day walking around, lost in thought, and studying some subject deeply.

During the day Roch concluded that Maroney was going to make a decided move. But what would it be? He had no one to advise him; none from whom he could seek counsel, and he was at a loss what to do.

In this strait he telegraphed to me, in Chicago, detailing his predicament, and asking instructions. He was much surprised at receiving an answer from Philadelphia, where I then was. I telegraphed him in cipher, congratulating him on his success so far, and told him not to mind the loss of his baggage; but to change his disguise, and rig himself up as a dashing Southerner. Accordingly, the first thing in the morning, he took a bath, had had his face clean shaven, and, going to the clothing and other furnishing stores, soon procured a fashionable outfit.

When he was dressed in his new clothes, what a metamorphosis had he made, from the clod-hopping Dutchman to the gay, genteel and courteous citizen! I telegraphed to him that I thought success was almost in his grasp, and to keep a constant lookout.

He took a room in the City Hotel, and was very much pleased, on coming into the breakfast room, to find Maroney there. He had to look twice before he was certain of his man, as Maroney had also changed his appearance. He had donned a suit of city clothes, had changed the cut of his whiskers, had had his hair cut short, and had altered his entire appearance. Now commenced the chase in earnest.

Maroney walked around the hotel, with his hands in his pockets, occasionally glancing out of the window. Finally he went out on the street and walked rapidly around. He would walk hurriedly up one street, cut across, and come down another, and then pass to the point from which he started, always retracing his steps, and doubling on his track.

The thought at once flashed through Roch's mind that he was endeavoring to discover if he was followed; and, seeing through his movements, Roch took up his position at the base of operations, and, as Maroney started up one street, he waited quietly on the corner, and always found that Maroney would come around past him in a short time. Maroney spent the whole morning at these manœuvres, trying to discover if he was followed, Roch having much the advantage of him, in being able to keep watch of him by walking only a fourth of the distance.

I kept the telegraph working, and Roch would take advantage of Maroney's doublings on his track, to rush to the telegraph office, send a despatch to me, and, in a short time, rush back for the answer. I informed him that I did not believe that Maroney had any suspicions of him, but was keeping a sharp lookout for any of the employés of the Adams Express Company who might know him, and who were numerous in New Orleans. He knew the New Orleans detectives who had been employed

on the ten thousand dollar robbery, and had everything
to fear from them.   He might run across the General
Superintendent of the Southern Division at any moment,
and wished to avoid him if possible.

I impressed on Roch the necessity of the strictest
watch.   I must confess that I felt feverish and excited
at having Roch all by himself watching the movements
of Maroney, in a place of the size of New Orleans, and
if it had been possible I should have placed more men
around him; but that was now out of the question, and
all I could do was to rely on Roch.   I communicated all
the facts, as I received them, to the Vice-President, who
was with me.

In the afternoon Maroney strolled down the street and
turned into the Adams Express office.   Roch knew no
one in the office, and, as this last move of Maroney's
greatly puzzled him, he telegraphed to me for instructions.   I consulted with the Vice-President, and replied:
"Trust no one.   Rely on yourself alone."   Roch got the
answer in about an hour, during which time Maroney
remained in the Express office.

On leaving the Express office, he went to a daguerrean
gallery, remained some time, and then went to the hotel.
On Saturday Maroney again went to the daguerrean gallery and received a package, which Roch supposed contained his pictures.   He telegraphed me to this effect,
and, on a moment's consideration of the incident, I
ordered him to procure a copy of the picture from the
gallery if he possibly could.   From the gallery Maroney
proceeded to the amphitheatre of Spaulding & Rogers,
on St. Charles street, and Roch, feeling certain that he

"As he gaily entered the gallery, flourishing his handsome cane, he was welcomed by a pleasant smile from a young lady, an octoroon."—Page 73.

would remain at least an hour, went to the telegraph office, sent the above despatch, and as soon as he received the answer, went directly to the daguerrean gallery.

He was now the dashing Southerner, and as he gaily entered the gallery, twirling his handsome cane, he was welcomed by a pleasant smile from a young lady, an octoroon, who was the only occupant of the room. Although of negro extraction, it was scarcely discernable, and moreover she was possessed of most engaging manners. Roch entered into conversation with her, in the course of which he asked if his friend who called up the day before, and whom he described, did not have his picture taken. She said he did, and that she had one left, which was not a very good one. Roch asked leave to look at it, and she hunted it up and handed it to him. He immediately recognized it, and giving her a five dollar bill, became its owner. So much for brass. Thanking the lady, and also thanking his stars that the proprietor of the gallery was out when he called, he returned to the amphitheatre. Maroney came out and went to the hotel, where they both took dinner. After dinner Maroney walked up and down the reception room, pondering deeply over some subject, and then took some paper and a pencil from his pocket. Roch watched him closely as he seated himself to write, and concluded that he was trying to disguise his hand-writing. Maroney finished and folded the note, and taking his hat, walked out on the street. As soon as he reached the sidewalk, he began to limp badly, as though it was almost impossible for him to get along. "Strange," thought Roch, "he cannot have met with an accident!" In a short time a colored boy came along. Maroney stopped him, talked to him a moment, then gave him the note and the boy ran off, while he remained in the same place.

What would Roch now not have given to have been able to cut himself in two, leaving one part of himself to watch Maroney while the other followed the boy? This, however, being one of the few things that he could *not* do, he was obliged to let the boy go while he watched Maroney. The affair seemed to have come to the sticking point. Maroney's face showed deep anxiety, and his limping was all a sham. The boy had taken a note to some place, but where, was the question.

In about twenty minutes the boy returned and said something to Maroney, but what it was Roch could not find out. Maroney handed the boy some money and he immediately ran off, while the former dropped his limp, walked to the hotel, and went at once to his room.

CHAPTER IX.

ROCH walked carelessly past the door of Maroney's room and saw him busily engrossed in packing up. He lost no time. Where Maroney was going he did not know. He rushed to the office, paid his bill, went to his room, changed his clothes, and in less than ten minutes issued from the hotel, again the plodding Dutchman. Alladin with his wonderful lamp, could not have brought about a much more rapid transformation. As he reached the sidewalk, Maroney had just stepped into a hack, and he heard him order the driver to get to the steamboat landing as soon as possible. Roch, with his long pipe and old satchel, followed on behind, and the citizens he met gazed in wonder to see a sleepy Dutchman travel at such a rate.

The "Mary Morrison," one of the fast boats of the river, was just casting off from the wharf as they arrived, and they had barely time to get on board. Roch had taken up his old quarters in the steerage, and thoroughly enjoyed the beautiful view as they steamed up past the famous Crescent City. He had now time to wipe the sweat from his brow, and wonder what place Maroney was going to. He concluded that he was going back to Montgomery by way of Memphis. True, it was rather an out of the way route, but such seemed to be the sort that Maroney preferred. He could not tell to what point

Maroney would pay his fare, but as Memphis seemed to be the objective point, he took a through second class ticket to that place. The first one hundred and fifty miles of the journey up the river is though the richest and most beautiful part of Louisiana. This part of the river is known as the coast, and is lined on both sides by waving fields of cane, interspersed with orange groves. Alligators lie basking in the sun, and the whole scene speaks of the tropics. Beautiful as was the country, it had no charms for Maroney. His mind was occupied with other thoughts, and he paced up and down the deck as if anxious to get to the end of his journey.

All went quietly until they reached Natchez, "under the hill," when Roch was again astonished to see Maroney's trunk being placed on the wharf boat. He could not understand this move, but had nothing to do but to follow. Maroney loitered around the wharf-boat, seeming to have no business to attend to, but when the Morrison steamed up the river, he advanced to the agent of Jones' Express, had a brief conversation with him, paid him some money, and an old trunk was delivered to him. Maroney did not seem to place any value on the trunk, and had it put carelessly along with his other baggage. Strange indeed, thought Roch, what can he want with that old trunk? It was an old box, painted black, and thickly studded with nails. It was a shaky looking affair, and did not look as if it would stand much of a chance with a modern "baggage smasher." It had some old tags pasted on it, which showed where it had been. One which was partly scraped off, read Montgomery, another Galveston, and still another New Orleans.

There was nothing to show that it was of any consequence, and Roch looked carelessly at it, as Maroney had left it carelessly on the wharf-boat, along with his other trunk, and sauntered up the hill. Maroney put up at the hotel, still leaving his baggage in charge of the agent of Jones's Express,—who was also proprietor of the wharf-boat.

Roch followed Maroney up town, but, as he did not know when the boats arrived going up or down the river, and as it began to grow dark, he concluded he had better stay on the wharf-boat and keep track of the luggage. Maroney might leave at any hour of the night, as, on the Mississippi it is not an uncommon occurrence for an unexpected boat to land or take off passengers with little or no delay, even at the dead of night. So he got some lunch, and lay around the wharf-boat, as many poor people do while travelling. Maroney did not come down during the night, but Roch felt perfectly easy, so long as he kept the trunks in view.

In the morning a steamer came along, bound down the river. Maroney made his appearance, but paid no attention to the poor immigrant, whom he considered beneath his notice. He had his trunks placed on board, and took passage for New Orleans. Roch was all amazement, and could not understand why such a chase should have been made after an old trunk. He was inclined to think that Maroney must have had some business with the store-keeper in Natchez, but what sort of business he could not determine. He was sure something had been done in New Orleans or at Natchez. It might have been with the *ladies* on the hill, or with the negro and the lame foot. Whatever it was, it was completely covered up.

He managed to telegraph these particulars to me, at one of the places where the steamer stopped, and I instructed him to keep right on, and that I would answer more fully in time.

On arriving in New Orleans, Maroney again put up at the City Hotel, while Roch went to a neighboring restaurant, to get some refreshments, intending afterwards to change his clothes, and make his appearance as the dashing Southerner. He had just finished his meal, when, on looking over to the City Hotel, he saw Maroney getting into a carriage, on which his two trunks were already placed. He rushed out as Maroney drove off in the direction of the depot where passengers take the cars for Pontchartrain, and then go by steamer to Mobile.

He had to make quick time again, and was fortunate enough to secure the services of a negro drayman who had a fast horse. With this assistance he got to the station "on time," and, securing a second-class ticket to Mobile, was soon away on another route.

After reaching Pontchartrain, and embarking on the steamer, Maroney seemed happier than he had yet been, and walked around the deck, singing and whistling, apparently overflowing with good spirits. As his spirits rose, Roch's fell in a corresponding degree. He was unable to understand the cause of this change; everything seemed confused to him, and he did not know what to do. He finally concluded that Maroney had left Montgomery, going to Atlanta, Chattanooga, Nashville, Memphis, etc., merely to see if he would be followed, and now, finding he had not been, he was returning home in a perfectly easy frame of mind.

So much at least had been done. Roch knew that all his actions had met with my approval. I was the responsible party, and if I was satisfied, he was. In the meantime, I was unable to form a definite opinion as to the reason for the change which had evidently taken place in Maroney. There was no denying but that something had happened to give him more courage, and it flashed through my mind : Has he got the money?

I thought nothing about the old trunk, as, if he had had anything valuable in it, he would not have left it so carelessly exposed, at the stations, on the wharf-boat, etc. All I could do was to carry out my old plan : "Watch and wait."

Roch, on the journey to Mobile, took a seat on this identical trunk ; he saw nothing suspicious about the old thing, which was not even locked, but tied up with ropes. Had it entered his mind that the trunk contained the money he was after, the battle would have been a short one. But he knew nothing, positively nothing, which would lead him to suppose that this was the case ; so he had nothing to do but to wait, and wait he did.

On Saturday, the thirtieth day of April, the steamer arrived at Mobile, and the passengers speedily disembarked. At three in the afternoon a steamer started up the Alabama river, for Montgomery, and on this boat Maroney took passage. Among the passengers going to Montgomery were a number of his friends. There were many ladies among them, and he was well received by all of them. He took no notice of his baggage, and his trunks lay carelessly amidst a pile of luggage.

On board all was life and hilarity. Fun and frolic were the order of the day. There were several horse fanciers on board, with whom he was acquainted, and he got into a conversation with them, his spirits rising higher and higher still.

When the boat touched at Montgomery he sprang ashore, where he was welcomed by a crowd of his friends, and gave orders to Porter to have his trunks taken up to the hotel. Porter, during his absence, had been appointed clerk of the Exchange. He was on the wharf when Maroney arrived, and shook hands with him. He told him he was now at the Exchange; that it was the best house in town, and that Mr. Floyd would be glad to welcome him as a guest. Maroney was pleased to hear this, and told Porter that when his trunks came up to the house he would give him some splendid cigars to try — some that he had bought on his trip. Porter saw Roch, but dared not speak to him.

Roch seeing Maroney placed under the espionage of Porter, proceeded to his Dutch boarding-house and gave himself a thorough cleansing.

Porter had a carriage at the wharf, which Maronry and he entered, and drove up to Patterson's. They took a few drinks and then went over to the Exchange, where they arrived just as Maroney's trunks came up. He directed Porter to send the large trunk to his room, but to place the old one in the baggage room, and to mark it plainly with his name, so that no one would take it by mistake.

In the evening Maroney and Porter stepped over to Patterson's and there met Charlie May, a wealthy harness-maker and a very prominent man. He was one of Maroney's best friends and was so convinced of his innocence of the crime he was charged with committing that he had gone on his bail-bond. They went into a private room and had a social chat, interspersed with an occasional drink. Several of Maroney's friends came in and joined the party.

Maroney spoke of the splendid cigars he had bought on his journey, and told the assembled company that when he opened his trunk he would give them a chance to prove their quality. All went pleasantly with him, and Porter was unable to notice any change, with the exception that he was perhaps a little livelier than before.

He recounted the incidents of his journey, the routes he had taken, the places where he had stopped, etc., and Porter found it varied little from the truth. He alluded to the girls he had visited in Chattanooga, said the stock was splendid, described the situation of the house and advised them to pay it a visit if they ever went to the town. He spoke of the fine horses he had seen at Cook's livery stable and of Cook's being a fine fellow. He also spoke of inspecting the live stock in the stables at Nashville and at the pleasant dwelling at Natchez, on the hill, and wound up by declaring he had had a splendid time, and ordering in Champagne for all the party.

In the morning, after breakfast, he told Porter to have the old trunk sent up to his room and he would get the cigars he had spoken about. Porter ordered the colored boy to bring the trunk up, and at Maroney's request went

6

to the room with him to assist in the opening. When the trunk was brought up the negro and Porter took off the ropes and Maroney carelessly opened it. There were four boxes of cigars in it. Maroney opened one of them, took a handful of cigars from it, gave a number of them to Porter to try, and when Porter had lit one, said:

"What do you think of that? don't you call that a splendid cigar?"

Porter admitted it was an unusually fine-flavored weed. Maroney then put some, from each of the boxes, into his pockets, and said he was going to drive out with " Yankee Mary."

Porter having no good excuse for remaining longer, returned to the office, whence he was soon recalled by Maroney, who requested him to have the trunk roped up and placed in the garret, where unclaimed baggage was usually stored. While this was being done, Porter observed the four cigar boxes lying carelessly on the bureau. Shortly after he saw Maroney and Charlie May pass rapidly up the street behind "Yankee Mary."

CHAPTER X.

WE will now return to the North, where we left Mrs. Maroney enjoying herself as the guest of Mr. Moore. Green shadowed her closely, and she did not make a move that was not reported to me. I thought it best to see Mrs. Maroney myself while she was North, and proceeded to Philadelphia for that purpose, bringing George H. Bangs, my General Superintendent, with me. I had concluded to give Mr. Bangs full charge of all the operatives employed in the case. He was to keep fully informed of all the movements of Maroney and his wife, receive daily reports from all the operatives, then daily report to me, and I would direct him how to proceed, and he would transmit the orders to the operatives. I had many other cases under way, and could not devote all my time to this one. Bangs was to remain in Philadelphia, where all the operatives would send their reports. He was a young man of great abilities; he had been promoted from the ranks, and I had full confidence in his capacity. He was cautious — sometimes a little too much so, or more so than I would be, but still with firmness enough to carry him through all emergencies.

The reader knows that I was determined to win. The Adams Express Company had furnished me with all the backing I wanted, and under such favorable auspices, I said, "Win, I must! Win, I shall!" I did not doubt

that Maroney was the thief.   The question now was
How can I find the money?

Philadelphia, at that time, was where the main offices
of the Adams Express were located, and the Vice-President was in charge. I held a consultation with him, and
he advised us to remain in Philadelphia and see Mrs.
Maroney; and while the interview was progressing, a
dispatch came to me, from Green, stating that Mrs. Maroney had left New York for that place. We were all
anxious to see her, but I concluded to send Bangs alone
to the station, as different persons had seen us with
the Vice-President, and it might excite comment if we
all went.

The train arrived in Camden, opposite to Philadelphia,
at eight o'clock in the evening, and Bangs, who was waiting, had Green point Mrs. Maroney out to him. He got
a good look at her as Flora and she stepped into a carriage. She was a medium sized, rather slender brunette,
with black flashing eyes, black hair, thin lips, and a rather
voluptuously formed bust.

Bangs and Green followed her to the Washington
House, on Chestnut street, above Eighth, where she and
Flora went into the reception room. She sent for the
landlord, who assigned them a suite of rooms, and they
retired.

It will be remembered that Maroney was observed to
post a letter while in Memphis. Roch managed to see
the address as it lay on the rack in the hotel, and found
it directed to Mrs. M. Cox, Jenkintown, Montgomery
County, Penn. When I arrived in Philadelphia, I concluded it would be a good plan to find out who Mrs. M.

Cox was, and accordingly detailed Mr. Fox to procure the information. "His orders were : Go slow ; be careful ; be sure not to excite any suspicion." Mr. Fox had been a watch and clock maker, and was a thorough hand at his trade. I provided him with a carpet-sack and the necessary tools, and also a few silver watches, of no great value, which I purchased at a pawn broker's. Thus equipped as an itinerant clock repairer, and having a few watches to "dicker" with, he started on foot for Jenkintown, a small place twelve miles from Philadelphia. He sauntered slowly along with his satchel over his shoulder, going into a farmhouse occasionally, and finally reached Jenkintown. Here he passed from house to house, enquiring if they had any clocks that needed repairing. As he was a good hand, and his charges most reasonable, only twenty-five or fifty cents for each clock, he soon had doctored several. He was of a talkative nature, and drew from the old gossips whom he encountered on his rounds, full descriptions of the members of different families who lived in or around Jenkintown ; and there is no doubt but that he was much better posted as to their business and weaknesses than they were themselves.

Toward evening, having done a good day's work, he went to the tavern, kept by a man named Stemples, and made arrangements to stop with him while in town. He found that a man named Cox lived in Jenkintown, and that he was a carpenter by trade. During the evening he was much surprised to meet Cox at the tavern. Fox was a genial fellow, and, after a paying day's work always made himself agreeable to those whom he met at the tavern where he put up. He had the knack of getting

easily acquainted, and soon was on the best of terms with
Cox and his friends.   He did not force the acquaintance,
but during the evening paid much more attention to Cox's
friends than to Cox.

Fox went through about the same routine the next day,
and toward evening, finding that he had made a dollar
and a half, he packed up his tools and went up to the
tavern.   Here he found Cox and his friends again.   He
told them how successful he had been, and received their
hearty congratulations — they feeling that there was no
doubt but that they would be gainers by his good fortune.
Cox and his friends joined in having a good time at the
tinker's expense, and pronounced him the "prince of
good fellows;" though I much fear, had Fox suddenly
importuned them for a small loan, they would have
changed their tune; but as he did not, "all went merry
as a marriage bell."

Cox had two bosom friends — Horton and Barclay.
They were held together by ties stronger than those which
bind kindred — they were fellow–topers, and could drink
about equally deep.   They generally concluded an evening's entertainment in somewhat the following manner:

Cox would say, "Hic, Barclay, you'r drunk; better go
home, hic."

Barclay would insist that he was never more sober in
his life, but that Horton and Cox were "pos-(hic)-tively-
(hic)-beasley."   All three would then start off, bent on
seeing one another safely home, and, like the blind leading the blind, generally fall into the ditch.   Three irate
women would then make their appearance on the scene,
and they would each be led home, declaring they were

Cox and his friends joined in having a good time at the tinker's expense, and pronounced him "the prince of good fellows."—Page 86.

never more sober in their lives. Fox found that Cox was
known by his friends as Josh. Cox, and he was what
might be called a lazy loafer, as were also his friends.
Horton and Barclay. Fox did not try to get any information from Cox, but got all he possibly could from his
friends, Horton and Barclay, who proved easy talkers and
kept nothing back. He now concluded it was a good
time to find out about Cox. He discovered in the course
of the evening that Josh. had a clock that needed repairs
but did not care to go to the expense of getting it fixed.
So he said: "Josh., you are a pretty good sort of a man,
and I'll tell you what I will do for you; I am not going to
work in the morning, and so I will come down to your
house in the course of the forenoon and fix up your clock
for you and not charge you a cent for the job." Cox was
so much pleased at this liberal offer that he took another
drink at Fox's expense and went home highly delighted.
In the morning Cox called for Fox, and again drinking at
his expense, conducted him to his house and gave him
the clock to repair. Fox now saw Mrs. Cox for the first
time. She seemed a very civil woman and a great talker.
She was of middle stature, with black hair and eyes, and
dark complexion. When I received this description, I
immediately said she must be a relative of Mrs. Maroney's, and so she eventually proved. In the course of
the conversation Fox gleaned that Mrs. Cox had some
relatives living in Philadelphia, which was nothing astonishing, and he got very little information from her. Cox
was out of employment, but expected work soon; his
house was commodious and very neatly kept, and Mrs.
Cox seemed a good housekeeper. Having finished the

repairs to the clock, Fox returned to the tavern, where he found Barclay and Horton, and soon had the glasses circulating. The pleasant liquor caused all the parties to grow familiar, and Fox was regaled with many a rare bit of scandal. He finally spoke of the Coxes from whom he had just returned, and was at once given their history so far as it was known in Jenkintown. The family had been in the town about four years, and had moved there from Morrisville, N. J. Josh. was not inclined to work, and just managed to scrape enough money together to live on. They had three children, and Mrs. Cox was a native of Philadelphia. Fox concluded, from all he saw and heard, that the people of Morrisville would be able to give him full information of the antecedents of the Coxes, and came into Philadelphia on the following day to get instructions. I was perfectly satisfied with what he had done so far, and on the next day sent him to Morrisville. Fox plied his trade in Morrisville with great success, and soon got acquainted with many of its inhabitants. His disguise was a splendid one to travel with, as at that time the clock-maker was welcomed everywhere, and while engaged at his work would amuse his patrons with thrilling stories of his adventures, or with the details of city life. In this way Fox got acquainted with many people who knew the Coxes when they were living at Morrisville, and they unanimously gave Josh. the character of a "ne'er do weel," although there was nothing against him but his laziness. Josh. had lived for three years in Morrisville, and but very little was known of his previous life. His wife was known as a hard-working woman, and that was all that could be learned about her.

Fox discovered, incidentally, that Josh. had a brother living at Centreville, near Camden, in the State of New Jersey. After a while he got around there, travelling all the way by the wagon road, and occasionally repairing a clock on the way. It would not do while assuming his present character to travel by rail.

On getting to Centreville he at once proceeded with his "dickering," being ready to either mend a clock or trade a watch. He found there was a Jim Cox in town who had a clock to fix, so he went to his house and got the job. He entered into conversation with Jim while engaged in repairing the clock, but found him a surly, uncommunicative, unsocial man, but Fox was a thoroughly good fellow and did not mind an occasional rebuff. So he took up the conversation, explained what was the matter with the clock, gave an interesting description on the works of clocks in general, and finally partially thawed Jim out. "By the by," said Fox, "I repaired a clock for a man of your name in Jenkintown; it was in a very bad condition, but I fixed it up as good as new; so I will this one. Do you know this Cox? they call him Josh. Cox.

"Oh, yes!" laughed Jim, "he is a brother of mine!"

"I am glad to hear it!" remarked Fox, "he is a mighty fine fellow! His wife is a very superior woman. Let me see, who was it her sister married down South? She has a sister there, hasn't she?"

"Yes," said Jim.

"Where?" enquired Fox, as he put a pin in the clock.

"I don't remember the name of the place; used to know it. Her husband is agent for the Adams Express at — at — yes — Montgomery! that's it, Montgomery! Don't remember her husband's name."

"You are like me in having a bad memory for names," said Fox, and then, having got the information he wanted, he turned the conversation to other subjects, all the time keeping busily engaged at his work.

He made a first class job of the clock, so that no enquiries should be afterwards instituted, and collecting his bill, slowly wended his way to Camden. From Camden he crossed the river to Philadelphia and reported to me at the Merchants' Hotel. Bangs and I were seated in a private room when Fox came in. After hearing his report I turned to Bangs and said:

"The plot thickens! Every day we are nearing success! We have the woman treed at last, and in the North, among our friends! Depend upon it we shall have the money ere long!"

CHAPTER XI.

ON Saturday I removed to the Washington House, as Mrs. Maroney was still there. I found she did not go out much, seeming to prefer to remain in her room with Flora. Sunday morning I went to the breakfast room with the determination of seeing her, but although I waited and waited, she did not come, and I afterwards found that she had taken her breakfast in her room.

I loitered about the house till after twelve, noon, at which time I was standing near the main entrance when I noticed a carriage drive up and stop. A gentleman alighted and walked into the hotel. In about twenty minutes Mrs. Maroney appeared escorted by the gentleman — a tall, handsome man, about forty-five years old — entered the carriage with him and was driven rapidly off, unaccompanied by Flora.

I was completely nonplussed, as she was gone almost before I knew she was there. As it was mid-day and in the heart of the city, it would not do for me to run after them, as I would soon fall into the hands of the police by having the cry of stop thief raised after me. I felt very much like following and standing my chances, as at that time I was young and supple, but before I could come to a conclusion the carriage was whirled around the corner of Tenth street and lost to view.

I loitered around for some time and then started towards my room. As I reached the head of the stairs, I saw a little girl playing in the hall, and, from the description I had received, concluded that she must be Flora. As she came past me I patted her gently on the head and calling her a sweet little girl, had a few seconds conversation with her. Glancing down the stair-way, I saw a lady looking out from the door of the reception room:

"Oh, my dear!" said I, "there is your ma; she seems to be looking for you!"

"That ain't my ma!" she answered. "My ma has gone for a drive with Mr. Hastenbrook!"

"Oh, indeed! Where is she going?"

"She's gone to Manayunk! You can't catch me!"

And Flora, who was full of fun, darted down the hall.

I had gained a point and I hurried to the Merchants' Hotel, saw Bangs, posted him, and started him off in a carriage for Manayunk to note the actions of Mrs. Maroney and her escort. Bangs soon had them under his eye and was enabled to get a good, full look at her escort, Mr. Hastenbrook. He found, afterwards, that Mr. Hastenbrook was the head of one of the largest shirt manufactories in the city. He carried on an extensive business with the South, and, outside of his business, was known as a great ladies' man. He was very gallant to Mrs. Maroney, and Bangs concluded, from their actions, that they also "loved not wisely."

At five o'clock they returned and Hastenbrook took supper at the Washington House. At supper I had a good full view of them, but neither of them noticed me, as I was dressed in coarse, rough clothes — a common occurrence with me. She little thought how closely I held her fate in my hands. Mr. Hastenbrook remained in her room till after midnight, Flora having gone to bed long before he left.

On Monday morning I left her in charge of Green and went to talk over matters with the General Superintendent. Suddenly Green burst in upon us and said that Mrs. Maroney and Flora had gone to the North Pennsylvania station.

I was much annoyed at his having left her to report and ordered him to go as quickly as possible to the station. If she had gone he must follow her on the next train and get off at Jenkintown. I described Cox and his residence and told him to watch and see if he could not find her somewhere in the neighborhood.

I told the Vice-President that I did not doubt but that Mrs. Maroney knew the particulars of the robbery, and I had some idea that she had the money with her. Jenkintown was a small place, where she felt she could hide securely, and remain covered up for an indefinite time. There, almost directly under our noses, the money might be concealed.

I mentioned the necessity of having a "shadow" sent down to Jenkintown, to watch all her movements, and if she moved to follow her, as we must know all she did. I mentioned that it would be necessary to get into the good graces of the postmaster at Jenkintown, so that we could tell where all the letters she received were post marked, and to whom her letters were directed.

In regard to Mr. Hastenbrook, I thought his attentions were those of a "free lover," but that if he was seen with her again I would have him watched. I drew the Vice-President's attention to the benefits which would result from putting a female detective on, to become acquainted with Mrs. Maroney at Jenkintown, as she would undoubtedly be the best one to draw her out.

At that time I had in my employ, and at the head of my establishment, one of the greatest female detectives who ever carried a case to a successful conclusion. She had been in my employ for two years, and had worked up the cases given her in an astonishingly able manner, proving herself a woman of strong, clear discernment. As she takes a prominent part in bringing to light the facts which follow, and in clearing away the mystery that overhung the disappearance of the forty thousand dollars, a short description of her may not prove uninteresting.

Two years prior to the time of which I am now writing, I was seated one afternoon in my private office, pondering deeply over some matters, and arranging various plans, when a lady was shown in. She was above the medium height, slender, graceful in her movements, and perfectly self-possessed in her manner. I invited her to take a seat, and then observed that her features, although not what would be called handsome, were of a decidedly intellectual cast. Her eyes were very attractive, being dark blue, and filled with fire. She had a broad, honest face, which would cause one in distress instinctively to select her as a confidante, in whom to confide in time of sorrow, or from whom to seek consolation. She seemed possessed of the masculine attributes of firmness and decision, but to have brought all her faculties under complete control.

In a very pleasant tone she introduced herself as Mrs. Kate Warne, stating that she was a widow, and that she had come to inquire whether I would not employ her as a detective.

At this time female detectives were unheard of. I told her it was not the custom to employ women as detectives, but asked her what she thought she could do.

She replied that she could go and worm out secrets in many places to which it was impossible for male detectives to gain access. She had evidently given the matter much study, and gave many excellent reasons why she could be of service.

I finally became convinced that it would be a good idea to employ her. True, it was the first experiment of the sort that had ever been tried ; but we live in a progressive age, and in a progressive country. I therefore determined at least to try it, feeling that Mrs. Warne was a splendid subject with whom to begin.

I told her to call the next day, and I would consider the matter, and inform her of my decision. The more I thought of it, the more convinced I became that the idea was a good one, and I determined to employ her. At the time appointed she called. I entered into an agreement with her, and soon after gave a case into her charge. She succeeded far beyond my utmost expectations, and I soon found her an invaluable acquisition to my force.

The Vice-President placed such full reliance in me that I had no hesitation in giving him the above sketch of Kate Warne, and advising that she be sent to Jenkintown, accompanied by a young lady who should have no direct connection with the case, but simply act as Kate's companion and friend. I knew this would greatly increase the expenses, but, as he well knew, we were now dealing with an uncommonly smart man and woman, and in order to succeed, we must be sharp indeed !

As I had previously said, when a person has a secret, he must find some one in whom to confide, and talk the subject over with him. In this case Maroney had evidently confided the secret of the robbery to his wife, and now, while they were apart, was the time to draw it out. What was wanted was a person who could ingratiate herself into the confidence of Mrs. Maroney, become her bosom friend, and so, eventually, be sure of learning the secret of her overwrought mind, by becoming her special confidante.

I also suggested the propriety of placing a handsome, gentlemanly man at Jenkintown, who should be provided with a span of horses and a handsome carriage, and deport himself generally as a gentleman of leisure. His duties would be to get up a flirtation with Mrs. Maroney, prevail on her to drive out with him, and, if possible, entice her to quiet, little fish-suppers, where he could ply her with champagne, and, under its exhilarating influence, draw from her portions of her secret. A woman of Mrs. Maroney's stamp, while separated from her husband, would most likely desire gentlemen's company, and as she, like most of her class, would put up with none but the handsomest, it was necessary to select as fine a looking man to be her wooer as could be found. She seemed to have already provided herself with a lover, in the person of Hastenbrook, and it was necessary to get some one able to "cut him out."

The company had a gentleman in their employ, named De Forest, whom I thought admirably adapted for this purpose, and if the Vice-President would allow me, I would assign to him the task of becoming Mrs. Maroney's lover. The instructions I would give him would be few and simple, and he need know nothing of the case, further than that he was to go to Jenkintown with a carriage and span of horses, make himself acquainted with Mrs. Maroney, and report daily all that took place.

I had already given Mr. Bangs entire charge of the detectives employed in the case, so that he would remain in Philadelphia, while I would keep up a constant communication with him by telegraph and mail.

The Vice-President coincided with me in all my plans, and said the Adams Express were going to let me have my own way, and that they had unbounded confidence in me. I felt that their placing such entire confidence in a young man like me was indeed flattering, and I was determined to prove to them that their confidence was not misplaced. Having made all necessary arrangements in Philadelphia, I left for Chicago to prepare Mrs. Warne and her friend for the case.

De Forest was given the necessary instructions, and drove out to Jenkintown with his team. He was a man about thirty-five years old, five feet eleven inches in height, remarkably good looking, with long black hair, and full beard and mustache, and in Philadelphia he was known as a perfect "lady-killer."

7

On getting into Jenkintown he put up at the tavern, and made arrangements to spend the summer. He then drove back to Philadelphia, reported to the Vice-President and Bangs, got his trunk, and drove back to Jenkintown.

CHAPTER XII.

D E FOREST loitered around Jenkintown, and found
that a gentleman who owned beautifully laid out
grounds allowed the public to frequent them at certain
times, so long as they did no damage to the walks or
the flowers. The garden was a charming place, and Mrs.
Maroney and Flora would often pass the morning in
strolling through it. De Forest discovered this, and made
the grounds a place of constant resort. The first day or
two, as he passed Mrs. Maroney and her daughter, he
would politely raise his hat to them. Then he would
meet Flora as she ran around the grounds, and by paying
her little attentions, soon caused the mother's heart to
warm toward him, and made the daughter the medium of
forming the mother's acquaintance. At the end of three
or four days Mrs. Maroney remarked to Mrs. Cox:
"What a fine man Mr. De Forest is!" All worked well.

When she went to Philadelphia, Green, who was shadowing her, entirely unknown to De Forest, found that she
frequented a famous restaurant on Eighth street, where
she met Mr. Hastenbrook. In the evening, on her return
to Jenkintown, she always met De Forest and strolled
around with him. What with the gallant Hastenbrook,
with his splendid mustache, on the one hand, and the sentimental De Forest, with his long hair and full beard, on
the other, she had her hands full, and felt that her lot was

cast in pleasant places. We will leave her to enjoy her-self, and turn our attention to Chicago.

On my arrival, I selected Mr. Rivers as the best man to go to Jenkintown, and lie quietly in wait, keeping a sharp lookout on the movements of Mrs. Maroney. He was born and brought up in Philadelphia, and was well acquainted with it and the surrounding country. I gave him full, clear instructions as to the part he was to per-form in this drama of real life, and he started the same day for Philadelphia, where he was to report to Mr. Bangs. I also saw Kate Warne, told her I wanted her to make a trip, and to get ready as soon as possible. She was also to get a Miss Johnson to be her companion.

In the morning she came to me for instructions. I gave her a full history of the case, and of all the steps that had been taken up to the time; described Mr. and Mrs. Maroney, stated that I thought they were not mar-ried, and, so far as pomp and splash made fine society, they frequented it. I then said: "You remember Jules Imbert, of Bills of Exchange notoriety?"

She answered, with a smile, that she remembered him well.

"Then," said I, "you had better assume to be his wife. Mrs. Maroney will most likely wish to remain in retire-ment for some time. She will probably remain in Jenkin-town all summer and spend the winter in Philadelphia. You know all about Jules Imbert's operations, so you will arrange for a permanent stay in Jenkintown, get acquainted with Mrs. Maroney, and when you get thor-oughly familiar with her, make her your confidante, and to show her how implicitly you rely on her friendship, disclose to her that you are the wife of a noted forger, who is serving a term in the penitentiary. As confidence begets confidence, Mrs. Maroney will, most certainly, in time unbosom herself to you."

I described the different persons engaged on the case: De Forest, the lover; Green, the "shadow," etc., and instructed her that not even De Forest was to know who she was or what her errand.

In a few days handsome toilets were ready for Kate Warne — whom we will hereafter know as Madam Imbert — and Miss Johnson. As soon as possible I started for Philadelphia accompanied by the two ladies, and on arriving in the city took rooms in the Merchants' Hotel. Kate Warne felt sure she was going to win. She always felt so. and I never knew her to be beaten.

Mr. Bangs reported that he had sent Rivers on to Jenkintown, where he obtained board in a private family. He pretended that he had a very sore arm, which prevented him from working and obliged him to go up to Philadelphia to get it dressed. As he was doing nothing he concluded he would live in Jenkintown, where board was much cheaper than in the city.

Green had been ordered to Philadelphia to take charge of Mrs. Maroney when she came up to the city, or to follow her if she started on another trip.

Madam Imbert and Miss Johnson drove out to Jenkintown and passed a couple of days at the tavern. They found that the rooms, though plain, were very neatly kept, and that the table was abundantly supplied with good, substantial food. Madam Imbert expressed herself well satisfied with the town, the purity of the air, and its beautiful drives and walks; and as her system had become rather debilitated by a long residence in the South, she thought she would spend the summer there and recuperate her failing health. She made an arrangement with the landlord to spend the summer at his house, drove into Philadelphia and reported to me. She had her baggage sent out, and the following day returned with Miss Johnson and they took up their abode in the tavern.

The reader will observe that Jenkintown is having a large increase made to its population, principally of male and female detectives. Stemples, the landlord of the tavern, had seldom had so many distinguished guests, and visions of Jenkintown becoming a fashionable summer resort floated before him, and he felt that the day was not distant when his humble tavern would, in all likelihood, be turned into a huge caravansary, filled to overflowing with the élite of society.

All went smoothly with De Forest and Mrs. Maroney in their love-making. Every day they met and strolled through the shaded walks of the garden. He lavished a great deal of tenderness on Flora, which he would gladly have bestowed on the mother, and Flora was no more charmed with him than was Mrs. Maroney.

One day, as they strolled through the most secluded part of the grounds, De Forest, with a beating heart, presented a beautiful bouquet to her. Mrs. Maroney accepted it with a pleasant smile, held down her head a little and blushed most charmingly. De Forest was more than elated, he was fascinated. He met me in Philadelphia a day or two after and said with much feeling:

"Why, Pinkerton, why *do* you keep watch of such a

woman? She is the most beautiful, most charming lady
I ever encountered! By heavens! I am in love with her
myself!"

I advised him to be careful, as the woman might be
very beautiful, but still be a serpent! I found he made
a truly devoted lover, and so I had nothing to complain
of in that respect.

When Madam Imbert and Miss Johnson arrived at
Stemples's, the inhabitants of Jenkintown were agog to
know who they were and whence they came. They
evidently belonged to a high class of society, and all sorts
of stories were circulated about them. The taller of the
two ladies was quiet, not given to conversing much, and
was very kind and considerate with the servants at the
hotel.

De Forest had managed to scrape up a slight acquaintance with them at the breakfast table, and when Mrs.
Maroney, who, like everyone else, had heard of their
arrival, casually remarked that she wondered who they
were, he was enabled to inform her that the tall lady was
from the South and that her name was Madam Imbert.

This was enough for Mrs. Maroney, she loved the
South. Maroney was a Southerner, and her heart
warmed toward any one from there, so she determined
to avail herself of the first opportunity of getting an
introduction to Madam Imbert.

She entered into a dissertation on Maroney and his
virtues; did not exactly say that he owned any negroes,
but hinted that he would soon do so. She spoke of
Maroney as a man who had plenty of money. De Forest
turned the conversation from Maroney as soon as pos-

sible, for, to tell the truth, he was as much in love with her as was the gallant Hastenbrook, and "my husband" was a term that grated harshly on his ear.

De Forest learned that she was going into Philadelphia on the following day, and determined to ask her to let him have the pleasure of driving her in. He had the proposition several times at his tongue's end, but held back from uttering it, for fear she should decline. At length he summoned up courage enough to disclose his wish. Mrs. Maroney had a habit of blushing. She blushed very sweetly, and accepted his kind offer with many thanks.

De Forest was now all animation. He went to the tavern, had his buggy and set of harness cleaned and scoured till they were bright as new, and gave orders to the groom to bring up his horses in the morning without a hair out of place. When a lady and gentleman go out for a drive they like to be by themselves, and generally find a child somewhat *de trop.* De Forest sincerely hoped that Flora would not be brought along, but, oh! deceitful man, he expressed a wish to Mrs. Maroney that the darling child accompany them. Mrs. Maroney very much relieved him by deciding that Flora had better remain at home and amuse her auntie, who would be *so* lonely without her!

Bright and early in the morning De Forest was up, and in the stable, seeing that everything was just as it should be about his turn-out. He then dressed himself carefully, ate a hurried breakfast, put on a stylish driving coat, and, jumping into his buggy, drove down to Cox's.

Mrs. Maroney looked perfectly bewitching as she

appeared, dressed in a bright spring costume, and De Forest tingled in every vein, as he helped her into the carriage and took a seat beside her. He grasped the reins, and the handsome bays were off with a bound.

What would have been Maroney's feelings if he could have seen his wife and her gay cavalier?

It was a beautiful April morning; the breeze was fresh and exhilarating; the fields were clothed with verdure, and the trees loaded with buds. From every side the birds poured forth their song. It was the season of love, and who could be more completely " in season " than was De Forest? The roads were in splendid condition, and they bowled along rapidly, carrying on an animated conversation. When they arrived in Philadelphia, De Forest drove to Mitchell's restaurant, opposite Independence Hall, where Mrs. Maroney alighted, and he drove off to stable his horses, intending to return at once and order a hearty dinner.

CHAPTER XIII.

DE FOREST, after stabling his horses, proceeded to the Adams Express Office and reported his success to the Vice-President and Mr. Bangs. He was highly elated, and they laughed heartily to see how well the play worked.

"By-the-by!" said De Forest, "I promised to go right back and meet her. Oh! I almost forgot! two ladies have lately arrived in Jenkintown; I think they are rich, at least the taller one is so reported. Her name is Madam Imbert, and she is from the South. They don't go out much; go to the gardens occasionally, and Mrs. Maroney is anxious to form their acquaintance; I think I will get thoroughly acquainted with them by-and-by."

The Vice-President and Bangs paid no attention to this, knowing that Madam Imbert could take care of herself. They instructed De Forest to attend to his own business, let other people alone, and with this admonition sent him off.

What was De Forest's astonishment on returning to the restaurant to find the *lady* gone! He did not like it, but concluded the only thing he could do was to wait. There are plenty of loafers around "Independence Hall" at any time, day or night, so drinking a mint julep and lighting a cigar, he joined the throng. He fumed and fretted for over an hour and a half, when he saw Mrs.

Maroney coming down the street, looking very warm. He met her and she excused herself by saying that she had called on a lady friend who lived on Spruce street, just above Twentieth, and finding her sick had been unable to get away; that she had walked back very fast and felt completely exhausted.

De Forest felt very sorry, and tenderly said she must not over-exert herself. He then ordered dinner, which was served up regardless of cost, and which they washed down with a few bottles of champagne of the very best brand. They were soon the happiest of friends, and all thoughts of separation had vanished from De Forest's mind.

It is strange what a difference there will sometimes be in reports. About two hours after De Forest made his report, Green came in and reported that according to orders he had "shadowed" De Forest and Mrs. Maroney when they drove into the city.

De Forest had left Mrs. Maroney at Mitchell's and driven off while he remained and kept his eye upon her. She left Mitchell's, walked over to the Washington House and went into a room where she remained for over an hour and a half. She left the hotel with Mr. Hastenbrook, who politely bade her good-bye at the corner of Eighth street, while she went down to Mitchell's and met De Forest, poor De Forest! but, "where ignorance is bliss, 'tis folly to be wise." After dinner De Forest ordered up his horses, and the happy pair, rendered extremely sentimental by the mellowing influence of the wine, started on their homeward journey. They stopped at a wayside inn a few miles out of the city, had a mint julep, and then proceeded on their way home, both very happy, and De Forest decidedly *spooney.*

Rivers had an easy time of it at Jenkintown. He got well in with Josh. Cox and his friends Horton and Barclay. In fact any one with a little money to spend on drinks could easily form their acquaintance. He became so thick with Josh. that Josh. would gladly have taken him into his house as a boarder had it not been for the fact that Mrs. Maroney and her daughter were boarding with him and had taken up all the spare room.

Rivers did not become acquainted with Mrs. Maroney, as she was proud and arrogant, and would disdain to form the acquaintance of any low "white trash" like him. Whenever Mrs. Maroney went to Philadelphia he followed her and excused his frequent absences to Josh. by stating that he went up to get his arm dressed. That arm was indeed a very sore one, and his physician must have made a small fortune out of him alone. When Rivers found that Mrs. Maroney was going into town with her escort, he would go in on the train and get to the outskirts of the city in time to meet them as they drove in. She was generally accompanied by De Forest, who had become her constant attendant. After they reached the city they had to drive slowly, and so he could follow them with ease. De Forest had been ordered to always drive to Mitchell's when he came in with Mrs. Maroney, and Green was there ready to take charge of her when they arrived, relieving Rivers, who would return by the evening train to Jenkintown.

Mrs. Maroney had a great desire to become acquainted with Madam Imbert and Miss Johnson. Madam Imbert appeared very sad, and it was currently reported that she had brought the lively Miss Johnson with her to console her and keep her in good spirits. The desired introduction was brought about by an accident. Mrs. Maroney was taking her accustomed stroll through the pleasure grounds, accompanied by De Forest and Flora. Flora, as usual, full of fun, was running far ahead of her, when she saw two ladies coming down a cross-path. As she turned her head to look at them, still running at full speed, she caught her foot in the grass borders of the walk and was thrown violently to the gravel pavement. The ladies, who proved to be Madam Imbert and Miss Johnson, rushed to her, and the Madam picked her up. Flora had scratched her hands badly, and Madam Imbert had partially bound them up before her mother and De Forest arrived. This led to an introduction, and Mrs. Maroney was not slow in following it up.

The next day Madam Imbert received a call from Mrs. Maroney, who wished to more fully return her thanks for her kindness to her daughter. The acquaintance progressed slowly, Mrs. Maroney making all the advances. There was something about Madam Imbert that seemed to draw one toward her. Mrs. Maroney felt that the Madam was a better woman than she, and that it did her good to pass an hour in her company. As she became more familiar with her, she discovered that Madam Imbert received many letters through the post, and often found her crying over them. The Madam would put them hurriedly to one side, and greet her with a forced smile which showed the efforts she made to hide her grief. Mrs. Maroney deeply sympathized with her, as she compared her own gay and happy life, free from care, to Madam Imbert's, from which every ray of sunshine seemed to have been blotted out.

On one of the trips which Mrs. Maroney made to Philadelphia with De Forest, Rivers, who had headed them off, as usual, at the outskirts of the town, and was following them in, was observed by De Forest. De Forest had seen the man with the sore arm just before they left Jenkintown, and he now noticed him following them from block to block. He had no idea that the man could be following Mrs. Maroney, and supposed he must be following him. The idea flashed into his mind that it must be some inquisitive boor, who was following him merely out of prurient curiosity to see how he conducted himself with Mrs. Maroney. He did not mention the matter to her, but as he saw the man still following him his anger overflowed, and he determined that when he left Mrs. Maroney at Mitchell's, he would find out what the fellow wanted with him. When he arrived at Mitchell's Mrs. Maroney went in, and he drove to the stables with the horses. Rivers met Green here, and turning Mrs. Maroney over to him, came to the office of the Adams Express and reported to Bangs.

Bangs gave him his instructions and he went out of the office by the rear entrance. He saw De Forest in the alley, but as he had nothing to do with him, let him go. He went down Chestnut street, turned into Third, where the cars start from, and, as he had a few hours to spare, determined to see some of his old friends. He had been loafing around about an hour when one of the detectives of the city force stepped up to him, and, tapping him on the shoulder, said : " You are my prisoner."

" What have I done to deserve arrest ? " demanded Rivers, completely dumbfounded.

" Never you mind that ! you're my prisoner, and if you don't come along quietly, you'll pay for it ! " was all the consolation he got from the detective.

" But I haven't done anything," pleaded Rivers.

" There, just shut up, now ! I don't want any of your talk. I know my business, and you're my prisoner ; so just you come along."

Rivers, finding resistance useless, went with him. At the same time he saw De Forest looking on, and seeming to rather enjoy his predicament. As the detective was taking him up Chestnut street toward his headquarters, they passed the Adams Express Office. Bangs happened to step out at this moment, and was much amazed to see Rivers under arrest. They said nothing, but Rivers looked steadily at Bangs, and Bangs at him. Without a moment's reflection, Bangs rushed off to report the arrest of Rivers to me. I was holding a consultation with Madam Imbert and Miss Johnson, at the Merchants' Hotel. Everything was working well, and I felt particularly happy, when Bangs rushed in and dispelled my happiness by stating that Rivers had been arrested. At the news, my heart fairly jumped into my mouth. I had felt success almost within my grasp, and now my plans had fallen through entirely.

The thought at once flashed through my mind that Hastenbrook was at the bottom of the trouble. He must be a friend of Maroney's in disguise. I left Madam

Imbert and the rest of the party at the Merchants' and proceeded to the Adams Express Office, where I met the Vice-President. I informed him of Rivers's arrest, and my fears that Maroney had checkmated me. The Vice-President said that he thought he could entirely remove my fears; that De Forest had come in from Jenkintown with Mrs. Maroney, and had reported to him. He stated that he had fixed a fellow nicely. A fellow had been loafing around Jenkintown for three or four weeks. De Forest had observed him just before starting for the city, and when he reached the suburbs discovered him dogging his movements wherever he went. He drove to Mitchell's, and came over to report, and the impudent fellow still kept on his track. He thereupon went to the city detective's headquarters. The employés of the Adams Express were well known, so that he had no difficulty in getting a detective, and, walking out with him, he pointed out the man, and said he would like to have him arrested, as he had been following him all the morning. The detective kept watch of the man for over an hour, and then, finding that he continued to loaf around, arrested him on the charge of vagrancy and took him to the office, where he had him locked up until he could prefer charges against him.

As may be easily imagined, I felt greatly relieved when I heard this. The ridiculousness of the whole transaction crossed my mind, and as the Vice-President equally appreciated the joke with me, it was some time before we could control our risibles sufficiently to make arrangements for the release of Rivers. I asked the Vice-President if he knew some lawyer whom he could get to volunteer his services in behalf of Rivers. He suggested one, and soon afterward a lawyer called at the detective's office and demanded the charge on which Rivers was held. He found that it was only a nominal one, and effected his release without any one's being the wiser as to his business.

When De Forest returned to Jenkintown that evening, he was greatly surprised to find Rivers there, as large as life, and drinking with his friend Cox as if nothing had happened. De Forest could not tell how he got out, but supposed he must have been let off on paying a fine; all he knew was that the dirty loafer had completely spoiled his pleasure.

We will now leave Jenkintown for a time, and return to Montgomery.

8

MARONEY passed the time very pleasantly. Mr. Floyd, of the Exchange, was on friendly terms with him, notwithstanding the little difficulty they had had in regard to Mrs. Maroney. He had no business to attend to and passed a good deal of time in the office of the hotel, talking with Porter and furnishing him with an abundant supply of good cigars.

Porter was a thoroughly good fellow, and had an inexhaustible fund of stories and anecdotes, some of them rather "smutty," but they were just the sort that suited Maroney, so that they had become the thickest of friends. Sometimes Maroney would take a hand in a social game of euchre at Patterson's, at other times he would take Porter or May out for a drive behind "Yankee Mary," and as they drove along expatiate on her many good qualities.

He seldom went into the express office, as, although he knew the employés well, he felt that when he called they kept a sharp lookout on his movements, and he did not appreciate such courtesy. He would occasionally go into the express car to see the messenger, and it was noticed that he always looked at the money pouch, though at the time nothing special was thought of it.

He seemed never to tire of relating the incidents of his journey, and would raise a hearty laugh by the manner in which he would describe his adventures at Natchez, on the hill, or of his visit to the amphitheatre of his friends, Spaulding & Rogers, in New Orleans. He was, to all appearances, the happiest man in town. He often talked over with Porter, his plans for the future, saying that, after his trial, he intended to go into the livery stable business, and wanted Porter to become his clerk. There was very little talk about the robbery in Montgomery, and when any one would mention it to Maroney, he would say, "You will see how it will end by-and-by," and always intimated that he would sue the company for heavy damages after his vindication by trial. Very little was said about Mrs. Maroney. She had few friends, indeed, yet these few seemed to have warm feelings towards her; most of the ladies seemed pleased that she had gone, leaving Maroney still with them.

Maroney passed a good deal of time in his lawyer's office and seemed to be making elaborate preparations for his trial. He would often walk out on the plank road towards the plantations, and Porter, by great exertions, found that he was attracted by a lovely girl who lived some three miles from the city. He never came into town with her; it would have been considered improper for her to receive the attentions of a married man, and a scandal would have been the inevitable result. There appeared to be nothing wrong between them, and Porter became convinced that it was a genuine love affair. The girl must have known she was doing wrong in permitting attentions from a married man; but Maroney was most enticing when he wished to be, and in this case loved the girl with what he thought a pure love, and easily overcame any scruple she might have in this regard.   He was very friendly with Gus McGibony, the Montgomery detective, and was always willing to do him a favor.

McGibony being the only *known* detective at Montgomery, was considered a big man in his way.   Maroney always treated him as such, played cards with him and called him up to take a drink when he treated.   Gus always spoke in the highest terms of Maroney, and had evidently taken sides in the case, for, when he was asked his opinion in regard to the robbery, he would say that Maroney was bound to win.   In this opinion he was supported by the whole community.

Porter would sometimes talk over the case with Watts, Judd & Jackson, the legal advisers of the company.   They were firmly of the opinion that Maroney had committed the robbery, yet still they must say that there was no proof by which he could be convicted when the case was brought for trial.

Roch was having an easy time of it, for as long as Maroney remained in Montgomery he had nothing to do but smoke his pipe and drink lager.   He was taking a good rest after his arduous labors "shadowing" Maroney on his lengthy tour.   At least the duties would have been arduous to any one but Roch, who, however, rather enjoyed them, and longed to prepare for another chase.

I knew that something decisive must soon be done, as the time set for Maroney's trial was rapidly approaching. We—the Adams Express and I—must move something.

Maroney was evidently preparing for his defense, and all was resting quietly.   As the reader well knows I

had a sharp watch set on the operations at Jenkintown
and on all that occurred in Montgomery.

On the first of May, Maroney announced his intention
of going North on a visit. He was with Porter at Patterson's at the time and seemed to have suddenly formed
the resolution. He said he had consulted with his
counsel and they had informed him that he might as
well go if he wished, as there was nothing to detain him.
He desired to see his wife and a few friends, and so had
determined to make a short visit to the North. His old
trunk, up in the garret of the hotel, amongst the unclaimed baggage, was never looked at.

Every one knew it was Maroney's, and even the colored porter, who sometimes went up into the garret with
Porter, to look up some article that had been sent for,
would say: " Dat's Massa 'Roney's trunk."

The day before Maroney started for the North he
packed up everything he needed for his journey in his
large trunk, and then said to Porter, who was assisting
him : "Let's go up to my old trunk, I still have some
cigars in it, and I think it would be well to get some of
them to smoke on my journey."

Porter sent for Tom, and they all three went into the
garret. Tom unbound the trunk; Maroney took out
some cigars and articles of wearing apparel, and, having
it tied up again, returned to his room. No further notice
was taken of the trunk by any one.

To place me on my guard, Porter immediately telegraphed me, in cipher, of this intended move. The
dispatch reached me in Chicago, and was indeed news to
me. What he intended to do in the North I could not

tell. I thought myself nearly blind in trying to solve the reasons of his movement, and in arranging plans for his reception in the North. What could we do? I was not a lawyer, but understood a good deal of the law, and felt that now was the time to work something in our favor. I soon made up my mind what course to pursue, and started the next day for Philadelphia, to lay my plans before the Vice-President personally; telegraphing Porter to get Roch ready to shadow Maroney. He was to retain his Dutch disguise, as it had done good service before, and had not been "spotted."

I arrived safely in Philadelphia, and found that I had not much preceded Maroney.

On the second of May, Maroney, having everything in readiness for his departure, went to the depot, accompanied by a great many friends, and took the train for the North. Roch had reached the depot before him, and had bought a through second-class ticket to Philadelphia, *via* Baltimore. Nothing of any consequence took place until they reached Baltimore. Maroney came through the cars only twice, seeming to be confident that he was not followed. He took an occasional walk to stretch his legs, but kept quietly to himself the whole of the journey.

At Baltimore Roch was met by Bangs and Green, who relieved him from duty when they got the "spot" on Maroney. They found Roch pretty well exhausted, as he had not slept on the journey, and had been obliged to sit in a very cramped position.

On getting into Philadelphia, Maroney went to the Washington House, while Roch went to the Merchants'

Hotel, where he immediately retired, and had a good long sleep.

At Jenkintown all went quietly. Mrs. Maroney was well loved by De Forest, well "shadowed" by Rivers and Green, and greatly benefited by the pure society of Madam Imbert. She said to Madam Imbert, a few days before the arrival of Maroney: "I am happy to state that my husband will be with me in a few days. I am *so* delighted at the prospect of meeting him once more, as he has been separated from me a great deal. We shall have a splendid time in Philadelphia and New York; perhaps spend the summer in Jenkintown, and then go South, *via* Cincinnati and Louisville; passing through Kentucky and Tennessee, into Alabama, and stopping at all the cities on the way."

On the fifth of May she packed up her trunks, and Flora and she were driven to the Jenkintown station. De Forest offered to take them into the city in his buggy, but the offer was declined, with thanks, and they left for Philadelphia without escort.

At Philadelphia she called a carriage, and, with Flora, was driven to the Washington House. In a short time Maroney arrived, entered his name on the register, and was shown to his wife's room, and the two after an eventful separation, were thus once more united.

Having no need of Rivers's services at Jenkintown, he was called to Philadelphia, to "shadow" the parties there. Madam Imbert and Miss Johnson of course remained.

On the sixth of May, Maroney mailed a letter, which the "shadow" discovered was directed to "William M.

Carter, Locksmith, William st., N. Y."   A note was taken
of this, and as soon as possible Bangs left for New York,
to interview Mr. Carter.   He found that Carter was one
of the best locksmiths in the city, and inclined to be a
good fellow.

Bangs, representing the New York office of the Adams
Express, gave him some jobs, making keys, etc.; and
finally brought him a key to the lock of the pouch used
by the company, and asked him to make two just like it.

Carter said he could make them, and after examining
the key for some time, said: " But stop a little; a friend
of mine, now in Philadelphia, sent me a draft of a key he
wanted made, and it is almost exactly like this!"   Pro-
ducing the draft, he exclaimed, "it is exactly the same!"
He handed it to Bangs, who found it a finely executed
drawing of the pouch key, made by Maroney.   Bangs
paid no attention to this circumstance, but Carter said he
would not make the key, as he did not know to what use
it might be put.   He would return the draft to his friend
and say he could not make it.   Bangs managed to get a
copy of the draft before it was returned.

On discovering this, I saw through Maroney's plan at
once; he wished to have a key made similar to the pouch
key, and introduce it as evidence in his trial that others
than the agents might have keys to the Company's
pouches.   Two days before Maroney met his wife in
Philadelphia, I held a consultation with the Vice-President and Bangs in the office of the Express Co.   I maintained that it was the Company's duty to arrest Maroney.
They had a right to bring suit against an agent of theirs
wherever found.   I urged him to lay the matter before

the Company's counsel in Philadelphia. If we could get
him in prison here all would be well, and the expense
and trouble of following him from place to place would
be entirely avoided. It was our duty to keep him in jail,
where I could introduce a detective, disguised as a fellow-
prisoner, whose duty would be to get into his confidence
and finally draw from him his secret and learn his plans
for the future. I presented my ideas so clearly that the Vice
President was convinced that the plan was a good one,
and he at once saw St. George Tucker Campbell, the
eminent lawyer, laid the whole case before him and asked
his opinion. They looked the whole case over, and he
admitted that my plan was a good one. He said we
might be able to hold Maroney for a short time, but he
really did not think we could long do so. He might be
able to fight it out for three or four weeks, but by that
time Maroney would be sure to effect his release. He
would be so excited over his daily expectation of effect-
ing his release that it would be impossible for me to make
a proper effort to mould his mind to my purpose. He
produced sufficient evidence to prove to me that it would
be bad policy to try my plan in Philadelphia. This was
a crushing blow, and I felt as if a load had been
placed upon my breast. Mr. Campbell left me one ray
of hope by stating that he was not fully posted in the
laws of the State of New York, and that I might be
enabled to carry out my purpose there. Leaving Bangs
in charge at Philadelphia, the Vice-President and I started
for New York. We had a meeting with the President
and other officers of the Company, and determined to
lay the matter before Clarence A. Seward, the Company's

counsellor in New York. He had just been engaged by
the Company, as I had been, and so far had attended
only to some small matters for them. The Vice-President notified him to' meet us at the Astor House, where
the case was laid before him. After looking up the points
of law involved, he decided that we could hold Maroney
in New York. We then instructed him to get the papers
in readiness, so that the moment Maroney stepped into
New York he should be arrested. How happy did I now
feel! All care was gone, the weight of sorrow had been
lifted from my breast as if by the hand of magic: hope
had taken the place of despair, and I returned to Philadelphia with renewed energy and firmness, bound to win
beyond a peradventure.

I now assigned to Green the duty of shadowing Mrs.
Maroney, and to Rivers the duty of shadowing Maroney.
I gave them strict orders to keep separate, and to make
a move only when the persons they were shadowing
moved. After Maroney had washed himself and removed
his travel-soiled garments, he had a long confidential talk
with his wife, played with and caressed Flora, and then
walked out with them on Chestnut street. They proceeded
as far as Eighth, apparently amusing themselves by looking into the shop windows, and then returned and did
not leave the hotel during the evening, passing the time
in their rooms. At eleven they retired, thus allowing
their "shadows," Green and Rivers to retire also.

CHAPTER XV.

SATURDAY, the seventh of May, was a busy one for my operatives. Maroney left the hotel, followed by Rivers, walked around, visited different stores, and finally stopped at the corner of Vine and Third streets. In five or ten minutes, who should come along and meet him but Mrs. Maroney, shadowed by Green? It seemed strange to Rivers that they should have taken this roundabout way of meeting, and he could not understand the reason for it. When Mrs. Maroney came up, Maroney took her arm, and together they walked to the office of Alderman G. W. Williams. They remained in the office some fifteen minutes, and on coming out went directly to the Washington House. In a few minutes they again appeared, accompanied by Flora, and getting into a carriage were driven to the ferry, crossed over to Camden, and took the train for New York.

Rivers, who was the fastest runner, started on a keen run for the Adams Express Office and reported to me that the Maroney family were under way for New York. Bangs was in New York, so I telegraphed to him, informing him of their departure for that city. He immediately found Mr. Seward and had everything in readiness to give them a warm reception.

But what had they been doing at Alderman Williams's?

It was better to find out at once. I supposed ᷉ had been executing some deed. I consulted with the Vice-President about the person most likely to procure the desired information from Alderman Williams. After due consideration, we decided that Mr. Franklin, head of the city detectives, was the best man for the purpose. Franklin had always been square and honest in all his dealings, but I determined not to put too much confidence in him. I am always suspicious of men until I know them thoroughly, or have them employed in my establishment; I therefore instructed Rivers to watch Alderman Williams, and learn all that he could.

The Vice-President sent for Franklin, and employed him to find out what had transpired at the Alderman's. Franklin was a genial man, a good talker, and devoted to his duty. He proved himself to be the best man we could have procured for our purpose. He was well acquainted with Alderman Williams, and strolled along past his office. The Alderman was seated with his feet cocked up on the window-sill, smoking a cigar, and, not having much to do, hailed Franklin as he went by, asking him to come in. Franklin accepted the invitation, and lighting a cigar which the Alderman handed him, took a seat.

The Alderman had witnessed an amusing scene, and, knowing Franklin's fondness for a good story, related it to him. Franklin thought the story a good one, laughed heartily at it, and then told one or two of his own. He finally turned to the Alderman, and said; "I say, Williams, this is rather dry work. What do you say to going

"Franklin gave his orders and the delicious bivalves were soon smoking before them. He called for champagne, and under its exhilarating influence grew wittier and wittier, and kept the alderman in such roars of laughter that he could scarcely swallow his oysters."—Page 125.

down to the restaurant with me, and having some oysters and a bottle of champagne to wash them down?"

Williams, like most Aldermen, was fond of the good things of this earth, and accepted the proposition without waiting for a second asking. He locked up his office, and they went down to the restaurant. Franklin gave his orders, and the delicious bivalves were soon smoking before them. He called for champagne, and under its exhilarating influence grew wittier and wittier, and kept the Alderman in such roars of laughter that he could scarcely swallow his oysters. At length Franklin told a story of a man by the name of Maroney, who had come to the city, and getting into rather questionable company, had been fleeced of quite a large amount of money. He had sought Franklin's aid in ferreting out the thieves, but finding it would be necessary to disclose his name and the circumstances in which he was robbed, and that the facts would find their way into the daily papers, he concluded to bear the loss and say no more about it.

As he finished this little story the Alderman laughed heartily, and remarked: "I'll bet five dollars it is the same man."

"Why, what do you mean?" inquired Franklin.

"Well, a man named Nathan Maroney came to my office yesterday with a wealthy widow, Mrs. Irvin, and I married them. I got a good big fee, too, and I'll bet five dollars he is the same man that called on you. Of course he would not want it known that he frequented such places just as he was going to be married, and so did not prosecute. Don't you see?"

They both laughed heartily, and Franklin, having learned all he wanted to, soon took his departure. He reported to the Vice-President that Maroney had been married the day before, and the Vice-President immediately communicated the news to me.

I hurriedly thought the matter over. I had all the points on Mrs. Maroney that I wanted. I could see that there was some cogent reason for Maroney's marrying Mrs. Irvin. He wanted to place her where she would tell no stories. There were only two ways to do this. Maroney, the thief, had either to murder his mistress, or to make her his wife. I could see plainly through the whole transaction. Maroney, after committing the robbery, had, in exact accordance with my theory, found that he needed some one in whom he could confide, and with whom he could ease his overburdened mind by disclosing the facts of the robbery. Who could be a safer person than his mistress? Her interests were identical with his; he had gained her the entrée to good society; had taken her from a house of infamy, where she was shunned and scorned, and by allowing her the use of his name, had placed her in a position to *demand* respect.

In all things she seemed devoted to his interests, and so far as he knew, her conduct while with him had been beyond reproach. What could be more natural than his selecting her and pouring into her ear the details of his crime?

How well it must have made him feel to find in her not a stern moralist who would turn from him with scorn and point to the heinousness of his crime, but a sweet enthusiast, with ideas moulded to suit his, who would encourage and renew his feelings of ultimate success and almost rob crime of its horrors!

What a happy moment it must have been to her to hear Maroney give vent to his pent-up feelings! How she must have looked forward with delight to the coming time when Maroney, rich with his ill-gotten spoils, should place her in a position *far* above what she had ever anticipated reaching! How her eyes must have flashed as she thought how she could then return with redoubled force the scorn that had been shown to her! She had only one more step to take and then her life of shame would be completely covered up: Maroney *must* marry her!!

She now had him in her power; she would be true to him if he would be to her; but if he *refused* her request to make her an honest woman in the eyes of the world, woe be to him!!

> " Hell hath no fury like a woman scorned."

She did not at once force the matter on Maroney, but waited until she reached the North, and then gradually unfolded to him the necessity of his marrying her. It was a bitter pill for him to swallow, but unless he chose to add murder to his other crimes, was his only means of safety.

The necessity was rendered all the more distasteful by the fact that he was now really in love with a girl who possessed all the qualifications which render the sex so dear to man. He had formed a plan to get rid of his mistress, Mrs. Irvin, as soon as possible after his trial, and then to marry the girl he loved, but he was doomed

to disappointment. As he had not the courage to kill
Mrs. Irvin, he had been forced North to marry her. He
therefore was determined to kill two birds with one
stone, and while North have some keys made to fit the
company's pouch.

I sat for some hours in the office of the General Superintendent, cogitating over the matter, and finally concluded to have the notice of the marriage published. I
wrote out the notice in the usual form and sent it to the
Philadelphia Press. It read :

"MARRIED.

"MARONEY — IRVIN — At Philadelphia, on May 7th,
1859, by Alderman G. W. Williams, Nathan Maroney, of
Montgomery, Ala., to Mrs. Irvin, of Jenkintown, Penn.

"Montgomery papers please copy."

I sent copies of the *Press* containing this notice to all
the Montgomery papers, enclosing the usual one dollar
note to pay for its insertion in their columns, and in a few
days the news was blazoned forth in Montgomery. But
I had not finished with it yet. I got the names of all the
ladies with whom Maroney was acquainted in Montgomery and the surrounding country, also of all his male
friends, and, buying a large number of the *Press* containing this notice, I had copies directed to these persons ;
and also to his friends in Atlanta, Chattanooga, Nashville,
Memphis, Natchez, New Orleans and Mobile, not forgetting the *highly respectable* ladies at the pleasant house at
Chattanooga, or at Natchez, on the hill. These papers I
sent to Porter by express, directing him to mail them.
Wherever I could learn of any of Maroney's friends, I

furnished them with copies of the *Press.* They must have thought some one very kind to take so much interest in him, or more likely thought he had sent them himself. I knew I was making capital for the company by having the notice so fully circulated in Montgomery. The inhabitants were amazed when they saw it, and terribly indignant at Maroney's conduct.

While it was true that Maroney and his wife had never mingled much in society in Montgomery, still he had brought a woman there and openly lived with her as his wife, who had not only led a life of infamy prior to her meeting with Maroney, but who, even then, was but his mistress. It was an outrage upon decency, and as such was felt and resented. From Maroney's personal popularity and agreeable manners, there were many who believed in his innocence, still more who did not desire his conviction. His marriage thinned the ranks of the latter and entirely wiped out almost every trace of the former. The man who would live with and introduce a prostitute as his wife, was regarded as never too good to be guilty of robbery or any other crime.

The sympathy which had been felt and expressed for Maroney by those who regarded him as fighting single-handed against a wealthy and powerful corporation, was now regarded as having been worse than thrown away. It was at once and permanently withdrawn. My move had proved a perfect success and I now felt much easier about the result of the final trial to be held in Montgomery.

We left Maroney, his wife and Flora on the cars, bound for New York, to enjoy their honey-moon. They were

9

shadowed by Green, and he noticed that Mrs. Maroney appeared supremely happy. She had accomplished her purpose; she was now a legally married woman. Maroney was in good spirits, but must have had a hard battle to keep them up. He was now enjoying some of the sweets of crime, being forced to leave the girl he loved and marry a common prostitute. He had sold his freedom for gold, and although outwardly he appeared calm and happy, inwardly he was racked with contending emotions. What would he now not have given to be back in his old position, free from the taint of crime, free to do as he wished? But the fatal step had been taken; he could not retrace it, he must go on, and when he won, as he now felt sure he would, could he not find some quiet way to get rid of his wife? They were rapidly nearing Jersey City, and when they reached there Mrs. Maroney grasped Maroney's arm, and taking Flora by the hand, walked aboard the ferry-boat. No newly-married bride ever felt more exultant than she. She glanced with scorn at the hurrying crowd, and as they roughly jostled her, felt contaminated by the touch. They little dreamed of the reception that awaited them in New York. The news of their marriage had been flashed over the wires to Bangs, and he had made all preparations to give them a warm reception. Bangs had called for Mr. Seward, and he having all the papers ready, drove to the Marshal's office. Seward was a great favorite with every one, and had no trouble in getting United States Marshal Keefe and a deputy to accompany him. They were all engaged when he called, but readily postponed their other business to attend to him. They, with Bangs, proceeded to the ferry

"You are my prisoner!" said he. "Nathan Maroney, I demand that you immediately deliver to me fifty thousand dollars, the property of the Adams Express Company."—Page 131.

and crossed over to Jersey City, to meet the train coming
from Philadelphia.

When Maroney and his wife stepped on the ferry boat
they did not notice the consultation of Green, Bangs and
Marshal Keefe. When the boat touched the wharf in
New York, all was hurry and bustle. Maroney, with his
wife and Flora, stood one side for a few moments, waiting for the crush to be over, and then stepped proudly
out for the wharf. He had taken scarcely three steps on
the soil of New York before he was confronted by Marshal Keefe.

"You are my prisoner!" said he. "Nathan Maroney,
I demand that you immediately deliver to me fifty thousand dollars, the property of the Adams Express, which
you feloniously have in your possession."

If a thunderbolt had fallen at his feet he could not
have been more astonished. The demand of the Marshal, delivered in a loud, harsh tone, and coming so
unexpectedly, completely unnerved him, and for a moment he shook like a leaf. His head swam around, and he
felt as though he would drop to the ground. By a desperate effort he gained control of himself. His wife hung
speechless on his arm, while little Flora grasped her
mother's dress, and gazed with a startled, frightened look
at the Marshal and the rapidly gathering crowd.

"I have no money belonging to the Express Company!" said Maroney, and supposing that that was all
that was wanted with him, he attempted to force himself
past the Marshal.

"Not so fast!" exclaimed the Marshal, taking hold of
one of Maroney's arms, while his deputy stepped forward

to assist him, if Maroney made any resistance. "Not so fast, you must come with me!"

Maroney could scarcely realize his situation; it was to him a horrid dream. In a few moments he would awake and laugh at it. But the jeering crowd, the stern officers of the law, his weeping wife and her frightened child, formed a scene which was indelibly stamped on his memory never to be obliterated. His wife insisted that her husband should be allowed to accompany her to the Astor House, and the Marshal finally consented. At the Astor House he saw his wife and Flora in their room, in the presence of Marshal Keefe, his deputy, and Bangs. No words passed between them. His new-made bride of only six hours was bathed in tears — what a honeymoon! Maroney was almost in tears himself, but he choked them back. He kissed his wife and Flora, and motioning to the officers that he was ready, followed them to Eldridge street jail.

How terribly must he have felt when the heavy door of his cell was bolted upon him, and he was left in solitude to brood over his position. How he must have cursed the moment when he married Mrs. Irvin. He did so merely to save himself, and now he was in prison! What would he not have given to undo what only six hours before he had been so anxious to consummate! What a blow it would have been to him if he could have known the efforts I was then making to disseminate through the South the news of his marriage; but this I did not intend he should know. Mrs. Maroney thought that Maroney would soon be out of jail, but wondered why he had been arrested in New York. She concluded that the

Company had determined on the plan of suddenly con-
fronting him and charging him with the crime, hoping
that if guilty he would break down and make a confes-
sion. He had passed through the trying ordeal unscathed
and most likely would be liberated in the morning. She
little thought they had been separated never more to be
united.

CHAPTER XVI.

M R. SEWARD had done his work well. I had little fear that Maroney would get out, as his bail was fixed at one hundred thousand dollars — double the amount of the robbery.

The question now arose : What shall we do with Maroney? I held a consultation with the Vice-President, Seward, and Bangs, and suggested the propriety of placing one of my detectives, named White, in jail with him. White was in Chicago, but I could send for him and have him in readiness for the work in a few days. White was a shrewd, smart man to act under orders, and nothing more was required. I proposed that he be introduced to to the jail in the following way : He was to assume the character of a St. Louis pork-packer. It was to be charged against him that he had been dealing largely in hogs in the West, had come to New York with a quantity of packed pork of his own to sell; and also had had a lot consigned to him to sell on commission ; he had disposed of all the pork, pocketed all the proceeds, and then disappeared, intending to leave for Europe, but had been discovered and arrested. The amount involved in the case should be about thirty-seven thousand dollars. It was part of my plan to introduce a young man, who should pretend to be a nephew of White's, and who should call on him and do his outside business. I had a good man for this work, in the person of Mr. Shanks. His duties would be to call at the jail daily, see his uncle White, carry his letters, go to his lawyers, run all his errands, etc.

White was not to force his acquaintance on Maroney, or any of the prisoners, but to hold himself aloof from them all. He was to pass a good deal of time in writing letters, hold hurried consultations with his nephew and send him off with them. Shanks was to be obliging, and if any of the prisoners requested him to do them favors, he was to willingly consent.

Very few people outside of a prison know how necessary it is to have a friend who will call on prisoners and do little outside favors for them. No matter how popular a man may be, or how many true friends he thinks he has, he will find if he is thrust into prison, that all of them will very likely desert him, and he will then keenly feel the necessity of having some one even to run his errands. If he has no friend to act for him, he will have to pay dearly for every move he makes. A man like Shanks would soon be popular with the prisoners, and have his hands full of commissions.

There were a good many objections made to my plan, but with Mr. Seward's assistance, all its weak points were cleared away, and it was made invulnerable.

I telegraphed, ordering White and Shanks to come on to New York, and, leaving Bangs in charge there, I started in a few days for Philadelphia.

Green was still employed in "shadowing" Mrs. Maroney, and kept a close watch on her movements. On the morning after Maroney's arrest she visited him in the

Eldridge street jail, leaving Flora in the Astor House. They had a long, private interview, after which she enquired of the Marshal the amount of bail necessary to effect her husband's release.   He informed her that the bail had been fixed at one hundred thousand dollars.   She seemed surprised at the large amount, returned and conversed with Maroney, then left the jail, and getting into a carriage, was driven to Thirty-first street.   Green hailed a passing cab and followed at his ease.   When she stopped, he had his hackman drive on a few blocks and turn down a cross street, where he stopped him.   He told the driver to await his return, and getting out of the hack, walked slowly down the street, keeping a sharp lookout on the house she went into.   Mrs. Maroney remained in the house about half an hour, and then came out and was driven to Pearl street. Here she went into a large building occupied by an extensive wholesale clothing establishment, remained some time, and then came out with a gentleman who accompanied her to the Eldridge street jail.   Green remained in his carriage.   Mrs. Maroney and the gentleman soon came out; he bade her good-bye, and she drove to several business-houses in the city.

Maroney received several calls during the day: he was very irritable, and seemed much depressed in spirits.

Mrs. Maroney returned to the Astor House at dark, weary, depressed, and despondent.

Green reported to Bangs that it was easy to read what she had accomplished.   Maroney had a number of friends in New York, and she had been to see if they would not go on his bail-bond.   They had all refused, some giving one excuse, some another, and the desired bail *could not be procured.*

For the purpose of finding his prospects, I had some of his friends interviewed, and managed to learn that the friend on whom Maroney principally relied to furnish bail, was one whom he had met in the South when he was a drummer, but who had now become a partner in the house.

Mrs. Maroney called on him; he expressed great sympathy for Maroney and her, but could not go on his bond, as the articles of association of the firm forbade any of the partners signing bonds, etc. In two days it was discovered that Maroney had no prospects of getting the required bail. Some of his friends, whom he importuned to assist him, called at the express office to find the reasons for his incarceration. They were generally met by the President or by the General Superintendent and informed that Maroney had robbed the company of ten thousand dollars at one time and forty thousand dollars at another, and it was for this that he was now in prison. The gentlemen saw at once the risk they would run in going his bail and concluded not to venture.

I was convinced that if the public knew he had stolen fifty thousand dollars and that the company were bound to prosecute him, he could not procure bail, and so it turned out.

Mrs. Maroney called at the jail several times and did everything in her power to procure bail, but finally gave up in despair. She had a long interview with Maroney, then drove to the Astor House, paid her bill, and, getting into a carriage with Flora, went to Jersey City and took the train for Philadelphia.

I had sent Roch to New York to "shadow" her and had brought Rivers to Philadelphia with me, as no shadow was needed for Maroney. When Mrs. Maroney left New York, Green turned her over to Roch and he accompanied her to Philadelphia. I had been informed of her departure and had Rivers ready to meet her in Camden on her arrival.

She arrived safely. Rivers relieved Roch and he reported to me. I supposed she would remain for the night in Philadelphia, but was disappointed, as she went directly to the North Pennsylvania station and took the cars for Jenkintown.

I was not quite prepared for this move, but by four in the morning I was in a buggy on my road to Jenkintown. When I arrived I put up at Stemples's, had an early breakfast, and seized upon a favorable opportunity to have a short conversation with Madam Imbert. I hurriedly instructed her to try and meet Mrs. Maroney, and if possible draw from her an account of what had happened and learn her plans for the future. I then got into my buggy and drove back to the city. It was a beautiful, bright morning, and the drive was very delightful.

Madam Imbert, accompanied by Miss Johnson, went for her accustomed stroll in the garden. They walked around for some time and were about returning when they met Mrs. Maroney and Flora. Miss Johnson took charge of Flora, who was her special favorite, and drew her to one side to have a romp while Mrs. Maroney and the Madam strolled along together.

Mrs. Maroney asked very anxiously about the Madam's health and seemed to be much pained when she learned that she was very poorly.

"Mrs. Maroney," said Madam Imbert, "I fear you find me poor company, indeed. Your life must be happy beyond expression. You have a kind husband, a sweet child, everything that makes life enjoyable! while I am separated from my dear husband, far away, with no one to love me! no one to care for me! I have bitter trouble, rendered all the harder to bear by the fact that I have to brood over it alone. I have not one friend in this wide world to whom I can fly for consolation. No! not one! My life is unspeakably lonely. You will forgive me for not being more gay; I cannot help it! I strive to be, but it is impossible. I often fear that my melancholy has a chilling effect on those around me, and that they think me cold and heartless!"

"Madam Imbert, my dear Madam, don't say that you are thought to be cold and heartless! Every one feels that you are suffering some great sorrow, and all are drawn towards you. As for me I have always tried to secure the sympathy of my lady friends, but I have only half succeeded. You are the first one in whom I have ever felt that I could confide, the first whom I wished to be my friend. If you are in trouble and feel the need of a friend, why not rely on me? make me your confidante."

"Mrs. Maroney, you do not know what you ask! My story is a sad one, indeed. I already value your friendship too highly to risk losing it. If you were to know my history, I fear you would turn from me in disgust."

Madam Imbert's tears flowed freely; she leaned on

Mrs. Maroney for support. Mrs. Maroney turned into one of the side paths and they took a seat on a bench. After much persuasion, Madam Imbert was prevailed on to disclose her secret.

She described to Mrs. Maroney the many virtues of her husband; told how wealthy he was, and then, with many sobs, and much apparent reluctance, stated that he was enticed into committing forgeries; that he was arrested, tried, convicted and sent to the State prison for ten years, and that now she was debarred from seeing him.

She was greatly relieved when she found that Mrs. Maroney did not turn from her in horror on discovering that she was the wife of a convict. On the contrary, Mrs. Maroney said :

" It was *too* bad, indeed ! "

She had suffered also, worse even than Madam Imbert, as her husband was innocent. Things looked bad for him at present, but all would be bright by-and-by. They had plenty of friends, but when they wanted them, they were not to be found.

She said that she was going South soon, but did not intend to stay long. She did not say that her husband was in jail, but merely that he was in some trouble.

Madam Imbert replied that it was very hard ; that there seemed nothing but trouble in this world, and they were both shedding tears copiously, when who should come in sight but De Forest ?

De Forest was truly in love with Mrs. Maroney. He had heard that morning that she had returned, and, finding that she was in the garden, had started in pursuit of her, and arrived at a most inopportune moment. As he came in view, Mrs. Maroney exclaimed: "Here comes that awkward fool! He is such a hateful creature! I'd like to poison him!"

De Forest came gaily along, expecting to be received with open arms, but instead found both the ladies in tears. "O ladies, what's the matter? Crying!" The ladies said nothing, but Mrs. Maroney gave him a scornful look which made him tremble. He had, however, broken up the interview, and the party separated, Madam Imbert saying that she would call in the afternoon.

De Forest walked off with Mrs. Maroney, but he found that she had changed wonderfully, and he got nothing from her but cold looks and sharp answers. He could not understand her conduct, and the next day came into the Express Office, and mournfully reported that Mrs. Maroney had acted in a manner he could not understand, and that he feared some one had cut him out.

Rivers kept a close watch on Mrs. Maroney, and in the afternoon called at the house to see Josh. He found the house in confusion, and an improvised washing of Mrs. Maroney's and Flora's clothing going on. Josh. was carrying water, and doing all he could to help the washing along. "D—d busy to-day," said he; "the old woman got an idea into her head to wash, and although I protested against it, I had to give in and haul the water."

"Oh!" said Mrs. Cox to Josh., "you are always in my way."

Rivers took this as a rather broad hint to him that he was in the way, and so asked Josh. to come up town with him. Josh. willingly acquiesced, and they started out. On the way they met Barclay and Horton, and adjourned

to Stemples's. Rivers treated, and then endeavored to
find out from Cox the reasons of his wife's hurry and
bustle. Cox told him that his wife had taken a sudden
notion to wash, and although he had strongly objected,
she had impressed him into the service, and set him at
work doing the chores and hauling the water.

Rivers tried to get more explicit information, but could
not. Cox, with all his shiftlessness, knew when to hold
his tongue; and so, after plying him with several drinks,
Rivers was obliged to let him go, without finding out
what he wanted. Rivers felt that something important
was under way. He had followed Mrs. Maroney on her
hurried journey to Jenkintown; had seen her hold a long
confidential interview with Madam Imbert, which was
broken up by the unwelcome appearance of De Forest,
and knew of the preparations going on at Cox's. So he
was on the alert.

CHAPTER XVII.

IN the afternoon Madam Imbert called on Mrs. Maroney, leaving Miss Johnson at home. Mrs. Maroney met her kindly, and poured into her ear a tale of sorrow. She told Madam Imbert that she was going South for a short visit, but that she would soon return, and then they could comfort each other. She did not mention where she was going, or allude in any way to Montgomery.

Madam Imbert did not deem it good policy to ask questions too closely, and, although she very much wished to get information, she remembered my strict orders against running any risk, and did not ask.

In the evening Rivers went up to Stemples's and took a seat in the bar-room, as it was the best place to gain information of what was going on. He had not been long there before Josh. Cox came in and asked for Stemples. "He is in the stable," said Rivers; "I will go and get him for you."

"No," said Cox, "don't disturb yourself," and started for the stable himself.

Rivers very politely accompanied him, but was unable to overhear what was said, as Cox drew Stemples to one side and spoke to him in a low tone. Stemples said, "All right!" and Cox started off. Rivers stopped him, and asked him to take a drink.

"I don't mind if I do," answered Josh.; and after

drinking he said : "I am in a d—d hurry," and was gone. "There is one drink gone to no purpose," muttered Rivers, as he made his way to the barn. He found Stemples hurriedly harnessing up his team, and turned in to help him.

"Strange fellow, that Cox!" remarked Stemples. "He wanted to get my team and not let me know where he was going. I told him he could not have it if he did not say where he was going, and he then said he was going to Chestnut Hill, a few miles this side of Philadelphia, but I'll bet he is going into the city. He said he would have the team back before morning, so I finally consented to let him have it."

This was startling news to Rivers. There were no horses in the town that he could hire, and he had no time to harness them if there had been. He managed to see Madam Imbert, and reported to her his predicament.

"They are going into the city," said she, "and you must follow them at all hazards, even if you have to run every step of the way."

Rivers had no time to lose. Stemples's team was at the door, and in a few minutes Josh. came for it and drove down to his house. Mrs. Maroney and Flora were waiting for him, and, as he drove up, got into the wagon, while Josh. hoisted up their trunks.

Rivers had no conveyance, but he was determined not to be outdone; he was young and athletic, and as they drove off he started after them on a keen run. He knew he had a twelve-mile race before him, but felt equal to the task. The night was very dark, and he had to follow by sound. This was an advantage to him, as it compelled

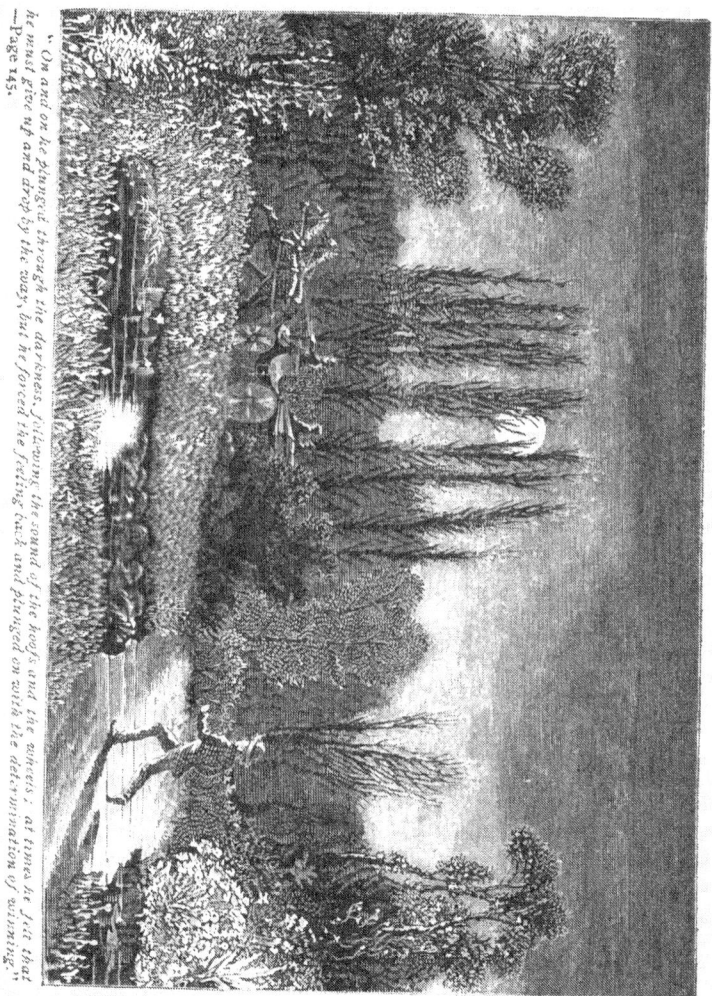

" On and on he plunged through the darkness following the sound of the boys and the *arreers* ; at times he felt that
he must give up and drop by the way, but he forced the feeling back and plunged on with the determination of winning."
—Page 145.

Cox to drive somewhat slower than he otherwise would have done, and rendered it impossible for them to see him from the wagon. On and on he plunged through the darkness, following the sound of the hoofs and the wheels. The moments seemed to have turned to hours; when would they ever reach the city? At times he felt that he must give up and drop by the way; but he forced the feeling back, and plunged on with the determination of winning. When they reached the outskirts of the city Josh. reduced his speed, so that Rivers easily followed without attracting attention. Josh. drove to the corner of Prime and Broad streets, to the depot of the Philadelphia, Wilmington and Baltimore Railroad, and assisted Mrs. Maroney and Flora to alight. As usual, there was a great crowd at the depot, and Rivers, mixing with it, followed Mrs. Maroney and Flora to the ticket-office without being observed by them, and went close enough to them to hear her ask for tickets to Montgomery. Rivers knew no time was to be lost; it was a quarter past ten, and the train left at ten minutes past eleven. He rushed out of the depot, where he saw Josh. getting the baggage checked, and hailing a hack, said to the driver: "Here is a five-dollar bill for you if you will drive me to the Merchants' Hotel and back in time to catch the train."

"All right," said the driver, and springing to his seat he put his horses to a full gallop, and whirled off toward the hotel.

Bangs had run down from New York the same evening to consult me on some matters, and he and I were sitting in a room at the Merchants', smoking our cigars, preparatory to retiring after a hard day's work, when Rivers

10

rushed in, and gasped out: "Get Roch up. Mrs. Maroney and daughter are on the train bound for Montgomery."

We threw our cigars out of the window, and had Roch up, dressed as a Dutchman, his trunk packed, and he into the carriage with us on the way to the P., W. & B. R. R. before he was fully awake. I turned out all the money I had with me — not a great deal, as it was so late — and rapidly gave him his instructions as we drove along. We arrived at the station just in time. Roch rushed to the ticket office, said "Second-class, Montgomery," received and paid for his ticket, and sprang upon the last car of the train as it slowly drew out of the station. There were no sleeping-cars at the time, which was fortunate for him, as, if there had been, he might not have been allowed to get on the train. In a moment the train disappeared in the gloom, and Mrs. Maroney and Flora were kindly provided with an escort, in the person of Roch. Leaving them to pursue their journey, we will now return to Maroney, in the Eldridge street jail.

White and Shanks soon came on from Chicago, and Bangs gave them full instructions as to their duties. White was ordered to follow his instructions implicitly, and not to attempt to move too fast. Bangs arranged a cipher for him, to be used in his correspondence, and he learned it thoroughly, so as not to need a key.

Having thoroughly posted them, Bangs turned his attention to procuring the arrest of White. He secured the services of a common, one-horse lawyer, and placed the case in his hands. The lawyer felt highly honored at being employed in a case of such magnitude, involving thirty-seven thousand dollars, and remarked that he would soon have Mr. John White secure in prison. He procured the necessary papers and placed them in the hands of the Marshal to execute.

Bangs knew just where White was to be found, but gave the Marshal a big job before coming across him. He searched the hotels, saloons, lawyers' offices, etc., going up to the different places, peeping in, and then going off on not finding him. He was doing an immense business hunting for White. Toward evening White was discovered talking to Shanks. The Marshal took him into custody and conducted him to the Eldridge street jail. Shanks, being a stranger in New York, accompanied him, so that he might know the place afterwards. White was booked at once, and while going along with the jailer was asked whether he wished to go to the first or second-class, the jailer judging that he would not take the third-class. The first-class was composed of those fortunate mortals who had money enough to send out to the neighboring restaurants and order in their meals. Of course Maroney was in the first-class, so White followed suit. He gave the jailer the usual *douceur* for introducing him to the prison, and then had his cell pointed out. White sent Shanks, who had accompanied him so far, to fetch his carpet-bag and some clothes. He then retired to his cell to meditate over his painful situation.

He glanced around amongst the prisoners, and soon picked out his man. Maroney did not seem to be doing any thing particular, but sat musing by himself. In this manner, brooding over their misfortunes, White and Maroney spent the evening until the hour of retirement. The next day White kept by himself, pondering over what he should do. In the course of the day his nephew, Shanks, who was a young man of about twenty, came with the satchel, and made himself very useful to White by carrying several messages for him. Some of the prisoners noticed this and asked White if he would not let his nephew do little outside favors for them. White said "Certainly, I shall be only too happy to assist you in any way I can."

Shanks was soon such a favorite with the prisoners that he greatly reduced the perquisites of the jailor. Maroney gradually became quite familiar with White. He would bid him good morning when they were released from their cells, and take an occasional turn in the hall with him. They were shut in together, and it became necessary to get acquainted. White wrote frequent letters to his lawyer, who was Bangs, under another name, and received regular replies, Shanks being the medium of communication. This was a great convenience, as lawyers are not always able to visit their clients when they wish them to. Maroney appeared to have few friends. Mrs. Maroney had gone, and he had no one to pay him regular attention. A few friends would call occasionally, but their visits seemed prompted rather by curiosity than by a desire to assist him, they gradually grew fewer and farther between, and finally ceased altogether. He received letters from the South, from Mrs. Maroney, who was on her journey, and from Charlie May, Patterson, and Porter, at Montgomery. These friends kept him well posted. The letters sent by Porter were copies of those I sent him, and were on the general topics of the day. Porter said he was sorry to have to address him in

Eldridge street jail, and wished he could be of some assistance to him. He alluded with anger to the report which had been circulated of his, (Maroney's) marriage. Of course all his friends at Patterson's knew he had been married for years, and that the report was a dodge of the Express Company to make him unpopular. Outside of his friends at Patterson's, every one in Montgomery seemed to believe the slander, and many said they always thought there was something wrong about Mrs. Maroney, and they expected nothing better from her. Many, also, said they had a poor opinion of him and believed he had committed the robbery. Porter concluded by stating that McGibony, the detective, seemed completely non-plussed, and had but little to say about the matter. He, (Porter) had conversed with him, and McGibony seemed of the opinion that it was a move of the Adams Express to place him in an odious position with the inhabitants of Montgomery.

After the receipt of this letter, Maroney appeared to be exceedingly down hearted. White noticed it, and so reported to Bangs. As Mrs. Maroney had not yet arrived in Montgomery, she was of course entirely unaware that the news of their marriage had been spread broadcast, and her letters were quite cheerful.

White was occasionally drawn into a game of cards. Euchre was the game generally played; he was well able to hold his hand, and seldom lost. The stakes were generally for the cigars, or something in a liquid shape, and the supplies were brought in by Shanks. Maroney would sometimes take a hand, but it was a careless habit with him, and he did not care how he played. As time passed away the prisoners became well acquainted, and would talk over the various reasons for their imprisonment. At certain times of the day they would be visited by their lawyers. Maroney had no lawyer engaged, but keenly watched those that came, in order to see which was the smartest, so that he might know whom to employ should he require one's services. Maroney was a smart man, and he gradually came to the conclusion that a lawyer named Joachimson would be the right man for him. White observed that he began to nod to him, and that they always exchanged the compliments of the day. This was as far as he went at present, it being evidently his intention not to employ counsel until Mrs. Maroney returned from the South. At least these were his thoughts so far as White could fathom them.

Leaving Maroney for the present, we will glance at Jenkintown. Here everything was quiet; in other words, quotations were low and no sales. Madam Imbert had little to do. She walked in the pleasure grounds with Miss Johnson, or called at Mrs. Cox's, with whom the Madam was now on the best of terms. Mrs. Cox had a number of children and the Madam often bought them little presents and exerted a kindly influence over them. Whenever Miss Johnson and she met Josh. on the street they would notice him, and the attention would make him feel quite proud. De Forest acted the same as before, and was becoming rather sweet on Miss Johnson. Madam Imbert was sad and melancholy, and repelled all his advances with quiet dignity. We will leave them to enjoy their easy times, having to make only two reports a week, while we follow Mrs. Maroney and Roch.

CHAPTER XVIII.

NOTHING worthy of record occurred on the journey and they arrived at Montgomery in due time.
Roch telegraphed to Porter from Augusta, Ga., that they
were coming, and he, having been previously informed
of the fact, was, of course, at the station to meet them.
He was now Maroney's bosom friend, and as such paid
much attention to Mrs. Maroney. He met her at the
depot with a carriage when she arrived, and conducted
Flora and her to the Exchange Hotel and gave them a
room.

The difficulty with Mr. Floyd had been smoothed over
and she soon felt at home. But something strange
seemed to have taken place in Montgomery. Porter, of
course, paid her great attention and gave her one of the
best rooms the house afforded ; but all the ladies she met
during the day passed her very coolly. The gentlemen
were all friendly, but not so cordial as usual. She could
not understand it.

She did not go out much the first day, but called up
the porter, and, going to the garret with him, pointed out
the old trunk and had him take it down to her room.
The following day she called at Charlie May's. Something unusual must have happened, as she left there in
bitter anguish. The house was near the hotel and Porter
had seen her go in and come out. She wore no veil and

the traces of her grief were plainly visible.   She returned
to the hotel and went to her room.   Porter, in a short
time, stepped up, knocked at her door and enquired of
Flora how her ma was.   Flora said her ma was not well,
that she had a bad headache.   He was bound to get in,
so he pushed past the child and saw Mrs. Maroney lying
on the bed crying.   Being the clerk of the hotel, his
coming in would not be considered unusual.

He enquired if there was nothing he could do for her,
and she said no.   He surmised what had happened and
concluded he could find out all about it at Patterson's.
He went over to Patterson's and met Charlie May.
Charlie said that Mrs. Maroney had called on his wife,
but had been roughly handled — tongued would be the
proper word.   Mrs. May informed her of what she had
read and otherwise heard about her getting married at
this late date.

Mrs. Maroney denied the report and declared that they
had been married in Savannah long before; that they
had afterwards lived in New Orleans, Augusta, Ga., and
finally had settled in Montgomery.

Mrs. May replied that it was useless for her to try and
live the report down; that the ladies of Montgomery had
determined not to recognize her, and that she had been
tabooed from society.   Mrs. May grew wrathful and
warned Mrs. Maroney to beware how she conducted herself toward Mr. May.

Mrs. Maroney rose proudly from her chair, and giving
Mrs. May a look that made her tremble, said:

"Mr. Maroney is as thoroughly a gentleman as Mr.

May or any one in Montgomery, and he is capable of protecting himself and me."

She then flounced out of the house and returned to the hotel.

She remained in her room all day, but on the following morning went to the office of her husband's counsel, where she remained some time, and then returned to the hotel.

Porter was summoned to her room, and on going up she asked him if McGibony was around. Porter said he presumed he was at the Court House. Mrs. Maroney then said :

"I would like to see him! My poor husband is in trouble and I need the assistance of all his friends, not but that he will eventually prove himself innocent and make the company pay him heavy damages for their outrageous persecution! but he is, at present, in the hands of the enemy. If he were only in the South, it would be very different. Here he would have many kind friends to assist him; there he has not one who will turn a finger to help him. Mr. Maroney and I are aware of the scandal that has been spread about us, but we will soon put our timid friends to the blush. They think it will be hard for Maroney to fight a wealthy corporation like the Adams Express, and, instead of helping him, seem inclined to join the stronger party. With them 'might makes right,' and when Maroney gains the day, how they will come crawling back to congratulate him and say, ' We always felt that you were innocent.' O Mr. Porter, it is a shame. Why is Maroney held a prisoner in the North, when he should be tried before a jury of his fellow South-

erners? What will not money do in this country? But
I will show the Adams Express that they are not dealing
with a weak, timid woman. I have just been to see my
husband's counsel and have made arrangements to get a
requisition from the Governor of Alabama on the Governor of New York to have my husband brought here. I
want McGibony to go North and bring him down. Of
course he would not attempt to escape, but it will be
necessary to keep up the form of having him in the
charge of an officer, and I think McGibony the proper
man to send. If McGibony will not go I shall have to
ask you, Mr. Porter, to execute the commission."

Porter, not having any orders how to act, said: "I
will think the matter over, and have no doubt but that
McGibony will be well pleased to go. There is only one
difficulty, and that is, he may not have the necessary
cash."

"That need not deter him," she replied, eagerly. "I
have plenty of money, and will gladly pay him all he
asks."

"I will find him and bring him to your room," said
Porter, as he walked away.

He went down stairs and immediately telegraphed to
Bangs, in cipher, informing him of all he had learned,
and asking for instructions in regard to acting as Mrs.
Maroney's agent in bringing Maroney to Montgomery.

Bangs held a consultation with the General Superintendent. The reasons for Mrs. Maroney's trip South
were now plain, and it was necessary for the company's
counsel at Montgomery to give the matter immediate
attention. The General Superintendent telegraphed to

Watts, Judd & Jackson of Mrs. Maroney's intended coup d'état, and ordered them to take the necessary steps to checkmate her, while Bangs ordered Porter to avoid acting as Mrs. Maroney's agent.

In the meantime Porter found McGibony, and conducted him to Mrs. Maroney's room. He learned that Charlie May and Patterson had come up during his absence. Mrs. Maroney made her desire known to McGibony, and he at once accepted the commission. She thanked him, and remarked that she hoped to have all in readiness in a few days.

Charlie May was very attentive to her, and she seemed to thoroughly appreciate him, although his wife had treated her so *cavalierly* the day before.

After dismissing the rest of the party she had a long, private conversation with Patterson. In an hour Patterson came down and went to a livery stable where "Yankee Mary" was known to be kept, and soon after Mrs. Maroney had an interview with the proprietor of the livery-stable. Porter had become one of the clique, and found that Maroney had a large interest in the stable. "Yankee Mary" was Maroney's own property, and his business with the livery-stables in Chattanooga and Nashville was to examine and buy horses for his stables in Montgomery. In a couple of days Maroney's interest in the stable was disposed of to Patterson, and the money paid over to Mrs. Maroney. "Yankee Mary" was not sold, and still remained the property of Maroney.

All these transactions Porter duly reported to Bangs, and Bangs to the Vice-President. They decided to secure "Yankee Mary" for the company, and Watts, Judd &

Jackson were instructed to attach her. This they did, and she changed hands, being afterwards cared for in the stables of the Express Company.

Flora was much neglected, as Mrs. Maroney devoted all her time to business. She was continually out in the company of Charlie May, Patterson, the livery-stable keeper, Porter, or McGibony.

At last it was announced by her counsel that the "die was cast," and the requisition refused ; so McGibony was spared the trouble of going North. The Governor of Alabama came to the conclusion that he could not ask the Governor of New York to deliver up a man who was a prisoner of the United States government, charged with feloniously holding money, until judgment was rendered against him. Mrs. Maroney found she could do nothing in Montgomery, so she packed up and, with Flora, started for Atlanta. Porter had Roch at the depot, and as soon as she started, she was again under the care of the Dutchman. At Atlanta she put up at the Atlanta House, while Roch took quarters in a low boarding-house. He watched closely, but was careful not to be seen, or to excite suspicion. Mrs. Maroney and Flora remained in the hotel, not coming down, for twenty-four hours. She was, no doubt arranging something, but what, was a mystery.

What she did will be eventually disclosed. The first notice Roch had of her movements, was when she came out of the hotel with Flora, and was driven to the depot. He had just time to get to his boarding-house, pay his bill, seize his satchel, and get upon the train as it moved off. Mrs. Maroney acted much as her husband did when he left Chattanooga so suddenly. "They are as alike as two peas," thought Roch; "both are secret in all their movements, and make no confidants."

But *the eye of the detective never sleeps,* and Maroney and his wife were always outwitted. While they greatly exulted over their shrewdness, the detective, whom they thought they had bewildered, was quietly gazing at them from the rear window of the "nigger car."

Roch found that Mrs. Maroney had bought a ticket to Augusta, Ga.; but before reaching that city, she suddenly left the train at Union Point. There was a train in waiting, which she immediately took, and went to Athens. Roch knew nothing about the country they were passing through, and was following blindly wherever she led. They had not gone far on their new route when Athens was announced. Roch saw Mrs. Maroney getting Flora and herself in readiness to leave the train. When the cars stopped at the station Flora and she got out, stepped into an omnibus, and were taken to the Lanier House. Roch followed, and when they entered the hotel, went to a restaurant and got some refreshments.

Athens was a thriving inland town. After Roch had finished his meal he strolled around, and finally arrived in front of the Lanier House. Puffing away at his pipe, he took a seat on the verandah. Here he mused for some time, apparently half asleep, when he was aroused by the clattering of hoofs and the rumbling of wheels, and looking up the street he saw a stage approaching. It drew up in front of the hotel, and a knot of people gathered around it. While the horses were being changed, the driver rushed into the bar-room to take a drink. Roch listlessly looked at the hurry and bustle, but suddenly sprang to his feet, and almost dropped his inseparable companion—his pipe—from his mouth, for whom should he see escorted from the hotel, and assisted into the stage, by the landlord, with many a bow and flourish, but Mrs. Maroney and Flora? Her baggage was not brought down, so that he was certain she would return. He had no time to think over the best plan to pursue, but determined to accompany her at all hazards.

The driver came out, mounted his seat and Roch got up beside him. It must be admitted that he was badly off for an excuse to account for his movements, as he knew nothing of the country, and did not know where the stage was going. The driver was a long, lank Southerner, burned as brown as a berry by the sun. He always had a huge "chaw" of tobacco stowed away in the side of his left cheek, and, as he drove along, would deposit its juice with unerring aim on any object that attracted his attention. He was very talkative, and at once entered into conversation with Roch "Wal stranger, whar yar bound?" was his first salutation.

Roch looked at him in a bewildered way, and then said, " Nichts verstehe ! "

"Whar are yar gwine? Are yar a through passenger, or whar are yar gwine?"

"Vel, I vish to see de country. I vil go mit you till I see von ceety vot I likes, und den I vil get out mit it!"

"Oh!" said the driver, in a patronizing tone, "yar parspectin', are yar?" And so they kept up a conversation, from which Roch gleaned that the stage was bound for Anderson's Court House, S. C. Whenever the driver would ask a question he did not like to answer, he would

"Wa, stranger, whar yar boun'," was his first salutation. Rich looked at him in a bewildered way, and then said,
"Nichts-verstehe."—Page 158.

say, " nichts verstehe," and so tided over all his difficulties. The passengers, one lady and three gentlemen
besides Mrs. Maroney and Flora, amused themselves in
various ways as they drove along. The gentlemen
smoked and conversed, and the other lady seemed very
agreeable ; but Mrs. Maroney did not say a word to any
one but Flora. Roch as he occasionally glanced over his
shoulder at her, observed that she seemed to be suffering
from much care and anxiety.

Eight miles out from Athens the driver stopped to
change his horses, and Roch took advantage of this circumstance to get a little familiar with him. He found
this an easy matter. A few drinks and some cigars to
smoke on the road — which he treated him to — put him
in such a good humor that he declared, as they drove off,
that it was a pity his German friend was not a white man.
Roch wondered if all the negroes spoke German, but
said nothing.

They drove along through a rich agricultural country
until they arrived at Danielsville, about sixteen miles
from Athens. Here Mrs. Maroney touched the driver
and asked him if he knew where Mrs. Maroney lived.
Oh ! thought Roch, now I see her object in coming here.
The driver knew the place well, and drove up to a handsome mansion, evidently the dwelling of a wealthy planter.

Mrs. Maroney and Flora left the coach and walked up
through a beautifully laid out garden to the house; a two
story frame, with wide verandahs all around it, and buried
in a mass of foliage. She was met at the door by a lady,
who kissed both her and Flora, and, relieving her of the
satchel, conducted them into the house.

Roch in his broken way told the driver that he liked the appearance of the town so much that he thought he would stop over. They drove up to the tavern and Roch asked the driver in to have a drink with him. As they went into the bar-room they met the clerk, and Roch politely asked him to join them. He informed the driver that he might go back with him in a day or two. The driver did not pay much attention to what he said, as all he really cared for was the drink. After the stage left, Roch entered into conversation with the clerk, and, under pretense of settling in the town, made enquiries about the owners of several places he passed on the road. Finally he asked who the handsome residence on the hill belonged to. "That is Mr. Maroney's place. He is one of the 'solid' men of the town; worth a great deal of money; has some niggers, and is held in high esteem by the community, as he is a perfect gentleman."

In the evening he dropped into a saloon, where he formed the acquaintance of several old saloon-loafers, who were perfectly familiar with everybody's business but their own, and from them gathered much useful information of the surrounding country, and had the clerk's opinion of Mr. Maroney fully endorsed.

Roch was up early in the morning and strolling around. He met an old negro who informed him that the stage for Athens would be along in three hours. He sauntered carelessly to Mr. Maroney's, and watched the house from a safe position, but, as the blinds were closed, could see no signs of preparation within. He therefore returned to the tavern, with the determination of keeping a watch on the stage. He had waited about an hour, when a gentleman walked up the steps to the stage office, which was in the tavern. He heard the clerk say, "Good morning, Mr. Maroney," which immediately put him on the alert.

"Good morning," responded Mr. Maroney. "I want to secure three seats in the stage for Athens; want them this morning." Securing his tickets, he went home, leaving Roch once more at his ease, as he now knew exactly what move to make. When the stage drove up, he called in the driver, stood treat, and again took a seat beside him. The clerk told the driver to call at Mr. Maroney's for some passengers, and they started off. Mr. Maroney, Mrs. Maroney and Flora were at the gate when they drove up, and all three entered the stage and went to Athens. At Athens they stopped a short time at the Lanier House; sent their baggage down to the depot, and took the train on the Washington Branch Railroad, which connects with the main line at Union Point. Mr. Maroney bid them good-bye, and returned to the Lanier House. The train consisted of only one car, and Roch had to take a seat in the same car with Mrs. Maroney, but he went in behind her, and took a seat in the rear of the car, so that he remained unnoticed.

Mrs. Maroney was very restless, and after they took the through train at Union Point, would carefully scan the features of all the well-dressed men who entered the car. She seemed to suspect every one around her, and acted in a most peculiar manner. In a short time they reached Augusta, Ga., where Mrs. Maroney and Flora left the train and put up at the principal hotel. It was late when they arrived, so that they immediately took supper and retired. Roch found a room in a restaurant,

11

and after his supper strolled through the hotel, but discovered nothing, as Mrs. Maroney and Flora remained
quiet in their room.

The following afternoon Mrs. Maroney and Flora left
the hotel, accompanied by a gentleman, and once more
started for the North. The gentleman accompanied them
to Wilmington, N. C. During the whole of the journey,
Mrs. Maroney acted, metaphorically, as if sitting on
thorns. She did not seem at all pleased at the attention
paid her by the gentleman. When he would ask her a
question she would glance at him with a startled frightened look, and answer him very abruptly. She seemed
much relieved when he bade them good-bye. Roch was
sitting in the rear of the second-class car and could keep
a strict watch on her movements. Not a person got on
or off the train whom she did not carefully observe.
Two or three times during the night she fell into a restless sleep, but always started up with a wild look of agony
in her face. Day or night she seemed to have no peace,
and by the time they reached Philadelphia she had become
so haggard and worn as to appear fully ten years older
than when she started.

Roch telegraphed to Bangs from Baltimore, informing
him of the time he would arrive in Philadelphia, and
Green and Rivers were at the station to relieve him —
Green to "shadow" Mrs. Maroney and Rivers to see
what disposition would be made of her baggage, and if he
found it transferred to Jenkintown to follow it and be on
hand there when Mrs. Maroney arrived. Roch went to
the office and reported to Bangs. He said that he had
never seen so strange a woman; she had acted on the

whole journey as if troubled with a guilty conscience. He felt confident she had something concealed, but could take no steps in the matter until he was absolutely certain, beyond a doubt, that his suspicions were correct. My orders were clear on this point — never make a decisive move unless you are positive you are right. If you are watching a person, and *know* he has something concealed, arrest him and search his person; otherwise, no matter how strong your suspicions, do not act upon them, as a single misstep of this sort may lose the case, and is certain to put the parties on their guard, and in a few minutes to overthrow the labor of months.

CHAPTER XIX.

WHEN Mrs. Maroney left the cars at the corner of Prime and Broad streets, she accidentally ran across De Forest, who was in the city on some business of his own.

"Oh! I am so glad to meet you," exclaimed Mrs. Maroney.

"And I am delighted to hear you say so," replied De Forest.

The poor fellow had missed her sadly. She had parted from him in anger, and he felt cut to the quick by her cold treatment. He had at first determined to blot her memory from his heart, and for this purpose turned his attention to Miss Johnson, and tried to get up the same tender feeling for her with which Mrs. Maroney had inspired him, but he found it impossible. He missed Mrs. Maroney's black flashing eye, one moment filled with tenderness, the next sparkling with laughter. Then Mrs. Maroney had a freedom of manners that placed him at once at his ease, while Miss Johnson was rather prudish, quite sarcastic, and somehow he felt that he always made a fool of himself in her presence. Besides, Miss Johnson was marriageable, and much as De Forest loved the sex, he loved his freedom more. His morals were on a par with those of Sheridan's son, who wittily asked his father, just after he had been lecturing him, and advising

him to take a wife, "But, father, whose wife shall I take?"
Day after day passed wearily to him; Jenkintown with-
out Mrs. Maroney was a dreary waste. He felt that
"Absence makes the heart grow fonder," so when Mrs.
Maroney greeted him so heartily he was overjoyed.

"Have you been far South?" he asked.

"Yes, indeed? Flora and I have not had our clothes
off for five days, and we are completely exhausted; what
a fright I must look!"

"You look perfectly charming! at least to me you do,"
fervently answered De Forest. "Let me have your baggage transferred to the North Pennsylvania Railroad. In
that way you can send it to Jenkintown without any
trouble. You and Flora honor me with your company to
Mitchell's, where we will have some refreshments, and
then I will drive you home in my buggy."

After a little persuasion Mrs. Maroney consented to the
arrangement, and De Forest, once more himself, got their
baggage checked to Jenkintown, and calling a hackman,
as he had left his own team in the stable, they were
driven to Mitchell's. Green followed them up and
watched them from the steps of Independence Hall,
while Rivers mounted the baggage-wagon and was driven
to the North Pennsylvania station, and in less than an
hour was in Jenkintown. De Forest ordered a substantial
meal at Mitchell's, and when they had finished it, ordered
his team and drove gaily out of the city, closely wedged
in between Mrs. Maroney and Flora.

When he went to get his team he hurriedly reported to
the Vice-President that he had Mrs. Maroney at Mitchell's, and that her former coolness had vanished. As they

drove up to Cox's, Mrs. Maroney was much pleased to meet Madam Imbert and Miss Johnson. The ladies bowed, and Mrs. Maroney requested the Madam to stop a moment, as she had something to tell her. Madam Imbert told Miss Johnson to walk on home, while she went to Cox's, and was warmly embraced by Mrs. Maroney. How De Forest envied her! De Forest drove up to the tavern with his team, and the rest of the party went into the house, where they were cordially welcomed by Mrs. Cox.

Mrs. Maroney said she was tired almost to death, but wanted a few moments' conversation with the Madam before she changed her clothing. "Madam Imbert," she said, "you don't know how happy I am to meet you. I have just come from the South, where all my husband's friends are. He is now in deep trouble, and is held a prisoner in New York, at the instigation of the Adams Express Company, who charge him with having robbed them of some fifty thousand dollars. They charge him with committing this robbery in Montgomery, but hold him in New York. I went South for the purpose of getting a requisition for his immediate return to Montgomery. When I got there I was much surprised to find that nearly all his influential friends had taken the part of the company, and I now return almost crazed, without being able to get the necessary papers, and my poor husband must languish in jail, I don't know how long."

"Mrs. Maroney, I can sympathize with you thoroughly. When my husband was prosperous we had hosts of friends — friends whom I thought would always be true to us; but the moment he got into trouble they were gone, and the only friend I now have is the abundance of money he left me."

"In this respect I cannot complain," replied Mrs. Maroney, "as my husband gave me money enough to support me a lifetime; but it is so hard to be separated from him! I am fortunate in having found a friend like you, Madam Imbert, and I trust we may spend many hours together. I must write a letter to my husband to let him know I am again in the North."

"I will take it down to the postoffice for you," said Madam Imbert.

"Oh, no, I thank you, I will not put you to the trouble; Josh. is going down to Stemples's, and he will post it for me."

Madam Imbert could not well stay longer as Mrs. Maroney seemed very tired. So she bade her good-bye, Mrs. Maroney promising to call on her the next day.

She was not satisfied with what she had accomplished, and feared that Mrs. Maroney had some secret arrangement under way. As she walked musingly along, she met Rivers in a place where no one appeared in sight.

"Rivers, I wish you would keep a sharp lookout on Cox's to-night. I think they are up to something, but what, I can't find out. Will you?"

"Certainly," replied Rivers; "I am pretty well tired out, but I can stand it for a week, if necessary."

"There is another thing which ought to be attended to," said Madam Imbert. "Mrs. Maroney is writing a letter to her husband; I think it is an important one. Don't you think you could manage to get possession of it ?   She is going to send it to Stemples's by Josh., so you might get him drunk and then gain possession of it."

"Leave that to me.   I think I can work it all right," said Rivers, as they separated, no one being aware of their interview.

Rivers went to Stemples's, and calling up every one in the bar-room, asked them to have a drink.   Barclay and Horton were there, and as they swallowed their liquor, looked at each other and winked.   Horton whispered : "Rivers is a little 'sprung' to-day."

" D—d tight, in my opinion," replied Barclay.

In a few moments Josh. came in, and in a very important tone asked for Stemples.

"Stemple sout ! Hellow, Josh., that you ? " said Rivers, slapping him on the shoulder.   "I've taken a leetle too much bitters to-day, but I'm bound to have another horn before I go home.   Come and have something ? "

"Where is Stemples ? " reiterated Cox.

"Oh, he's up stairs.   Come and have a drink ? "

Josh. willingly assented, and with Barclay and Horton they went up to the bar.   Rivers seized the whisky-bottle as the barkeeper handed it down, and filled his glass to the brim.   Josh., Horton, and Barclay took moderate quantities of the liquor.   "Drink hearty, boys," said Rivers, "I am going to have a good horn to go to bed on."

Josh. looked closely at him, and then turned and winked knowingly to Barclay and Horton. The moment he turned, Rivers changed glasses with him, emptied out nearly all the liquor that Cox had put into his glass, and filled it with water.

"Here, boys, drink hearty! Ain't you going to drink up?"

Thus admonished, all four raised their glasses and drained them at a draft. Josh. swallowed down the brimming glass of pure whisky without a wink, and it must be admitted that, to his credit as a toper, he never noticed the difference. They had two or three drinks on about the same basis before Stemples came down.

Josh. was standing with the letter in his hand ready to give it to him when he came in. When Stemples came in Rivers snatched the letter from Josh's hand and said:

"Here, Stemples, is a letter for you!" and handed it to him.

Cox was in a condition not to mind trifles, and scarcely knew whether he did or did not give the letter to Stemples. So long as he had it, that was all he wanted.

Rivers, quick as a flash, had read the direction on the letter: "Nathan Maroney, Eldridge Street Jail, New York."

Stemples took the letter and placed it carelessly in a pigeon-hole, behind a small, railed-off place just at the end of the bar. Josh. started home with Barclay and Horton. Rivers accompanied them a short distance and then returned to Stemples's. He looked through the windows and saw that the bar-room was completely deserted. He peered around and found that both Stemples and the barkeeper were in the stable harnessing up the horses, bent on going to a ball at a neighboring town. He glanced around in all directions until he was sure there was no fear of detection, and then stealthily entered the barroom. He noiselessly crossed the floor, went behind the railing, pulled the much desired letter from the pigeon-hole and, with his treasure, returned safely to the street without detection.

He returned to his boarding-house, procured a lamp and went directly to his room. He then dexterously opened the letter in such a manner that no trace was left to show that it had been tampered with, and tremblingly proceeded to read it, filled with the hope that the mystery would be solved by its contents. He read as follows:

"MY DEAR HUSBAND:— I know it will pain you to learn that a notice of our marriage has been published in Montgomery. It has caused a great many of our old friends to turn away from us, among others Mrs. May, who was the first one to inform me, and who grossly insulted me and fairly ordered me out of her house. Who could have spread the news? I think the only true friend you now have in Montgomery is Mr. Porter. Patterson swindled me in the bargain for the livery stable, and Charlie May is, you know, as variable as the weather in the North; but Mr. Porter did me many kind turns without seeking to make anything out of me. Flora and I arrived in Jenkintown this afternoon thoroughly tired out. I could not get the requisition. I will write fully to-morrow or the next day.

"I have all safe in the trunk. Left ——— at hotel in Athens. I afterward found it convenient to alter my bustle and put paper into it and strips of old rags. It set well, but I was tired when I got home with it.

"Your loving wife."

Rivers scribbled off a copy of the letter and then sealed it up again. He walked back to Stemples's and found a party in the wagon waiting for the bar-keeper to close up and go to the ball with them. Rivers, still pretending to be drunk, staggered up to the door of the bar-room, which was just about to be closed, and walked in. There was no one present but the barkeeper; the people in the wagon were yelling to him to hurry up.

"Give me a drink," said Rivers.

"You have had enough for one night, it seems to me," remarked the barkeeper.

"No," said Rivers, "just give me one drink and I'll go!"

As the barkeeper turned to take down the bottle, Rivers flipped the letter, which he had in his hand, over towards the pigeon-hole; it just missed its mark and fell on the floor.

"What's that?" exclaimed the barkeeper, turning hastily around, "a rat?"

"No, a mouse, I guess!" said Rivers.

"I declare, if that mouse didn't knock a letter out of the pigeon-hole!" remarked the barkeeper as he picked it up and put it in its place. "Hurry up, Rivers, I want to go!"

Rivers swallowed his drink and went off well pleased with his success.

His work was not done yet, as Madam Imbert had requested him to keep a watch on Cox's house. He walked along in the direction of Cox's, and felt almost oppressed by the perfect stillness of the night. It was not broken even by the barking of watch-dogs. The whole place seemed wrapped in slumber. When he reached the house, he walked carefully around for about an hour, when a light in the second story — the only one he had seen — was extinguished. He then crawled up close to the house, where he could hear every movement within; but all he heard was the shrill voice of Mrs. Cox, occasionally relieved by snorts from Cox, and he concluded that all that was transpiring at Cox's was a severe curtain lecture, brought about through his instrumentality. At two A. M. he returned to his boarding-house, wrote out his report for Bangs, enclosing the copy of Mrs. Maroney's letter, and retired after an exciting day's work.

CHAPTER XX.

ON the following day Mrs. Maroney called on Madam Imbert, and together they strolled through the pleasure grounds. Each narrated her sorrows, and each wanted the support and friendship of the other.

Madam Imbert's story we will let pass. Mrs. Maroney dwelt on her husband's hardships, and her conversation was largely a repetition of what she had said the day before. She spoke of her husband as a persecuted man, and said : "Wait till his trial is over and he is vindicated ! Then the Adams Express will pay for this. The Vice-President has made the affair almost a personal one, but when Nat. is liberated the Vice-President will get his deserts. When he falls, mortally wounded with a ball from my husband's pistol, he will discover that Nathan Maroney is not to be trifled with. In the South we have a few friends left, and Mr. McGibony, a detective, is one of them. I think I can trust him. He was to have come North to escort my husband to Montgomery, if the Governor had granted the requisition ; but he would not, and Maroney will hear of my failure to-day, as I wrote to him last evening. De Forest is a useful friend, and I think him also a very handsome man. I left Montgomery, feeling very unhappy, and was obliged to go to Athens and Danielsville. I was so exhausted that I had to stop a day at Augusta to rest. I had some valuables concealed on my person, and they were so heavy as to greatly tire me. At Augusta I was forced to alter my arrangements for carrying them, and arrived in Philadelphia completely worn out. I can assure you it was with feelings of the greatest pleasure that I met De Forest. He very kindly took charge of my baggage, and brought Flora and me out in his buggy. I am so glad to be here once more."

As both ladies were tired, they walked over to some benches placed in a summer house, and took seats. Miss Johnson and Flora had been with them, but strolled off.

Mrs. Maroney kept up the conversation, on unimportant topics, for some time, and then suddenly turned to Madam Imbert and said : "You must have had to conceal property at times ! Where did you hide it ?"

Madam Imbert felt that now the trying moment for her had arrived. She knew that Mrs. Maroney had the stolen money in her possession, and that if she could only prevail on her to again conceal the money on her person, she could seize and search her; but Mrs. Maroney had said she could not carry it around, and so was obliged to change its hiding place. If she endeavored to prevail on her to secrete it on her person, she might suspect her motives, and hide it where it would be hard to find, so she answered in an indifferent tone ; "Oh, yes, I have often hidden valuables ! Sometimes I have placed them in the cellar, and at other times, waiting until all was quiet, I have stolen out into the garden, at a late hour of the night, and secreted them."

Mrs. Maroney looked her square in the eyes, but she did not alter a muscle under the scrutiny. "Your advice is good," she said, in a musing tone.

Madam Imbert would gladly have offered to assist her, but did not, at the time, feel safe in offering her services. She determined to act as quickly as possible, and to try and discover where she would secrete the money, as, from her actions, it was evident it was not yet hidden.

As they sat talking Madam Imbert pretended to be taken with a sudden pain in the neighborhood of her heart. She was so sick that Mrs. Maroney had to assist her to Stemples's. She explained to Mrs. Maroney that she was subject to heart disease, and was frequently taken in a like manner. When they got to the tavern she requested Mrs. Maroney to send Miss Johnson to her, which she did, and then walked slowly homeward.

In about three-quarters of an hour Miss Johnson called at Cox's, and reported that the Madam was much better, and was sleeping soundly. She had become lonely, and had started out to get Flora and take a walk. As soon as she entered the sitting room at Cox's, on her return, she found no one there but the children. In a moment Mrs. Cox came up stairs and joined her. She looked quite flurried, and seemed not to be particularly pleased at Miss Johnson's presence.

Miss Johnson had just made known her desire for Flora's company, when Rivers (whom Madam Imbert had seen and instructed to find out what Josh. was doing,) came in, in his usual rollicking way, and asked Mrs. Cox where Josh. was.

"He is out in the garden at work," said Mrs. Cox.

At almost the same moment Josh. yelled up from the cellar: "That you, Rivers? I'll join you at Stemples's, by-and-by."

It was immediately plain to Miss Johnson and Rivers that something was going on in the cellar which they did not want outsiders to know about. Miss Johnson remained with the children about half an hour, when Josh. and Mrs. Maroney came up from the cellar, perspiring freely, and looking as though they had been hard at work. Josh. started out to keep his appointment, evidently longing for a drink, and Miss Johnson, after a short conversation with Mrs. Maroney, went out with Flora. She did not remain long away, soon bringing Flora home, and then proceeding to the hotel to report to Madam Imbert. Rivers had already reported, and Madam Imbert was confident they were secreting the money in the cellar, so she determined to report to Bangs at once.

In the afternoon she had so far recovered as to be able to go to Philadelphia to consult her physician. At least she so informed Mrs. Maroney. Before going she walked over to see if Mrs. Maroney would not accompany her, but found her tired and weary, and in no humor for a ride. She therefore returned to Stemples's, hired his team and drove into the city alone. She reported to Bangs, and got back in time for supper. In the evening she called on Mrs. Maroney and had with her a long conversation.

What, with Rivers and De Forest, and Madam Imbert and Miss Johnson, very little happened at Cox's that was not seen and reported to Bangs.

Mrs. Maroney called the property she wished to conceal her own, but we concluded that it was the stolen money. For four days all went quietly in Jenkintown;

Mrs. Maroney made no allusions to her property, and passed the greater portion of the day either with Madam Imbert or with De Forest.

On the fifth day she received a letter from her husband requesting her to come to New York, and to bring a good Philadelphia lawyer with her. She made known to Madam Imbert, and De Forest, the contents of the letter. De Forest found that he wanted to go to the city in the morning, and made arrangements to accompany her with his buggy. At her earnest request Madam Imbert accompanied them. They drove to Mitchell's, had some refreshments, and then separated.

Green, of course, was at Mitchell's when they arrived, prepared to follow Mrs. Maroney. Madam Imbert went to the Merchants's Hotel and reported to Bangs, while De Forest reported to the Vice-President. Here were two persons acting in the same cause, and yet De Forest was profoundly ignorant of Madam Imbert's true character.

Mrs. Maroney proceeded to a lawyer's office in Walnut street. Green saw the name on the door, and knew that it was the office of a prominent advocate. I will not mention his name, as it is immaterial. She remained in the office for over an hour, and then returned to Mitchell's, where the party had agreed to rendezvous. After dinner they drove back to Jenkintown.

The following morning the rain poured in torrents, but Mrs. Maroney took the early train and went to the city, "shadowed" by Rivers. At Philadelphia he turned her over to the watchful care of Green. In Camden she was

12

joined by her lawyer, and on arriving in New York went directly with him to the Eldridge street jail.

All had gone well with White and Maroney. They had grown a little more friendly, though White was very unsocial, and seemed to prefer to keep by himself. Maroney had got Shanks to do several favors for him, and was very thankful for his kindness. Shanks was busily employed in carrying letters to White's lawyers, and bringing answers. The reader has already been informed with regard to the character of those communications.

White and Maroney were engaged in a social game of euchre when Mrs. Maroney and her lawyer arrived. Maroney did not have a very great regard for his wife, but any one, at such a time, would be welcome. He greeted her warmly, shook hands with the lawyer, and requested him to be seated while he held a private conversation with his wife. He drew her to one side, and they had a long, quiet conversation. In about an hour he called his lawyer over, and they consulted together for over two hours.

White was miserably situated. He could see all that went on, even to the movement of their lips as they conversed, but could not hear a word.

As soon as the interview was over Mrs. Maroney left the jail — the lawyer remaining behind — went to Jersey City, and took the train to Philadelphia.

Green telegraphed Bangs that she was returning, and he had Rivers at Camden to meet the train and relieve Green.

She arrived in Philadelphia too late for the Jenkintown

train, but hired a buggy at a livery stable, and had a boy drive her out and bring the horse back.

Rivers was looking around for a conveyance, when a gardener whom he knew, and who lived a few miles beyond Jenkintown, drove along. "Going out to Jenkintown?" he asked.

"Yes," replied the gardener.

"Give me a ride?"

"Of course; jump in." And he was soon being rattled over the pavement in the springless lumber-wagon. He tried to keep up a conversation, but the words were all jostled out of his mouth.

The weather had cleared up, and he had a delightful drive out to Jenkintown. He stopped the gardener twice on the road and treated him to whisky and cigars, and they arrived shortly after Mrs. Maroney. "There must be something up," thought he, "or she would not be in such a hurry to get home; what can it be?"

In Eldridge street jail, one day was nearly a repetition of another. White acted always the same, and said very little to any one except to Shanks, whom he always drew to one side when he wished to converse with him.

Maroney conversed with White a good deal, and was disappointed on finding that he could not play chess. White would occasionally join in a game of cards, but kept separate from the rest of the prisoners as much as possible. He had paid his footing, five dollars, the fee required to gain admission to "*the order*," as the prisoners call it. He found the "order" to be narrowed down to drinkables and smokables for all the prisoners initiated. Maroney had joined before, and said to White, "I don't think much of it. These people care for nothing but drinking and eating, while I have something else to think about."

By degrees Maroney conversed more and more with White; sometimes he would forget and talk loudly. White would look up and say, "Hush! walls have ears sometimes, don't talk so loud." At other times he would say, "Maroney, I am not a talking man; I keep my own counsel, and have discovered that the worst thing a man can do is to be noisy." Maroney would try and mollify him by saying, "Oh, pshaw! I didn't say any thing in particular."

"You can't tell who the spies are here," White would reply, "do you see those prisoners? well, how do you know but that some of them are spies? I would not trust one of them. I have a big fight under way myself; I know the men who are opposing me will take every advantage, and I propose to keep quiet and wait."

Maroney would remark, "But no one heard?"

"Hush," White would whisper, "how many times must I tell you that walls may have ears?"

In time he had Maroney afraid almost of his own shadow.

When White wanted to tell Shanks any thing, he would take him by the arm and draw him to one side; his lips would be seen to move, but not a word could be heard.

One morning Maroney said, "White, I would like to have a boy like yours to attend to my business; he is a good boy, never talks loud, and I could make him useful in many ways."

"Yes," replied White, dryly, "Shanks is a good boy,

and minds what I say. Suppose they should bring him on the stand to prove I said a certain thing, Shanks would be a bad witness, because he never hears any thing I don't want him to."

"I see he is shrewd, and I like him for that," said Maroney.

The days passed slowly away, White always attending to his own business, which seemed very important. One day Maroney said to White, "I'm tired, let's take a turn in the hall?" They made several trips, conversing on general topics, when Maroney lowered his voice and said:

"White, couldn't you and I get out of this jail?"

"I have not thought of it, have you?"

"Yes," answered Maroney, eagerly; "all we need is two keys. If we were to get an impression of the lock Shanks could have them made, couldn't he?"

"Yes," replied White, "you can get almost any thing made in New York if you have the money with which to pay for it. But if we made the attempt and failed, what would be the consequences? We should be put down and not allowed out of our cells, and I should be debarred from seeing Shanks; so suppose we think it over, and watch the habits of the jailors."

Every day Maroney broached the subject, but White always had some objections to offer, and Maroney finally abandoned the project in disgust. There is no doubt but that Eldridge street jail at the time could have been easily opened.

Little by little Maroney sought to place more confidence in White, but found his advances always repelled. White would say, " Maroney, let every man keep his own secrets,

I have all I can do to attend to my own affairs. My lawyer has been to see me and my prospects, as he presents them, are not very flattering. Shanks says they are likely to get the better of me if I am not careful. I feel so irritable that I can scarcely bear with any one." Maroney was more than ever desirous of talking with him, but White said: "I don't want to talk; let every man paddle his own canoe. If I were out of trouble, it would be a different thing, but my lawyer at present gives me a black lookout."

Shanks came in and White drew him to one side. They had a long talk and then White paced restlessly up and down the hall.

"What's the matter, White? have you bad news?" enquired Maroney.

"Yes, I am deeply in the mire, but let me alone and I'll wriggle myself out."

CHAPTER XXI.

I NOW determined to strike a blow at Maroney. Some idea of its power may be gained by imagining how a prisoner would feel upon receiving the news that, while he is languishing in prison, his faithless wife is receiving the unlawful attentions of a young gallant, and that everything indicates that they are about to leave for parts unknown, intending to take all his money and leave him in the lurch. This was exactly the rod I had in pickle for Maroney. I applied it through the following letter:

"Nathan Maroney, Eldridge Street Jail, New York:

"Ha! ha! ha! * * * * Your wife and the fellow with the long mustache and whiskers are having a glorious time, driving around in his buggy.

"You have heard of Sanford? He loves you well. He is the one who moves the automaton with the whiskers and long mustache, and gives *your wife* a *lover* in Jenkintown.

"You should *feel happy*, and so do I. The garden at night; honeyed words; the parting kiss! She loves him well! I *know you are happy!*

"Good-bye! * * * *   REVENGE!"

Having written the document, I had it mailed from Jenkintown, through the assistance of friend Rivers.

At Jenkintown all was going smoothly. De Forest was

more loving than ever, and Madam Imbert found it almost impossible to have a private conversation with Mrs. Maroney, as she seemed always with him. When De Forest came to Philadelphia I had it suggested to him that it would be advisable to get Mrs. Maroney to walk or drive out with him in the evening. He immediately acted on the suggestion, and before long could be found almost every evening with her.

Mrs. Maroney did not again allude to her valuables, and evidently felt perfectly easy in regard to them, considering that she had them safely secreted. One day, while Mrs. Maroney was in the cellar, Madam Imbert called. Mrs. Cox met her and said:

"Sister is in the cellar; I will call her up."

"Never mind," remarked the Madam, "I'll just run down to her," and stepped towards the cellar door.

Mrs. Cox quickly interposed and said:

"Oh! no; I will call her!"

This little incident showed Madam Imbert that something was going on which they did not want her to know.

Mrs. Maroney soon came up, said she was delighted to see her, and did not look at all confused.

Rivers, Cox, Horton and Barclay had formed themselves into a quartette club and were nearly always together.

Rivers's arm had not healed as yet, and he still wore it in a sling. Cox and he were on the best of terms, and the Jenkintowners regarded him, as well as the other detectives, as permanent residents.

De Forest was happy beyond expression, and Mrs. Maroney seemed equally so. She wrote letters daily to her husband and often spoke of Madam Imbert and how deeply she felt for her, bowed down with care and alone in the world. She very seldom alluded to De Forest and never spoke of his being her constant companion.

While all was passing so pleasantly in Jenkintown, a terrible scene was being enacted in Eldridge street jail. I had not posted White as to my intention of sending the anonymous letter to Maroney, as I wished to find what effect Maroney's conduct would have on him. The day after Rivers had posted the letter, Shanks brought it to Maroney when he came with the morning's mail. Besides my letter there was also one from Mrs. Maroney. Maroney looked at the letters and opened the one from his wife first. He read it, a pleased smile passing over his face, and then laid it down and picked up my letter. He scanned the envelope carefully and then broke the seal. White was watching him and wondered why he examined the letter so closely. As he read, White was astonished to see a look of deep anguish settle on his face. He seemed to be sinking from some terrible blow. He recovered himself, read the letter over and over again, then crushed it in his hand and threw it on the floor.

He sprang to his feet and walked rapidly up and down the hall; but returned and picked up the letter before the wily White could manage to secure it. White wondered what it was that troubled Maroney. He whispered to Shanks:

"What the d—l is the matter with Maroney? He has received bad news. I should like, in some way, to find out what it is. The old man will be wondering what is in that note, and when I report, will blame me for not finding out."

Maroney appeared almost crazed. He forced the letter into his pocket and went into his cell without a word; but his face was a terrible index of what was passing in his mind.

After a little, White and Shanks walked by his cell and saw him lying on the bed, with his face hidden in the clothes. He did not come out for over an hour; but when he did, he *seemed* perfectly calm. He was very pale, and it was astonishing to see the change wrought in him in so short a time.

White met him as he came out, but did not appear to notice any difference in him.

"Here, Maroney, have a cigar; they are a new brand. Shanks is a superior judge of cigars. I think these are the best I have yet had, and I believe I will get a box; I can get them for eleven dollars, and they are as good as those they retail at twenty cents a piece."

Maroney held out his hand mechanically and took one. He put it into his mouth, and without lighting it, commenced to chew it.

White, in one of his reports to me, says: "A man often shows his desperation by his desire to get more nicotine than usual." Maroney did not converse with White, and only said he wanted to write. He sat down and wrote a note, but immediately tore it up. He wrote and tore up several in this way, but finally wrote one to suit him. White quietly told Shanks that when Maroney gave him the letter he was writing, he must be sure and see its contents. Of course Shanks always obeyed orders, and never neglected anything his uncle told him to do, even if it was to forget something that had happened. In this way he was extremely useful. It was getting late, and the jailer had told him two or three times that he must go, but he did not take his departure until Maroney had sealed the letter and handed it to him.

Maroney was in a terrible condition, and White found that it would be impossible to get anything out of him that night, as the whole affair was too fresh in his mind; so he got some brandy he had in his cell, and asked him to take a drink. Maroney eagerly swallowed a brimming glassfull, and took four or five drinks in rapid succession. He seemed to suffer terrible anguish, and his whole frame trembled like a leaf. In a few minutes he retired to his cell, evidently determined to seek oblivion in sleep.

We will now follow Shanks to his hotel, where he is engaged in opening Maroney's letter. Although the letter was very securely sealed, he accomplished the task without much difficulty, and read as follows:

"MADAM: I have received a strange letter. What does it mean? Are you playing false to me? Who is this man you have with you? where does he come from? Are you such a fool as not to know he is a tool of the Adams, and that you are acting with him? I cannot be with you. If I had my liberty I would hurry to your side, snatch you from this villain, and plunge my knife so deep into him that he would never know he had received a blow!!! Why are you so foolish? Do you love me? You have often said you did. You know I have done all in my power to make you happy, and have placed entire confi-

dence in you. Why have you never told me about this
man? Listen to me, and love me as before, and all will
go well. Tell me all, 'and tell me it is not so bad as it is
told to me!' Spurn this scoundrel, and have confidence
in me forever!!!"   NAT.

Shanks hurriedly copied this letter, and mailed it after
making another copy, which he forwarded to me at the
same time. In the morning he gave White a copy of the
letter, which revealed to him the cause of Maroney's
anguish.

Maroney came to White in the morning, and found him
moody, and not inclined to talk. Still he clung to him as
his only hope. It was a strange fascination which White
had acquired over Maroney. Maroney appeared to feel
better, although he was still very pale, and seemed to be
comforted by White's presence, although he did not say a
word about his trouble.

We will now make a trip which Maroney would like to
make, and return to Jenkintown.

Maroney's letter arrived by the five P. M. mail, at Jenkintown, the day following the one on which Shanks
mailed it. In the morning Mrs. Maroney had spent some
time with Madam Imbert, and then had gone for a drive
with De Forest. They went to Manayunk, had a fish
dinner washed down with a bottle of champagne, and
drove back as happy and free from care as two children.
Mrs. Maroney left the buggy at Cox's at half-past four,
and found Madam Imbert waiting for her. The Madam
noticed that she was a little exhilarated. After they had
conversed for some time she asked Mrs. Maroney out for a
walk, and they strolled leisurely down to the station. The

train from Philadelphia had just passed through, and Mrs. Maroney said: "Let us walk up to Stemples's and see if any letters have come for us."

When they reached Stemples's, Mrs. Maroney went in and received a letter. Madam Imbert was not so fortunate. "Oh!" laughed Mrs. Maroney, "I have seen the time, when I was single, that I would receive half a dozen letters a day; but this is more valuable than them all, as it is from my husband. Heigh ho! I wonder what my darling Nat. has to say." At the same time she broke the seal, and then proceeded to read the letter.

Madam Imbert walked a little way behind her, as was her habit. She was a very tall, commanding woman, and made this her habit so that she could glance at anything that Mrs. Maroney might read as they walked along. It was a part of her business, and so she was not to be blamed for it. Mrs. Maroney flushed at the first word she read, but as she went on her color heightened, until she was red as a coal of fire. "Why," she muttered, "Nat., you're a d—d fool!" When angered she always used language she had acquired in her former life.

Madam Imbert heard her, and was anxious to see the contents of the letter, but could only catch a word here and there as she looked over Mrs. Maroney's shoulder.

Mrs. Maroney glanced over the letter hurriedly, and then read it again. She muttered to herself, and the Madam hoped she was going to tell her what it was that caused her hard words; but she did not, and soon folded the letter up and put it away. As they neared Cox's she said: "Please excuse me; I feel unwell, and fear I have been too much in the sun to-day."

At this moment De Forest walked out of Josh's. "Mrs. Maroney," said he, "will you come to the garden this evening?"

Madam Imbert turned to leave.

Mrs. Maroney looked him full in the face with flashing eyes, clenched her little hand, and in a voice hoarse from passion, exclaimed: "What do you want here, you scoundrel?"

If a thunderbolt had fallen at his feet, De Forest could not have been more astonished; he was struck speechless; his powers of articulation were gone. She said not one word more, but stalked into the house and closed the door with a bang that made him jump.

Madam Imbert wended her way to the tavern, but De Forest stood for fully two minutes, seemingly deprived of the power of motion. He then darted eagerly toward the door, determined to have an explanation, but was met by Josh., who said: "You have done something that has raised the d——l in Mrs. Maroney, and she will play the deuce with you if you don't clear out. If you try to speak to her, she will pistol you, sure!"

"But what have I done?" asked De Forest. "It is only an hour since I left her, and we were then on the best of terms. I have *always* treated her well!"

"Come, come!" said Josh., "don't stand talking here. People will see we are having a fuss." And he took De Forest by the arm and led him toward Stemples's.

Madam Imbert had met Rivers on her way, and sent him to find out how affairs were progressing. He arrived at this moment. "Hello," said he to Josh., "I was just coming to see you."

"Mrs. Harvey looked him full in the face with flashing eyes, extended her little hand, and in a voice hoarse from passion, exclaimed: 'What do you want here, you scoundrel?'"—Page 190.

"Yes! You have come at the wrong time. Mrs. Maroney is as mad as blazes, and would have shot De Forest if it had not been for me. I can't tell what for, but, by the Eternal, she would have done it!"

De Forest was all in a maze. He could not imagine what he had done to cause the woman he loved to become so excited as to desire to kill him.

They all three went to the hotel, and De Forest, although generally not a drinking man, called them all up and treated. The fun of the whole thing was that De Forest had not the slightest idea what it was that had caused the trouble. Only an hour before she was by his side in the buggy, and they were so happy and so loving! She had been cooing like a turtle dove, and now, "Oh, wondrous change," she wished to shoot him. He could not remember having uttered a single word that would wound the most sensitive nature.

After tea, Madam Imbert walked down to Cox's, first seeing Rivers and directing him to keep a close guard on the house that night, and especially to watch the cellarwindow, so as to know if anything took place in the cellar. On arriving at Cox's she was shown into Mrs. Maroney's room. Mrs. Maroney was in bed, but did not have her clothes off. She had not been crying, but fairly quivered with suppressed excitement. She rose and closed the door, and then burst out with, "Why, Madam Imbert, have you ever heard of so foolish a man as my husband? Who knows where De Forest comes from? Do you?"

"No," answered the Madam; "he was here when I came. Don't you know?"

"No. All I know is that I became acquainted with him here, when I first came, and I found him so serviceable that I kept up the acquaintance; But," she broke out in a wild, excited manner, " D——n him ! I'll put a ball through him if he dares to injure me."

" Keep cool, keep cool ! What does it matter? You are excited ; it is a bad time to talk," urged Madam Imbert.

" But I must talk : I shall suffocate if I don't. Madam Imbert, I must tell you all."

"No ! You must not talk now. Calm yourself! You must keep cool ! Think of your poor husband languishing in prison, and remember that any false move of yours may prove to his disadvantage."

" But what makes him charge me with receiving improper attentions from De Forest ? I know I have sometimes been foolish with him, but he is soft and I have moulded him to my purpose. He has been my errand-boy, nothing more; and now my husband thinks me untrue to him, when I would gladly die for him, if it would help him. It is too hard to bear, too hard ! !"

Madam Imbert had had the forethought to bring a bottle of brandy with her, so she advised : " Don't make things worse than they are; you had better say no more until morning. Here, have a little brandy ; I saw you were nervous, and so brought a bottle with me ; take some, and then go to bed. After a good sound sleep you will be able to see your way much clearer than now."

" Oh, thank you," said Mrs. Maroney, as she eagerly seized the glass and gulped down a large quantity.

Madam Imbert started to leave.

"Please don't go yet; I must tell you all," pleaded Mrs. Maroney.

"Wait till to-morrow," said Madam Imbert, "it is a bad time to talk."

"Madam Imbert, you are now my only friend, and I would like to have your opinion as to who it is that is writing these letters about me to my husband. If I knew the dirty dog, I would put a ball through him. I am not fairly treated. I am Maroney's wife, and he should not believe such slanders against me. As long as I live I will do all I can for him."

"Mrs. Maroney," said Madam Imbert, getting up, "I must not listen to you; I will go."

"Please don't! Who can it be that is writing these reports from Jenkintown?" again enquired Mrs. Maroney.

"That is a point upon which it is hard for me to enlighten you," replied the Madam; "it might be Barclay or some of Josh.'s friends. Josh. is a good clever fellow, for a brother-in-law, but I would not trust him too much; he is a little inclined to talk, and Barclay may have drawn something from him and written to your husband; I know De Forest don't like him."

"I will see Josh. at once, and find out about this Barclay," said Mrs. Maroney.

"You had better wait till morning," said Madam Imbert, as she rose to leave the room; "I must go to bed, and you had better follow my example."

Mrs. Maroney began to show the effects of the brandy she had been drinking, but she took Madam Imbert's arm and went to the door with her. It was now ten o'clock, but she requested the Madam to take a turn in the garden

13

with her. They had hardly taken two steps before Mrs. Maroney stumbled over a man concealed at the side of the house. It was Rivers, but he was up and off before the frightened ladies had a chance to see him. Madam Imbert screamed lustily, although she well knew who it was.

"D—n him," said Mrs. Maroney, "that's that De Forest; I will kill him, sure! What was he doing here?"

Madam Imbert remarked that it was either he or Barclay.

"I know what he is looking after," said Mrs. Maroney; "I see through the whole thing! De Forest is a tool of the Vice-President; he thinks he has got my secrets, but I'll be after him yet." Her voice was hoarse and dry, and plainly showed the effects of the brandy. Madam Imbert walked out of the garden and went to the tavern, while Mrs. Maroney went into the house.

Rivers, when he was disturbed in his watching of the cellar window, rushed straight to Stemples's, where he found Barclay, Horton and Cox. "How do you do, boys?" said he, "come and have a drink; I have just come in from seeing my girl; she is a good one, and I think will make me happy; had a long walk, though; over two miles, and I think I deserve a glass."

Josh. was telling about Mrs. Maroney's quarrel. Rivers heard him patiently through, and they had two or three drinks, when Mrs. Cox stalked into the room. All the women in Jenkintown seemed on the rampage, at least all those we are dealing with.

"Josh., you lazy, good for nothing fellow, I have been looking all over the village for you!"

"Why, you ought to know you could find me here," said Josh.

"Come home at once; sister wants you to watch the house to-night! some one has been lurking around there, and she wants you to find out who it is."

"Well," said Josh., carelessly, " I'll come."

Rivers now spoke up: "I am not very busy just now, and I will watch with you."

"Will you?" said Mrs. Cox, in a pleased tone; I would be much obliged to you if you would; Josh. has been drinking so much that I can't place much reliance on him."

"Certainly," said Rivers, and the trio started for the scene of action.

Mrs. Maroney was in bed when they arrived, but she hastily rose and came to the door in her night dress.

" Now, Josh.," she commanded, " I want you to keep a close watch, and if De Forest, or any one else comes by the cellar-window, just you think they are coming to rob your house, and fire! Here is my revolver."

" I will take care of that," said Rivers, " I am going to stay up and watch with Josh."

"Oh, thank you! Josh., you had better let Mr. Rivers have the revolver."

She went in, and Josh. turned the revolver over to Rivers. They then secreted themselves where they could see any one coming into the yard. In less than an hour Josh. was snoring. At three in the morning Rivers roused him up, got him into the house, and then, thoroughly tired out, started for home.

CHAPTER XXII.

IN the morning Jenkintown enjoyed the calm that always follows the storm. Madam Imbert called on Mrs. Maroney, and found her suffering from a severe headache. She said she feared she had taken too much champagne the day before, and believed that De Forest had attempted to get her drunk. She could not imagine why he watched the house. She was bound to have nothing more to do with him, as she was certain he was a tool of the Express Company. "And yet," she said, " I thought he was a man above that sort of business! I thought he would disdain to sell himself for such a purpose."

Madam Imbert advised her to be patient, and to be careful not to do De Forest an injustice by judging him wrongfully. "You don't know," she remarked, " but that he really loves you, and was only trying to see if you were receiving other company." They conversed for some time on the subject, and Madam Imbert finally found that Mrs. Maroney was very much inclined to take her view of the subject. She said she really thought De Forest loved her, and perhaps she had been too hasty with him. It was Madam Imbert's best plan to take this course, as it would show what a disinterested friend she was. She wanted to keep watch on Cox's house, but in such a manner as not to excite suspicion.

Mrs. Maroney said she would write to Nat. and explain the matter, but said she would like to find out who had written to her husband. Madam Imbert and she cogitated over the subject for some time, but could not decide upon any particular person. Finally Mrs. Maroney concluded she would take a nap, as she thought she would feel much brighter afterwards. She said she would write to her husband the first thing after dinner, and asked the Madam to call a little later and take a walk with her.

De Forest remained in the hotel all the morning. He did not call on Mrs. Maroney, and vainly puzzled his brain to determine the cause of her excitement. He came into the bar-room, where he found Rivers, as serene as ever, and willing to console any one. In a few minutes Josh., Horton and Barclay arrived. The *posse* talked over the trouble of the preceding night, and De Forest hoped that, as Josh. had come from the scene of action, he would be able to enlighten him as to the cause of Mrs. Maroney's strange conduct. But Cox was as much at a loss to account for her passion as he. Said he : " All I know is that she is a regular tartar, and no mistake ! Whew ! didn't she rave though ? "

The Vice-President and I received the reports in Philadelphia, and had a quiet laugh over them. All was working to suit us.

In the afternoon Madam Imbert walked out with Mrs. Maroney, who had just finished her letter to her husband. As they walked along she said, " I told my husband that I knew nothing about the man with the long mustache further than that he was living in Jenkintown before I left the South; that when I first arrived here he did several kind things for me, and had driven me into Philadelphia a few times when I could not get the train, but that you, Madam Imbert, had always accompanied me. I spoke of you as a perfect lady, and as being a true friend of mine, and that you often cautioned me against talking too much. I said that if it was De Forest he alluded to, I was perfectly safe in his company. I asked him if he thought it likely that I, whose interests were identical with his, would be likely to prove untrue to him, and told him he might rest perfectly assured that I would do nothing without his knowledge and consent."

They walked to Stemples's and posted the letter. On the way they met De Forest, but Mrs. Maroney took no notice of him. After mailing the letter, they strolled through the pleasure grounds for some time. At last they separated, each taking their respective way home.

At the tavern Madam Imbert was met by De Forest, who requested a private interview. She readily consented, and, after tea, met him in the sitting-room. De Forest related his sorrowful story, and asked her if she knew what had caused Mrs. Maroney to treat him so harshly.

She said, "these things will happen once in a while; it is part of a woman's nature to take sudden and unaccountable freaks; but all will be right by-and-by." She quoted Scott's beautiful lines:

> " O Woman ! in our hours of ease
> Uncertain, coy and hard to please,
> And variable as the shade
> By the light quivering aspen made :
> When pain and anguish wring the brow,
> A ministering Angel thou —"

De Forest fervently hoped that, as she had brought "pain and anguish" to his brow, she would now become his "ministering angel," and went off somewhat comforted. Madam Imbert saw Mrs. Maroney in the evening and told her of the interview with De Forest. This made her feel quite happy, and she even remarked: "I think I have been too hard on the poor fellow."

White and Maroney were together when Mrs. Maroney's letter arrived. Maroney read it carefully through and then went to his cell. In the afternoon, White observed him writing and directed Shanks to open the letter when he received it. Shanks did so and found it was to his wife.

He wrote that he was happy to hear that she was still true to him, and to find that he had been deceived. He felt assured that the blow must have been aimed by some of his enemies. If he were at liberty he would find the man, but as he was not he would have to wait. He directed her to endeavor to find out who had sent the letter. As she assured him she would do nothing without his approval, he was contented.

When I received a copy of his letter, I was convinced that he was trying to make the best of a bad bargain. He could not be spared from Eldridge street jail just at that time and had to trust his wife whether he would or not.

White and he lived quietly together. He told White that he was confined at the instigation of the Adams Express, who accused him of stealing fifty thousand dollars from them.

"But, of course," said he, "I am innocent!"

Still, as I have before mentioned, he was anxious to break jail — an unusual inclination for an innocent man.

About this time he happened to read in the papers an account of a robbery in Tennessee, in which a description of the stolen money and bills was given. As he and White were walking in the hall, he said to White:

"White, I wonder if it would not be a good move to try some game in my case? Of course, I am innocent! I think the messenger, Chase, the guilty party, and I want to arrange some plan to throw suspicion on him or some one else; but (in an amusing tone) there is no one else. Chase received the money from me and put it into the pouch! Still, I can't prove this, as there were no witnesses. It will be my oath against his, and as the company have taken his part, he will have the best of it. It a strange affair. Chase was at the counter checking off packages as I put them in the pouch. He now says he did not see all the packages, as they went in so quickly that he had all he could do to check them off. Strange, indeed! If I were checking off packages of such large amounts I think I should be likely to look at them, don't you? I wish in some way to prove Chase dishonest. At present it is even between us, but the company support him and leave me in the lurch."

"Yes," said White, "it is just about as you say, an even thing between you; but the company have undoubtedly sided with Chase because you have the most money, and they think they can recover the amount from you or from your friends! But I don't see how you can clear yourself. If Chase only swears he did not receive the money, it will go hard with you."

White thought that now Maroney would propose to him to get Shanks to have some duplicate keys of the company's pouch made; but apparently he did not yet feel fully certain that he could trust White. He broached the subject several times, but finally dropped it altogether.

A few days after, Maroney had another talk with White and treated him with much more confidence than before. White said little, and was a good man to talk to. Maroney made no admissions, but all his expressions and manners showed guilt. White at least did not accept them as showing his innocence. He always pointed to Chase as the guilty party. Maroney frequently brought up his troubles as a topic of conversation with White; but White was professedly so employed with his own business that he said but little. All that Maroney said to him seemed to go in at one ear and out at the other. When he made a remark it was a casual one and had no bearing on the subject. This caused Maroney to talk still more, devising plans for throwing suspicion on Chase. White casually said:

"What sort of a man is Chase? A smart, shrewd fellow who would pick up a money package if he saw it lying handy, and dispose of it?"

"No," replied Maroney, slowly weighing every word. "I don't think he would. He is a pretty fair man; but the company have no right to make him a witness against me!"

"Who are his friends?" enquired White.

"His father lives in Georgia; he is a whole-souled old planter; has a good many slaves; but his property is much encumbered. Chase is a good fellow after all!"

"By-the-by," asked White, "does he ever go to see the fancy girls?"

"Yes, he does, occasionally," answered Maroney.

"Would it not be a good plan to take four or five thousand dollars and get the girls to stuff it into his pants pocket; then get him drunk, and as he started away have some detective arrest him?"

"Yes," answered Maroney, "it might be done, and Gus McGibony is the man to do it. He is a good friend of mine. If I were only out, I might do something. White, your idea is a good one, you are a splendid contriver; but I must find some one to carry out the plan. I have friends in Montgomery, and I think Charlie May would help me. No, he is too much under the influence of his wife! Patterson would help me some; but I think Porter is the best man for me!"

"Porter? who is he?"

"He is the clerk of the Exchange Hotel," said Maroney.

"He would be a good man for you if you can trust him."

"I know I can do that! he would do anything in the world for me."

"He is just the man to be familiar with the girls. Clerks at hotels always are. Girls must often stop at the hotel, and he might arrange to get Chase into a room with one of them, and then the rest could be easily accomplished. Does Chase board at the Exchange?"

"Yes," answered Maroney. "White, you're a genius! I have a good mind to write to Porter at once and lay your plan before him."

White looked at him in astonishment. "Are you

crazy " said he ; " would you trust such matters on paper ?
I *never* do.'

"You are right again," exclaimed Maroney.

They talked the affair over for several days, the trouble
being to get a proper person to act as a go-between to
arrange matters with Porter. Maroney asked White why
he could not trust Shanks.

"You could ; but the trouble is he has never been in
the South."

"That would make but little difference."

"No, now I think of it, I don't know as it would. He
would only have to carry the messages, and Shanks
always obeys orders."

"Well, I will think it over," remarked Maroney ; and
the matter dropped, he evidently fearing that Shanks
would get the money and clear out.

One day he said : "White, I wonder if the Express
Company would not settle the matter with me ? I am not
guilty of the theft, but things look blue for me. I have
some money, and I think I will make a proposition to
them."

"You could not do a more foolish thing ; they would
at once conclude that you were certainly guilty, and make
you suffer for it," argued White.

White kept me informed of all that went on, and I had
instructed him that we would make no compromise. The
company did not care so much for the money, as of making an example of the guilty party. That would show
the other employés what would be their fate if they
were caught in similar peculations.

About this time Maroney's brother came to New York,

from Danielsville. He was a man of good standing, well-meaning, and honest in his intentions. Maroney had looked anxiously for his coming, as he supposed his brother would be able to effect his release on bail. He knew that his brother alone could not make the bail-bond good, as one hundred thousand dollars is a large sum to be raised, but supposed that by his influence he might get others to sign with him.

I placed "shadows" on his brother's track, and they, with White on the inside, and Shanks on the outside, kept me fully informed of what he was intending to do. He appeared to feel very bad at finding his brother in jail, and evinced a desire to do all he could for him. He had a long interview with Maroney and his lawyer, but everything appeared against him. Maroney's brother had no property in New York, and the only way he could raise the necessary bail was by giving a mortgage on his property as security to some man in New York, and have him go on the bond.

The matter was well canvassed between them, but finally, like all the other plans devised to effect his release, was abandoned as impracticable. The brother did not like to procure bail in this way, for if he did, and Maroney should run away, the Adams Express would prosecute the bondsmen, who in turn would foreclose the mortgage, and in all likelihood become the owners of his property. He would do a great deal for his brother, but felt that this was asking too much. His duty to his family would not permit him to run so great a risk, and he therefore returned home without accomplishing the object of his visit.

So far, all my schemes had proved successful.

White had weakened Maroney's confidence in his friends. I wanted him to see and feel that all those whom he considered his friends before the jail door closed upon him, were so no longer. One by one he saw them abandon him to his fate, till he had no one left on whom to rely, but White. His brother had come and gone without accomplishing anything. He feared that even his wife was untrue to him, and that she, instead of proving a safe guardian for his property, might at any moment leave with De Forest and the money. His wife had often spoken of a Madam Imbert, but he had never seen her, and knew not whether she was to be trusted. From his wife's correspondence, he was disposed to think favorably of her, and several times was on the point of sending word to his wife to pay him a visit and bring Madam Imbert with her. But what good would it do? After all, it was better to trust White.

One day White turned to Maroney, after writing several letters and holding a long interview with Shanks, and said: "Maroney, I think I can procure bail. My lawyers have been working hard in my behalf, and one of them went to St. Louis to see my prosecutors. He found they would do nothing unless they got all their money back. Of course I could not give them that," said he with a wink, "as I haven't it; and so my lawyer was unable to do anything for me. Shanks, however, has just been in, and he has not been idle during the five days he has been absent. He has made arrangements with a party to go my bail, provided I will advance a considerable sum as security. Nothing is needed now but security, and I think

I can manage it. I can give them some money, and they will then manage to get me out on straw bail. I can then loaf around town, enjoying myself, and if I cannot compromise the matter, or if I think that the trial will go against me, I can run away. In this way I shall lose my security, and my bondsmen will have to fight the bond; but still," said he, with a chuckle, the keen Yankee showing out, "but still I shall not do so badly, after all, as I shall have about twenty thousand dollars left to begin business with in a new place."

Maroney was more than ever impressed with his ability, and began to think that White was now his only true friend, and the best man to help him out of his difficulty. He had now been in jail several months, and it was time to get matters fixed up. Why could he not trust White to help him? He was a good contriver, and apparently could be trusted. Still it would not do to be too certain, so he would quietly feel his way along. He gradually broached the subject to White by saying, "White, I feel very bad at the idea of your leaving me; after you go, all my friends will be away from me. I might rely on Porter's help, or perhaps on Patterson's. McGibony is a good fellow, and would willingly help me, but I can't trust him too far, as he could be easily pumped. Moreover, the great trouble is, that they are all down South. I can not take my wife from Jenkintown, and yet I feel as though the Adams Express were watching her. What must I do? You are a keen fellow; can't you help me when you get out? I have some money of my own, and I would gladly pay you for your trouble."

"Well," said White, "I shall have all I can do to attend

to my own business for the first four or five days I am out, but after that I might help you. I don't know as I shall be able to do you any good, but if I make an effort, we must have a clear understanding that my connection with the matter must never be known. If I wish to communicate with you I will send Shanks, who will be at once admitted to see you as an old friend. If I were you, I would not talk to any of your New York friends about it. They don't seem to care much for you, and very seldom come to see you. Your lawyer is not doing much for you, and it would be just as well not to let him into the secret either. Above all, you must not let your wife or Madam Imbert know any thing about it. I have had much trouble once or twice through women, and have determined never again to trust them. It is utterly impossible for a woman to keep a secret. She may love you to distraction, but confide a secret to her and she is never satisfied till she divulges it." Maroney eagerly listened to all White had to say, and then replied: "White, depend upon it, you are the right man for me! If you will only figure for me as well as you have done for yourself, you will have me out of jail in a very short time."

"What do you want me to undertake?"

"The first thing is to carry out the plan you proposed the other day — of placing the money on Chase's person. I will make the blow more telling by getting you to have a key made similar to the pouch-key, and putting it into his pocket at the same time. I have a fine drawing of the key and you can easily have it made. I know Chase is the guilty party, and this move will exonerate me and bring the proper person to justice. I am sorry for Chase, but he can't expect me to suffer for his crime. I will furnish you the necessary money to put into his pocket, and give you a letter to Gus. McGibony, who will arrest Chase at the proper moment."

"That's easily arranged," said White, "and McGibony need not know any thing about the dodge. I shall need him only to make the arrest at the moment when the girl gives me the wink. The worst of the thing is, we shall be compelled to have a woman in the case any way; but I am acquainted with a splendid looking girl here, who may, perhaps, keep her mouth shut. I will send her to Montgomery, get her into the Exchange Hotel, and she will soon manage to draw Chase into her room. When he goes in I will get McGibony and have him arrested and searched as soon as he gets to his own room."

"Capital! capital!!" said Maroney, jumping up and walking across the hall, rubbing his hands with glee. "White, if you succeed in this I will pay you well for it."

"What kind of money was it the company lost?" asked White.

"Oh! of course I don't know; I never saw it!" quickly answered Maroney, at the same time looking into White's face with an expression in his eye which showed that he wished to read his inmost thoughts. White took no notice of this look, but went on with apparent unconcern. "Well, one of the first things we must do is to find out what kind of money was stolen from the Express Company, procure bills of the same kind, and when they are found on Chase, he is gone, and his conviction is certain."

"Yes! yes!" muttered Maroney, as the thought flashed through his mind, "can he really suspect me of having stolen the money?" "Yes, it would be a good plan. You might find out what banks the company received the money from and get some of their bills! It is a good thing to look after, any way."

Maroney was not fully prepared to trust White, although he would eventually have to do it. If he had been scanned by a close observer, there would have been discovered in his mind a doubt of White's fealty, caused by the home-thrust he gave when he asked about the money.

14

CHAPTER XXIII.

AT Jenkintown all was well. Mrs. Maroney had made up with De Forest and his present happiness was so great that he had entirely forgotten his past sorrow. He was very fond of Flora and enjoyed walking with her, especially when her mother was along. Madam Imbert sometimes drove into Philadelphia with Mrs. Maroney to do shopping, and De Forest was always their coachman. Mrs. Maroney was loyal to a promise she had made her husband, and never went out driving with De Forest unaccompanied by Madam Imbert.

De Forest had only one seat to his buggy, and it was rather irksome to be conveying two ladies around all the time. He had but little room, seated between them, and as the weather was warm, he was often very uncomfortable. He was tall, and his knees were jammed closely against the dash-board; but he bore all the inconvenience manfully.

It was always their custom to drive to Mitchell's when they went to the city. The ladies would alight here, while De Forest would stable his horses. At dinner time they would meet again and drive home. One day, while in the city, Madam Imbert said to Mrs. Maroney:

"Wait here a few minutes for me, I want to get some money changed."

She left Mrs. Maroney at Mitchell's and walked to

Third street. Here she went into a bank and drew five hundred dollars I had left there for her and came out. She then walked up Third street and went into the office of Miller Bros., brokers, where she had the money changed into Eastern funds.

Mrs. Maroney was smart. She had followed closely after Madam Imbert and acted the part of a "shadow." As the latter came out of the brokers' office and approached the corner of Chestnut street, Mrs. Maroney met her.

"I am glad to meet you," said she; "I am on my way to Second street to get some goods. Did you get your money changed?"

Madam Imbert was prepared.

"Yes," said she, "but I did not have much. I have the most of my money in a safe place. At the Third street bank, they told me they did not have any Eastern funds and looked very queerly at me, so I went to the brokers' office and they finally changed it. A person has to be cautious, as it is sometimes very difficult to succeed. People ask questions at times that it is impossible for one to answer. You have never had to do so much in this way as I have! have you?"

"No!" replied Mrs. Maroney, coloring deeply; "but I suppose I shall have to learn! I will tell you a secret of mine some time. You may be of great use to me, will you help me if you can?"

"Yes," said Madam Imbert, recalling her poor husband languishing in confinement. "Your husband is like mine, both are in prison. I feel strongly drawn toward you and will do all I can for you. Oh! why can't I succeed in getting my darling free!"

They had reached the dry-goods store and went in to make their purchases.

I was desirous of impressing upon Mrs. Maroney the difficulties in the way of changing money, and my plan was successful beyond my expectations. She saw the trouble Madam Imbert had at the bank and at the brokers, and learned that bankers and brokers were liable to ask very pointed questions when changing money. If she had any idea of changing her stolen money she might be frightened out of it, and prefer to rely for assistance on Madam Imbert, who seemed an experienced hand.

After they had made their purchases the ladies returned to Mitchell's and were driven home by De Forest.

Madam Imbert spent the evening with Mrs. Maroney, but nothing of interest transpired. A day or two after, as they were seated in the garden, Mrs. Maroney took Madam Imbert partially into her confidence and gave her a sketch of her life, which, it must be confessed, as narrated by her, made her appear very pure and spotless. She said that Maroney met her a heart-broken widow, and that she married him only to prevent him from committing suicide, so desperately smitten was he; that they came to Montgomery, where Maroney was appointed agent of the Adams Express—a very lucrative position—and then continued :

"Maroney had a good deal of money of his own, but did not talk much about it, in fact kept it a secret from every one but me. No one is obliged to state what he is worth. He was a very kind-hearted man and fairly idolized my little Flora. He was making arrangements to buy a plantation and a lot of slaves; had made money buying and selling horses, and owned a large interest in a livery stable in Montgomery. On a trip he made to the North he purchased a fast horse named "Yankee Mary," and used to take me out for a drive every day. Nat. is one of the best men that ever lived, but he is a little inclined to be careless. We were as happy and contented as could be, when — oh! unfortunate day for us! — the Adams Express was robbed and my husband was accused of the theft. He was arrested in Montgomery, but liberated on small bail. Soon afterward I came North on a visit, and when he came to bring me home he was arrested in New York and thrown into prison. I immediately went South, sold all his property and secreted the money about me, so that the Adams Express would not get hold of it. I have now the money secreted here; but there have been a great many small burglaries committed around here, and I am in constant dread of its being stolen. I don't dare leave Jenkintown for a night, and fervently wish my husband were out of jail to take care of it. What do you do with your money, Madam Imbert?"

"I take care of it in various ways. Sometimes I carry large amounts concealed on my person; but the last time I was away I placed the most of it in a safe place."

"I wish I knew of a safe place. If my husband were only out, he would soon find one," remarked Mrs. Maroney.

"What are his prospects for getting out?" asked the Madam.

"Well, I don't know, indeed; he is sometimes hopeful, sometimes in despair; he has been writing me lately of a friend of his named White, who was imprisoned a day or two after him. White has managed to make arrangements to effect his own release on bail, and when he gets out, has promised to assist Nat."

"If White managed to get himself out, I should think him just the man to assist your husband," said Madam Imbert.

"Nat. thinks so too; but he probably will not decide on any plan until White gets out, when they together may do something."

A day or two after this long conversation, Mrs. Maroney again alluded to the robberies taking place in Jenkintown, and expressed much anxiety for the safety of her treasure.

Madam Imbert informed her that she expected a friend of hers to come in a day or two to exchange some money for her. She had to have some to send to her husband's lawyer, who was making every effort to effect his release. "If your money is bulky, from being in bills of small denominations, he might exchange it for you and give you large bills, which you could easily carry with you. I have transacted a good deal of business with him, and have always found him careful and honest. If you wish, I will introduce you to him."

Mrs. Maroney was always very suspicious, and her fears were somewhat aroused by the proposition. "What sort of a man is he?" she inquired.

"I know nothing further of him than what I have told you; he has always acted honestly with me."

"Could you not manage to have the money exchanged for me without my being known in the transaction?" asked Mrs. Maroney.

"Yes, I could, but it would be better for you to see him."

"Oh, no; there is no necessity of his knowing me. You can introduce me as a friend, if you like, but get the money changed as if it were your own, and pay him well for it."

"Just as you please," answered the Madam.

Mrs. Maroney wished in this way to compromise Madam Imbert, and get her into the same boat with Maroney and her. I was doing everything possible to bring out the money, and was able to protect my detectives. I had placed tempting bait for both Maroney and his wife, and they were nibbling strongly. My anglers were experts, and would soon hook their fish, and after playing them carefully would land them securely.

Mrs. Maroney's confidence in Madam Imbert increased daily, until finally she said to her: "Madam Imbert, you would do me a great favor if you would take charge of some money packages I have. You could put them in a safe place, and let me have small amounts now and then, as I needed them. When my husband gets out we can use the money; but now we do not need it. The Adams Express might find out I have money, and they might try to get possession of it. It is not theirs, but they would make trouble for me if they could."

"No," replied the Madam, "that I could not do. I don't want to be bothered with other people's money. I have enough trouble with my own. If I should take yours, I should never have any rest, fearing it might be stolen; and if it should be, I could never forgive myself. No, it is better for you to take care of it. I will advise you all I can, but cannot take the responsibility of protecting your property."

Mrs. Maroney wrote to her husband and asked his advice. She informed him that she had followed Madam Imbert and had discovered her exchanging money, thus proving that she was telling the truth; and now she knew she could trust her. She spoke of the Madam's refusal to take charge of the money, but said she had agreed to get it exchanged, and asked him what she had better do.

Maroney talked the affair over with White, and asked his opinion as to the best course to pursue. "She may do very well," said he, "but I don't know as I would trust her. You never saw her. She may be a first-rate woman, or she may be the opposite. If I were in your place I should wish to see her before I trusted her. It would be well to have your wife bring her to the jail to see you. Some women are smart, and she may be. As a general thing women are very good as playthings, but trusting them is an entirely different matter."

Maroney carefully considered the matter, and finally wrote to his wife, directing her to induce Madam Imbert to accompany her to Eldridge street jail, as he wanted to see her and judge of her character before trusting her too far.

On receipt of this letter, Mrs. Maroney called on Madam Imbert, said she was going to New York to see her husband, and asked the Madam to accompany her. She said they would have a pleasant trip, and return home the same evening.

De Forest came up at this moment, and interrupted the conversation.

"Good morning, ladies," said he gaily, "I have come to ask you to take a fish-dinner with me at Manayunk."

Madam Imbert declined the invitation, but Mrs. Maroney concluded to go, and started off with the happy De Forest. Madam Imbert returned to Stemples's, hired his team, and drove into the city. She reported to me, and asked for instructions about going to New York with Mrs. Maroney. I told her to go; gave her full instructions, and then had an interview with the Vice-President. I told him that all was working well, and received his congratulations. Everything seemed auspicious, and pointed to speedy success. It was true that a good deal of money was being spent, but there was no other way to carry the matter to a successful termination.

Madam Imbert returned to Jenkintown in time for supper, and, after a hearty meal, called at Cox's. She found no one at home but Mrs. Cox and the children. Mrs. Cox said her sister had not returned from her ride, and she feared that she must have met with some accident. Madam Imbert conversed with her until between eight and nine, when Josh. and Rivers came in.

Mrs. Cox said, "Josh., Mrs. Maroney has not reached home yet. I fear she has met with some accident."

"Hasn't she? Well, I'll go and hunt her up. Come along, Rivers."

"Josh., you good for nothing fellow. You must wait here; don't you know you should not leave the house unguarded at this time?"

"Oh!" thought Madam Imbert, "danger in leaving the house, eh! So there are two more in the secret,—Josh. and his wife!"

Josh. said he would only step down the road, and would soon return.

Nine o'clock came, but no Mrs. Maroney or De Forest. Madam Imbert did not know what to make of it, and began to think something unusual was under way. She arose to leave, but Mrs. Cox said: "Please don't leave me alone. Josh. will soon be back. Won't you stay down and watch the house, while I put the children to bed? Flora is asleep, and I am lonesome. I do wish that shiftless fellow would come home."

"I am very tired," remarked Madam Imbert, preparing to leave, "and am afraid the tavern will be closed, as it is getting late; but I will see if I can find Josh., and send him home."

"If you don't find him, please come back," pleaded Mrs. Cox.

"Well, I'll do that," said she, going out. She walked to Stemples's, and without going into the bar-room, where she knew she would find Josh., went to her room and instructed Miss Johnson to find Rivers and tell him to keep Josh. for an hour. She then returned to Cox's.

Miss Johnson found that Rivers was with Josh., Barclay and Horton, in the bar-room. She walked by the door, and, unobserved by the others, gave Rivers a signal to come out. He slipped out, and as he passed her she said: "Rivers, keep Cox for an hour," and in a second he was back calling for more drinks, and getting off jokes which brought down roars of laughter.

CHAPTER XXIV.

M RS. COX was very much pleased when Madam Imbert returned, and started up stairs to put the children to bed. There was not a moment to lose. As soon as they left the room Madam Imbert rushed to the outer door and listened. She was satisfied. No one was coming, and so, grasping a lamp, she went down into the cellar. Her quick eye took in every thing at a glance, but she could discover nothing out of the way. The floor was a common earthen one, but no signs of recent digging were to be seen. She pitched in, and for a few moments worked like a Trojan; she removed and replaced all the barrels, crocks, dishes, everything under which articles might possibly be concealed, but found nothing She again searched carefully over the floor, and in the centre of the cellar saw slight signs of where the ground might have been lately dug up, and the soil carefully replaced. She knelt down to examine it more carefully, when she heard the rumbling of wheels. She sprang to her feet and rushed up stairs. She was none too soon, as she was hardly seated before Mrs. Maroney came in. She was greatly surprised to see Madam Imbert, and exclaimed: "What! you here? It is rather late for you to be out, is it not?" Madam Imbert saw at once that she was slightly intoxicated. She replied:

" Yes indeed it is ! I found your sister all alone, and she begged me to stay until she got the children in bed."

Mrs. Cox came in at this moment, looking very angry. "Where have you been all this time? You ought to know better than to leave me all alone. Josh. has gone out with Rivers, and I believe they must be drinking. I am angry with Rivers. Josh. is getting to drink more than ever since he came here. It is too bad in you to stay away so long ! I had to beg Madam Imbert to stay with me, and Flora has just gone to bed crying for her ma ! "

" Madam Imbert, I am very sorry I have been the cause of your late stay," said Mrs. Maroney. Then, pointing to some dirt on the Madam's dress — which had come from the cellar — she exclaimed : " What's that on your dress ? "

Madam Imbert looked carelessly at it, and said : " Why, I thought I had brushed that all off ! When I was out looking for Josh. I stumbled and gave my knee a terrible wrench." Then glancing at the clock, she said : " Why, how late it is ! Miss Johnson will think that I am lost. Good night ! "

" No, don't go yet; have a little brandy ? It will do you good, as the air is quite chilling. Do you know that De Forest is a very fine fellow ? I have a much higher opinion of him than ever before." She got the brandy and partially filled a tumbler with it. Madam Imbert just touched the liquor with her lips, and then passed it back to Mrs. Maroney, who drained the glass at a single draught.

"You are doing wrong," remarked the Madam; "you should remember your promise to your husband."

"Well, I shall not be going to-morrow. I shall suffer for this by having a severe head-ache. Was any one with you, down here, while sister was putting the children to bed?" asked Mrs. Maroney, looking full into Madam Imbert's face, but she saw nothing suspicious there. "No," answered Madam Imbert, as innocently as a lamb.

The two ladies walked out of the house together, and Mrs. Maroney accompanied the Madam a short distance up the street, when they met Josh. and Rivers. Mrs. Maroney went home with Josh., and Madam Imbert told Rivers to keep watch on Cox's house, as something was in the wind. Rivers informed her she would have to hurry back to the town, as Stemples would soon close up for the night. Rivers passed slowly around the house. He knew that Josh. had taken enough to make him sleep well, and that Mrs. Maroney was in about the same condition, so that Mrs. Cox was the only one he had to fear. After a while he crawled close up to the cellar window. He heard an animated conversation going on inside, but could not distinguish the words. Some one closed a door with a bang, and all sound ceased. He looked up and noticed a light pouring through a narrow window, which he knew lighted a closet opening off from the sitting-room. He climbed up to it and saw, what was to him at least, an amusing scene. Josh., his wife, and Mrs. Maroney, were seated in the room. Mrs. Maroney looked as though in a violent passion, and plainly showed that she had been drinking. Josh. was making desperate efforts to look and act perfectly sober, but in spite of his efforts he would occasionally give a loud hiccough, while Mrs. Cox sat bolt upright in her chair, looking in sober disgust on both of them. Rivers, in his new position, could see and hear all that was going on. Mrs. Maroney was talking in an excited manner.

"What brought that Madam Imbert here to-night? I am suspicious of that woman. She is very smart, and I saw dirt on her dress. It seems plain to me that she has been in the cellar, and down on her knees. What made you go up stairs and leave her here all alone?"

"You have confidence in her, but you have been drinking, and that makes you suspicious," replied Mrs. Cox.

"How dare you talk to me in this way?" yelled Mrs. Maroney. "I know my business! You know why I am living here, and supporting you and your worthless, good for nothing vagabond of a husband. He could never earn a living for himself, to say nothing of taking care of a family. All I want you to do is to obey me and keep your mouths shut, and I will pay you well for it; Josh. is always drunk and blabbing about."

Josh. attempted to say something.

"Hold your tongue, you fool! you are so drunk now you don't know what you are doing!"

"Why," said Cox, "I did take a drop too much, but I don't believe I have taken half so much as you!"

In a second Mrs. Maroney grasped a pitcher and smashed it over Josh.'s skull! Mrs. Cox sprang to assist her husband. For a moment there was a lively time, and the prospects were good for a regular scene, but quiet was soon restored, and Josh., muttering, went off to bed.

"I must go into the cellar the first thing in the

In a second, Mrs. Mahoney grasped a pitcher and smashed it over Josh's skull.—Page 222.

morning," said Mrs. Maroney. "Don't look at me in that way; my faculties are all clear. No one must go into it until I come down, as I want it to remain just as it is. I am suspicious of that Madam Imbert. There was no necessity of her being here so late, or of your leaving her alone, you fool! Be sure, now, not to let any one go down!" Mrs. Maroney then took a lamp and started for her room. Rivers listened for some time, and finding all quiet, went up to Stemples's.

He saw a light in Madam Imbert's room, and after listening around, and finding no one stirring, he went quietly under her window and threw some dirt against the panes. The light in the room was instantly turned down. Soon afterward, the window was noiselessly raised, and Madam Imbert poked her head out. "Who's there?" she asked, in a low tone.

"Rivers," he replied; "like to see you; important."

"Wait," said she; "I will be with you at the front door directly."

She was acquainted with all the modes of egress, and threading her way through the darkness, soon stood with Rivers in front of the house. He reported all that had taken place.

Madam Imbert said: "I think it is all right, but still I may be mistaken, and we must be sure. Can't you find some way to get into the cellar? There is a small window, about two feet by thirteen inches, which you might remove, and gain access in that way. It will be light at four o'clock; it is now twelve, and every one at Cox's will be sound asleep at that time. You can then slip in, and if I have disarranged anything, put it to rights. Be sure not to get caught!"

"I will certainly do it," said Rivers, as he started to return to Cox's.

During his absence some one had set loose a dog that Cox owned. It was a miserable cur, but was long-winded, like its master, and possessed of good barking qualities. Rivers got well concealed, but the dog was after him — bark, bark, bark; he tried all he could to quiet him, but could not. Soon a neighboring dog commenced to howl; then another, and another, until all the dogs in the village had joined in a grand chorus. He did not know what to do. He was concealed by the side of a fence, but did not dare strike the dog, which kept a few paces from him, barking incessantly. Mrs. Maroney heard the noise, and opening her window, said; "Sic, sic; good fellow, sic."

Rivers jumped up and got the dog to follow him until he reached a field some distance from the house, when, with a well-directed throw he stunned him with a large stone, and soon stamped all life out of him. He then took the "melancholy remains," placed them at Barclay's door, and returned to Cox's, where he found all quiet. He returned to his old position and remained until day began to dawn.

At dawn he crawled to the window, easily removed it, and slipped into the cellar. He examined everything carefully, found some marks on the floor where barrels had been removed, and in less than half an hour had obliterated all traces of Madam Imbert's operations. He then crawled out, replaced the window, and quietly returned to his boarding-house. He had made arrangements by which he could always let himself in or out at any hour of the night. The family he boarded with thought he was somewhat of a "rake," but as he always paid his bills promptly, liked him for a boarder.

In the morning Madam Imbert was on the lookout, and between nine and ten Rivers came along. He reported that he had replaced everything in the cellar, and described how he had killed Josh.'s dog and left his remains at Barclay's.

Madam Imbert strolled down to Cox's, and met Mrs. Maroney at the door. She was more polite than usual, having made an examination of the cellar and found her suspicions baseless. Soon Josh. and Rivers made their appearance. Rivers remarked that he had heard a strange dog barking the night before, and got up to find out what was going on, but could discover nothing.

"Yes," said Mrs. Maroney, "that was Josh.'s dog. A man was lurking around here before I went to bed, so I let the dog out. In a short time I heard it after some one, and opened my window and set it on. You see, Josh., how necessary it is for you to keep sober. If you had been up you might have shot that scoundrel. This morning I saw his footprints distinctly impressed in the walks."

"Well," said Josh., "if my dog got hold of him, he made a hole in his leg, I'll bet. I know he is a good dog."

"Yes, I think he is," said Rivers, as he and Josh. strolled over toward Barclay's.

Barclay met them on the way. "Josh.," says he, "that dog of mine is a splendid animal, by George! You ought to have heard him bark last night. A strange dog came

15

around my place; my dog tackled him, and 'oh, Moses,' how they *fit!* It ended by my dog's killing his antagonist. Come and see how he *chawed* him up!"

He led the way to where the dead carcass lay. As soon as they came in sight of it Josh. dashed forward, and raising the dead animal by its caudal appendage, angrily exclaimed: "That's my dog! You must be the man who was lurking around my house last night! You had better go down and explain to Mrs. Maroney what you were doing around there."

"What do you suppose I could be doing at your house?" asked Barclay, much perplexed. "Why, I was not out of my house once last night."

"I tell you," said Josh., "Mrs. Maroney will walk into you when she finds this out. You ought to have seen her last night. She smashed a pitcher over my head, and I believe she would have killed me, if my wife had not pitched into her. Of course I could not strike back, as she is a woman."

Rivers invited them up to Stemples's, and in less than an hour Cox and he had impressed upon Barclay the necessity of his seeing Mrs. Maroney and explaining to her that he had not been lurking around the night before.

They started off together, and arrived at Josh.'s residence just as Madam Imbert and Mrs. Maroney were coming out. Barclay immediately went up to her and assured her that he had not been loafing around the night before.

"Who said you had?" said Mrs. Maroney, now fully convinced that it *was* he. "Who said you had?" and she opened upon him with a perfect tirade of abuse.

Raising the dead animal by its caudal appendage, he angrily exclaimed, "That's my dog!"—Page 226.

Madam Imbert took her by the arm and drew her to one side. "Mrs. Maroney, don't take any notice of that man. He is a fool, and your best plan is to let him severely alone. Some people may be wiser than others, and will begin to suspect that something is wrong if you go on so. You know the old saying: 'Walls have ears.'"

"You are right, you seem to be always right," said Mrs. Maroney, and she let the matter drop.

CHAPTER XXV.

THE two women left Barclay perfectly dumbfounded and walked over to the garden. Mrs. Maroney said she was going to New York in the morning to see her husband, and begged the Madam to accompany her. Madam Imbert agreed to go, saying that she had some purchases to make. They concluded to hire Stemples's team in the morning and drive into Philadelphia, put it up at some livery stable, go to New York, visit Maroney, return to Philadelphia, and drive home in the evening.

Nothing of importance took place the day they visited New York. Green knew of their intended trip and "shadowed" them to New York and back. All he had to report was that nothing had transpired worthy of mention. It is quite as important to find that nothing takes place as to note what actually occurs, for thus the case is cleared of all uncertainty. The "shadow" reports truthfully of all things just as he finds them.

The women, on their arrival in New York, went directly to Eldridge street jail and Mrs. Maroney introduced Madam Imbert to her husband. She then had a long private conversation with him and afterwards re-joined Madam Imbert. The three had a pleasant chat, Maroney acting in all respects the part of a perfect gentleman. His face showed deep anxiety, but he talked very cheerfully and told Madam Imbert that he hoped soon to have the pleasure of meeting her at Jenkintown. He assured her that he would soon be free and would then take vengeance on his enemies.

He said he intended to go to Texas and buy a ranche. The Rio Grande country just suited him, and he expatiated at length on the beauty of the country and the salubrity of its climate.

After a few hours passed in social converse they parted. Mrs. Maroney went to visit a friend on Thirty-first street and Madam Imbert to do her shopping. They agreed to meet at the Jersey City ferry at four o'clock.

Green followed Mrs. Maroney. She visited her friend, stopped some time and then met Madam Imbert at the appointed place and time.

On the road to Philadelphia Mrs. Maroney spoke of her husband and said he was very much pleased with the Madam, and thought her a very fine-looking, intelligent woman, in fact just the person to help them; but he was about to carry out a plan which he knew would be successful. White was soon going to be released on bail and would then arrange everything for him. In the meantime, she was to wait quietly and do nothing, as he would shortly be with her.

On getting into Philadelphia they ordered their team and drove out to Jenkintown. The same day White came to Maroney and said:

"Congratulate me, old fellow. Shanks has just brought me some letters from my attorneys and I find that all has gone well. My affairs are in a much better condition, and now, after a long and irksome confinement, I am about to be liberated on bail. In two or three days, or by the end of this week, at farthest, I shall be at liberty."

"I am delighted to hear of your good fortune," answered Maroney in a hearty tone. "You must not forget me when you are out, but as soon as you can arrange your own affairs, turn your attention to mine. I am anxious to see the plan to entrap Chase at once set in operation. Won't it be a good joke when McGibony nabs him and finds the money on his person? Ha! ha! ha! what will the Adams Express say then? They will feel rather sore over their pet, I reckon."

He laughed over the idea for some time, while a fiendish expression of joy settled on his face.

"I'll attend to it as soon as possible," said White; "but you see I have no money of my own that I can use at the present time. I would gladly advance you the necessary amount if I could, but all my available cash will have to go as security to my bondsmen. I believe you a thorough good fellow, and will cheerfully do all in my power for you."

"I don't wish you to advance the money for me. I know you would if you could; but you and I are about in the same fix. We have plenty of funds, but can't use them at present. I believe I shall be able to raise the money in some way before long. If the job works well with Chase I shall be completely vindicated. Another thing, the suit against me will soon come up, and my counsel says that I am sure to win it. I shall be the only witness on the part of the defendant and shall have to swear that I never took any of the money. This will be the truth, as a cent of money never came wrongfully into my possession. It is a good thing they did not know I had an interest in the livery stable, or they would surely have seized that."

"I have a good lawyer," said White, "he has carried me through successfully, and as soon as possible after I get out I will help you."

The next day Bangs disguised himself and called at the jail as White's counsel. He had a long talk with him in his cell and then walked briskly out in the manner of a lawyer with a large practice, whose moments are precious; but lawyers have one object, while he had another. Bangs wished to avoid the scrutiny of the prisoners, as there might be some of them who knew him.

White came smilingly up to Maroney after Bangs left and said:

"My case is surely arranged, and I am off to-morrow."

"Are you, indeed?" exclaimed Maroney. "I am delighted to hear it;" but his voice sank. It seemed as if he wanted White out, so that he could help him, but was afraid to trust him. He turned and walked away, came back, and again congratulated White. White assured him that he was going in the morning. "So soon?" remarked Maroney; "well, I am happy to find you are. I don't want to see any man kept in jail. My own case will soon come up, and after I am cleared here, the trial in Montgomery will be a perfect farce. I shall write to my wife and tell her how well you have succeeded. Isn't it strange, White, that I have taken such a liking to you? You are the right man for me. There is not a soul in this jail but you whom I would trust." He walked into his cell and wrote a letter to his wife. Several times he came out and conversed with White. He seemed to have something on his mind which he wished to disclose, but lacked the courage to do so. He finally backed down entirely, and concluded to wait. He played several games of cards with White and the other prisoners, and then conversed with Shanks, who came to remove some of White's baggage. He found that White had taken a room on Bleeker street, and the moving of his effects showed how near at hand was the moment of his departure.

The next day was an eventful one, and clearly proved the soundness of my theory. After breakfast Maroney took White's arm, and walked around the hall several times with him, his manner plainly showing that he was very much embarrassed. He finally drew him into a quiet corner opposite to where the prisoners were congregated playing cards and amusing themselves in various ways. "White," said Maroney, "I am going to entrust to you my secret. I feel that I can trust you; I know I can. I have watched you closely, and find that you are true as steel. Now listen: I have invited you to take hold of my matters, and in order to give you a clear understanding of my case, it becomes necessary for me to divulge to you what at present is known only to my wife and myself. It is useless for me to ask, but still I wish you to give me your solemn promise to keep my secret inviolate."

"Oh, yes, I'll do that," said White, "but I have got a good deal of business of my own to attend to, and if you think you can't trust me, you had better keep it to yourself."

" No, no, nothing of the kind! I know I can trust you!" said Maroney, "and you have given the promise. Now, White, who do you think stole the fifty thousand dollars?"

" I am sure I don't know," replied White.

" Well, I did! I stole it from the company, and have been able to keep it so far. If you will assist me, I shall continue to do so. Would you have stolen it if you had been in my place?"

" Certainly," exclaimed White; "do you think I am a fool? I shall make a big pile in my operation."

" Then," said Maroney, "if we only join our forces, we shall make some one howl."

Neither spoke for some minutes. White acted as if the matter was a common, every-day occurrence; but he thought: " He has broken the ice; I shall soon hear it all."

Maroney was the first to break the silence. He said: " I first stole ten thousand dollars, which was brought to my office on Sunday, by the messenger from Atlanta. This package was intended for a party in Columbus, Ga. It had been missent, and forwarded by mistake to Atlanta, instead of to Macon, and from Atlanta to me in Montgomery. My duty was, on receipt of the package, to immediately telegraph to Atlanta of its arrival, and to send it off by the train that left that evening for Columbus. I had no right to the package, and should have immediately re-billed it and sent it off. I was certain that no one knew that it had been missent. It had evidently found its way into the pouch through a mistake, as it was not marked on the way-bill, or its presence known to the messenger. I never thought I should be guilty of theft till the time; but the moment I saw the package it flashed into my mind that if I took it I would never be detected. The temptation was too strong to be withstood. I yielded to it, and without any one's seeing me, dropped the package under the counter. The messenger did not see it, and as his way-bill checked up all right, soon left the office. I watched my chance and put the packet of money into my coat-pocket and went home.

"You see, White, that was my first offense, and I felt rather frightened. I felt sorry that I had yielded to the temptation, but could not part with the money, it seemed so completely to have infatuated me. I took it home and hid it, but did not tell my wife a word about it. In a short time despatches were sent all around to the different agents to find, if possible, where the package was. I received several of them, but reported that I had not seen or heard anything of it. I was so assured of the impossibility of my detection that I had lost all the fears that at first assailed me, and was as cool as a cucumber.

"The General Superintendent came around with several detectives, but they could not find the money. I was tried in many ways, but I never flinched, and they finally had to give the matter up.

"In a short time I asked for leave of absence to make a visit to the North. It was granted me, and I started off, with the ten thousand dollars in my possession. I soon found that I was followed by a detective, and I led him a wild-goose chase until I reached Richmond, Va., where I gave him the slip, and he never knew where I went. I did the same in the forty-thousand-dollar case. I gave them all the slip at Chattanooga."

" No matter about that," said White ; if you are going to give me a statement, give me a clear one, and not jumble everything together."

"Well, I gave the detective the slip at Richmond, and went to Winnsboro, S. C. There I passed myself off as a cotton buyer, but had great difficulty in making a purchase, as Robert Agnew, a prominent cotton-broker, held all the cotton in the neighborhood, and did not care to sell as he expected a rise in price every day. After some dickering I induced him to sell me seven thousand five hundred dollars' worth, which I paid for with the stolen funds of the company.

" I had the cotton shipped to R. G. Barnard, Charleston, S. C., to be sold, proceeds to be remitted to me, in Montgomery. The cotton was sold and the amount forwarded to me in two drafts on New York, one of which I had cashed in that city, and the other in Montgomery. I lost quite a sum by my speculation, as cotton did not rise, but fell. I was perfectly contented to stand the loss, as the stolen money was exchanged. I bought " Yankee Mary" with the two thousand five hundred dollars remaining, and returned to Montgomery, after having successfully disposed of all the stolen money.

"On my return I found everything quiet, and went on with my duties as usual; but one day the Superintendent came to me and said the company had concluded to change agents, and that I had better resign. I did so at once, saying that I was just about going into business on my own account. I must say that when I met the Gen-

eral Superintendent I did not like his looks, as he seemed
to suspect me.   He made many enquiries as to how I got
my money, but was unable to ascertain anything.

"The Superintendent of the Southern Division asked
me to take charge of the office until my successor arrived,
and I willingly consented.   The Superintendent had
much suavity of manner, and it was hard for me to tell
whether he considered me guilty or not.   I rather thought
he suspected me.   When I found that my time with the
company was to be so short I determined to make a good
haul, as I knew I could never get a situation in the business again, for the Adams Express was the only express
company in the South.   I began to look around to see
how I could best accomplish my purpose.   I studied the
character of the different messengers, and thought Chase
the best man to operate upon.   I determined to wait until
I had a good heavy run out, and then put my plan in
operation.   Chase was a good, clever fellow, but careless.
I tried him in several ways, and found that he could be
"gulled" more easily than any of the other messengers.
I could not do anything on the runs in, as the messengers
checked the packages over to me, but on the runs out I
checked over to them, and, with a careless man like
Chase, it would be the simplest thing in the world to call
off packages, and, as he checked them off, for me to drop
them behind the counter instead of into the pouch."

"As he stood outside of the counter, I was enabled to call off all the packages on the way-bill, but dropped the four containing the forty thousand dollars under the counter."—Page 237.

CHAPTER XXVI.

ON the twenty-seventh of January I had a very heavy run in, and among numerous other packages were four that attracted my attention; one for Charleston, S. C., for two thousand five hundred dollars, and three for Augusta, Geo., for thirty thousand, five thousand and two thousand five hundred dollars respectively. Chase was going out in the morning, and then was the time to act. I got an old trunk that was lying in the office, and packed it full of different articles, among other things four boxes of cigars. Early in the morning I was up and down at the office. Chase soon came in, drew his safe over to the counter, and began to check off the packages marked on the way-bill, as I called them off and placed them in the pouch. If he had obeyed the rule of the company he would have taken each package in his hand and placed it in the pouch, but he carelessly allowed me to call off the amounts and place the packages in the pouch. In this way, as he stood outside of the counter, I was enabled to call off all the packages on the way-bill, but dropped the four containing the forty thousand dollars under the counter amongst a lot of waste paper I had placed there for the purpose. The way-bill checked off all right; Chase said "O. K," so I locked the pouch, handed it to him, and he locked it up in his safe. He then went to breakfast, leaving me alone in the office. I immediately picked up the packages, distributed their contents into four piles of equal size, removed the cigars from the boxes, and placed a pile of money in each. I then filled the space above the money with cigars, nailed down the lid of the boxes, placed them in the trunk, tied it up and directed it to W. A. Jackson, Galveston, Texas. There was a wagon loading at the door. I had the box immediately placed on it, and within an hour of the time I had taken the money it was on its way down the Alabama river, for Mobile. The boat started down the river at the same time that Chase left for Atlanta. That is what I call sharp work. No one but me knew of the loss of the packages.

"Chase was in his car, perfectly at ease, but when he reached Atlanta he was destined to receive a shock he would not soon forget. As soon as he arrived there the loss was discovered, and the Assistant Superintendent of the Southern Division, who happened to be in the Atlanta office, immediately telegraphed to me for an explanation. I did not take the trouble of answering the despatch, and he came on to Montgomery that night to investigate. All I had to say was that I had checked the money over to Chase, and they would have to look to him for an explanation. Telegrams came thick and fast, but I was nerved up to pass through anything, and left them unnoticed.

"When Chase returned to Montgomery he was greatly excited and appeared much more guilty than I. The Assistant Superintendent was in the office when he arrived. I received the pouch from Chase, checked off the way-bill, found the packages all right, and throwing down the pouch, placed the packages in the vault. I then returned and picked up the pouch as if to look into it. I had my knife open, but concealed in my coat sleeve. As I raised the pouch to look into it, I slipped the knife into my hand and in a second cut two slits in the pouch and threw the knife back up my sleeve. I immediately said to Mr. Hall, who stood directly in front of me, 'Why, it's cut! How the messenger could carry the pouch around, cut in this manner, and not discover it, is astonishing!'

"The Assistant Superintendent examined the pouch and found it cut, as I had stated. This was a great point in my favor, and the Assistant Superintendent was at once convinced that I was innocent of any participation in the robbery. No one suspected me after this until the Vice-President and General Superintendent came. They looked at the pouch, and one of them said, 'I understand this,' and they had the pouch taken care of. This was the first thing that seemed to create suspicion in the General Superintendent's mind. He had me arrested, but could not prove any thing against me. My friends all stood by me, and I had to do an immense amount of drinking. My wife one day asked me about the robbery; I at first denied any knowledge of it, but she is smart and does not easily give up. She kept at me and I finally concluded that the best way to keep her still was to tell her all. So I owned up to her, and then gave her some money and started her for the North. It is hard for me to keep any thing entirely to myself, and especially hard to keep any thing from my wife.

"I remained in Montgomery, but was not at all lonely, as I always had a squad of friends around me. In fact I never knew before that I had so many. I knew that the trunk was safe, but felt at times a little apprehensive that some one might open it. Its contents were amply sufficient to pay all charges on it in case it should never be claimed.

"After my arrest, I was taken before Justice Holtzclaw. At the preliminary examination I was held in forty thousand dollars bail, but at the final examination the company presented so weak a case that I think I ought to have been discharged at once. The justice thought differently, but reduced my bail to four thousand dollars, in which amount I was bound over to appear for trial before the circuit court. I easily procured bail, and was soon at liberty. I remained in Montgomery after my release, keeping a sharp look out for detectives, as I felt sure the company would have plenty of them on my track, but I could not discover any. It was hard to believe they had none employed, as on the ten thousand dollar case they had a small regiment of them; but none were to be seen in Montgomery, and I concluded they must be looking for the money in another direction. I had a slight mistrust of McGibony, but soon proved to my entire satisfaction that he was not employed in the case. Every thing went on smoothly, and I could discover nothing suspicious going on around me. I at length determined to make an excursion to several of the large Southern cities, to ascertain, if possible, whether I would be followed. Before leaving, I wrote to the agent of Jones's Express, at Galveston, assuming the name of W. A. Jackson, and directed him to send my trunk to Natchez. I started out on my trip and visited

Atlanta, Chattanooga, Nashville and Memphis. I scanned the passengers who came on board or left the trains, all the guests who 'put up' at the various hotels where I stopped on my journey, but could not discover a sign of a detective. By the time that I got to Memphis I knew I was not followed, and so took the steamer 'John Walsh,' intending to get off at Natchez, gain possession of my trunk, which must have reached there, and go on down the river to New Orleans. When I reached Natchez, I enquired of the agent of Jones's Express whether he had a trunk for W. A. Jackson, shipped from Galveston, Texas. He examined his book and said that he had not received such a trunk, but that possibly it had been sent and detained in the New Orleans office. I was now in a quandary; I was afraid to go to New Orleans and ask for the trunk, as I knew the Adams and Jones's Express occupied the same office in that city. Could it be possible that the company had suspicions of the trunk and were holding it as a bait to draw me out? No! it was not possible! Still, I did not care to go to the office and ask for the trunk, as some one would be sure to know me, and my claiming a trunk as W. A. Jackson would be proof positive to them that something was wrong about it. They would seize and search it, and then my guilt would be apparent. I finally determined to go to New Orleans, put up at the City Hotel, and then carelessly drop into the office of the company and see if I could discover the trunk lying around. I did so, and on coming into the office was immediately recognized by the employés, some of whom were glad to see me. I did not stay long; glanced around, saw the trunk was not there, and returned to the hotel.

16

"I wanted to find whether the trunk had gone on to Natchez, so I wrote a note, asking whether a trunk directed to W. A. Jackson, Natchez, was in their possession or had been forwarded to its destination, and signed it W. A. Jackson. I then walked out of the hotel, limping as if so lame as to be scarcely able to walk, and met a colored boy standing on the corner. I hired him to take the note to the office for me and bring back the answer. He soon returned with a note which politely informed me that the trunk had been sent to Natchez. I immediately returned to Natchez, found the trunk, signed the receipt, paid the charges and left for Mobile *via* New Orleans, and I tell you I was more than pleased when I arrived there with my trunk.

"When I reached Montgomery a bevy of my friends came down to see me. Porter, one of my best friends — a splendid fellow — was amongst them, and as he was clerk of the hotel I had him order my baggage up. He had a carriage for me and we drove to Patterson's, and then went over to the hotel. In the morning I had him bring the old trunk into my room. I opened it before them all, carelessly took a few cigars from each of the boxes and gave to them to try. In this way their suspicions in regard to the old trunk, if they had any, were entirely dispelled.

"Mrs. Maroney was still in New York. I remained for some time in Montgomery, still suspecting that some one was on my track, but could find nothing to confirm my suspicions. It was getting time for me to make some preparation for my defense. I had formed a plan to overthrow the testimony of the company by having a key made to fit their pouch, introducing it at the trial and proving that outsiders might have keys as well as the agent. I was desirous of having the key made at once. It could not be made in Montgomery or at New Orleans, for, though there were plenty of locksmiths, their work was not fine enough to suit me; so I concluded to go to New York and have one made.

"I had some business to transact with my wife also, and wrote to her to meet me at a certain date in Philadelphia. I came North, met my wife in Philadelphia, where we stopped a day or two, and then started for New York. As I stepped ashore from the ferry-boat I was arrested. Never before in my life was I so dumbfounded. I can't tell you how they knew the time I would arrive. The detectives in Philadelphia must have been after me while I was there, and when I left for here they must have telegraphed, and thus secured my arrest. They brought me here and I told my wife to come and see me in the morning. I was too confused to say anything and my brain was in a maze. I never dreamed of the possibility of arrest in New York. I might have been prepared for it in Montgomery, but did not think it possible that anything of the kind could happen here. My wife spoke to me on the subject, but I was unable to do or say anything. I make it a rule, when I am confused and can't collect my thoughts, to say nothing until I am calm, when I plan what I had better do.

"In the morning I decided that it was necessary for my wife to go to Montgomery and bring the money North with her. I was in jail and might need the money to procure bail, which I would like to do now. Then, there was danger in leaving the money where it was secreted—in the old trunk in the garret—as Floyd might want to clear the garret out, and I had several times seen him sell unclaimed baggage. My old trunk might be sold for a trifle and some one take it home and find it contained a treasure.

"As soon as she could, Mrs. Maroney went to Montgomery for the money. I had informed her where it was concealed, and told her to get it and bring it North.

"The money was rather bulky, as although there were some large bills, there were a great many fives, tens, twenties and a few one hundred dollar notes. The whole of it made a large pile, but my wife proved a good hand. She fooled them all, and concealed the money in her bustle. It was a troublesome weight to travel with, and she was obliged to stop at Augusta, Ga., to rest herself. She also spent a day with my brother at Danielsville, who promised to come and see me. He came, and, as you know, accomplished nothing.

"My wife has now got the money concealed in the cellar of Josh. Cox's house. Cox is her brother-in-law, and from what she tells me of him is a good-natured fellow, but pretty shrewd. Mrs. Cox is very smart. They never leave the house entirely alone, one or the other of them always keeping watch.

"That Madam Imbert is said by my wife to be a fine woman. I was much pleased with her when she came here the other day. Mrs. Maroney managed well with her and discovered that her husband is imprisoned in Missouri. She also followed her in Philadelphia and found her changing money. My wife is smart, she sud-

denly confronted her and the Madam admitted all. A
man comes to see her who exchanges money for her. My
wife was about arranging with her to have the express
money exchanged, but you are going out and I prefer to
entrust my affairs to you. You see, White, I know I can
trust you. There is only one thing that troubles me
about Jenkintown: A fellow named De Forest is stopping
there and is quite attentive to my wife. I think he is an
agent of the Adams Express; but from what my wife
says, she is smart enough for him and can rope him in
long before he can her.

"Now I have told you all, and hope you will act in the
matter just as your judgment dictates. The fact of the
matter is, your knowledge of the North is so great that
you can act much better than I."

"Yes," said White, "I understand the ropes well, and
you may depend upon it I will handle them as well as I
know how. I think that as soon as I get clear myself —
which may take four, five, or six days — and have settled
up with my lawyers — I don't like those fellows, but
sometimes you can't get along without them — I think I
will try and get a key to the pouch made; I can do so
easily. Then I will go to Montgomery and see Chase,
study his movements on the cars and at the hotels. I
can at the same time arrange to get the girl, whom I
intend to bring from here, into the Exchange, and as soon
as possible get her acquainted with Chase. But see here,
don't you think it best to get some of the stolen money to
use in this case?"

"Certainly," said Maroney, "My wife will give you all
the money you need. I will give you a letter to her."

"No," said White, "I don't want to have anything to do with women. Your wife may be perfectly true to you, but if I come in I doubt very much whether she takes any interest in me, unless it be to thwart my plans."

"Why not?" asked Maroney. "My wife should know and take an interest in all my affairs. She will do all in her power for us, and she is so shrewd that she will be able to help us very much."

"Well," said White, "that may be all true enough, but women are sure to get strange notions. I don't like to deal with them; women seem naturally suspicious. I don't want to treat your wife with injustice, but at the same time if she has a finger in the pie, ten to one she will suspect me of trying to get the whole pile and intending to clear out with it."

"Don't you believe that for a moment," replied Maroney. "She knows I have entire confidence in you, and that will be enough for her. You need have no fears that she will interfere in the matter in any way. I trust you, and my word is law to her. I would prefer to have you take all the money; you can then select what you want for Chase, and try and work off the balance in small amounts. This will be a delicate operation, as the banks very likely marked some of the bills before they shipped them."

"Yes, there are a great many obstacles to be overcome in changing the money, but I think I can manage to work it off in some way."

CHAPTER XXVII.

WHITE, I will write a letter to my wife which will pave your way to gaining her implicit confidence."

"How will you do that?" asked White.

"I will write to her informing her that you are coming, and that you will identify yourself by presenting a letter from me."

"Yes, but suppose she won't give up the money? I could not go back again, as some of the detectives might suspect me and take me into custody."

"Oh, nothing of the sort will happen. I will write you a letter that will surely get the money; come, we will see what we can do." And they sat down at a table, where Maroney began to write.

In a short time he finished a letter, and read it to White. He wrote:

"MY DEAREST WIFE: I have confided all to Mr. White. He will be liberated to-day or to-morrow. He has some business to attend to, which will detain him four or five days, when he will call on you in the guise of a book-peddler. Now, I say to you, trust implicitly in him! I have trusted him with my secret. He will take care of all. Give him everything you have in the packages. Take no writing from him, whatever. He requires something to work off on Chase, and wants to use some of the stuff I got in Montgomery. When he succeeds in this, Chase will be in my place. Then he will begin to exchange all I have ; afterwards all will be easy. When I am at liberty, we can enjoy it in safety. I feel perfectly safe, and confident. Now, dearest, as I have before said, trust him implicitly, and all will be right.

Yours forever,   Nat."

White approved of the letter. Maroney, therefore, sealed it up, directed it, and gave it to Shanks, who was in the jail, to post. Of course the dutiful young man would not fail to do so.

He then wrote the following letter of introduction and handed it to White:

"My Dearest Wife : This is the book-peddler. You will want to buy books from him. Buy what you want. Give him the packages for me. He is honest. All is well.   Nat."

White scanned its contents, and said : "I suppose this is sufficient, but the question still remains : will she obey it ? I will do the best I can, but I have little faith in women."

"Oh, now !" said Maroney, "don't make me feel down-hearted. I have done the best I can, and I know she will obey me."

"Very well," replied White, "I will go as soon as pos-sible — in a week, more or less ; as soon as I can possibly arrange my own affairs. On my arrival in Jenkintown I will write to you at once and let you know how I am received."

"Agreed ; I have trusted you, and my wife must trust you."

Shanks had several commissions to attend to. He first came to my room in the hotel and handed me Maroney's letter to his wife. I opened and read the letter, and exclaimed. "Now the battle is ours! Victory is almost within our grasp." I saw the Vice-President and read the letter to him. He was highly delighted and said he could now see the wisdom of all my manœuvres.

The following day White was released from his long confinement. It must be admitted that his duties were extremely arduous, but such is often the fate of a detective. I have sometimes had my men in prison for a longer time than this, and they have often failed to accomplish any thing, being obliged to give up without discovering what they were looking for. White remained in New York attending to his *own* business after his release. He called once or twice on Maroney to show that he had not forgotten him, and to assure him that he would soon get a pouch-key made. This was easily accomplished, as all he had to do was to go the Express Office, get a key, file it up a little to make it look bright and new, and show it to Maroney as an earnest of his intentions in regard to Chase.

We will now leave the parties in New York and return to Jenkintown. Very little had taken place here and the various parties in whom we have an interest were conducting themselves much as usual. Mrs. Maroney and Madam Imbert went to Philadelphia on the same day that White was liberated. They spent most of the day in the city and came out on the cars in the evening. De Forest met them and drove them to Stemples's in his buggy. After tea Madam Imbert went down to Cox's and strolled

up to the post office with Mrs. Maroney. Mrs. Maroney
received a letter which she opened. She said it was from
Nat. She began to read it as they walked along. As she
read, Madam Imbert noticed that all color left her face,
and she became white as wax. She folded up the letter
and leaned heavily on the Madam's arm for support.

"What's the matter? are you sick?" she anxiously
enquired."

"No;" but I have received so strange a letter; walk
along with me; I am very weak; I will tell you its contents in a few minutes."

She did not go in the direction of Cox's, but led the
way to the garden. Here the two women took seats.
She read the letter over again and then handed it to
Madam Imbert. "Read it," she said. The Madam did
so. Neither spoke for some time. "What do you think
of it?" she at length asked. "I think it a little strange,
but at the same time have no doubt but that it is all right.
Your husband is of course the best judge in this matter,
and must have good reasons for taking the step. He has
full confidence in White; has been locked up with him
for several months; has seen him day and night, and
doubtless has thoroughly studied his character. White is
almost like his wife, and he knows what he is doing when
he consents to trust him so far."

Mrs. Maroney was rapidly getting better and said,
angrily, "No, I will never give him the money in this
way! it is all nonsense! 'What do I know about White?'
This is asking too much of me! Why did he not write
and consult me on the subject? He simply says, 'White
is out of jail now; give him the money!' and gives me

no chance to speak on the subject. Suppose White gets the money; how do I know but that he will run away with it and leave us to suffer without getting any of the benefit? Madam Imbert I must tell you all: you see that in this letter Nat. does not mention money, but he means money. As you are now the only one I can trust, I will talk plainly to you. My husband took the forty thousand dollars from the Express Company, and also ten thousand dollars previously. Now all is out! When he was thrown into prison in New York he sent me for the money which he had concealed in Montgomery, and I brought it here, and have it hidden in Josh.'s cellar. Now what am I to do? If I give it to this man White, I shall probably never see it again; in fact I am sure I never shall."

"You are mistaken, I think," said Madam Imbert; have confidence!"

"*Confidence!* It would be my best plan to run away myself!"—she was going on still further, but Madam Imbert stopped her.

"Don't say any thing more at present, my dear Mrs. Maroney. You are too excited to talk calmly; let the matter rest until morning."

They dropped the subject for the time, and as Mrs. Maroney expressed a desire for a little brandy to calm her nerves, went down to Cox's. Mrs. Maroney offered some brandy to the Madam, which she politely declined to take, but this did not in the least abash her, for she gulped down enough to stagger an old toper. Josh. was not at home, and so very little was said.

Mrs. Cox asked her if she had received a letter from Nat.

"Yes," she answered in a snappish tone, and said no more.

Madam Imbert had accomplished all she desired for that day, and so left Mrs. Maroney to herself. In the morning Mrs. Maroney sent Flora to her, with a request that she would accompany her to Philadelphia. Madam Imbert sent word that she would be happy to go and would come to Cox's immediately.

De Forest met Flora and commenced playing with her.

"I must go right home," said she, "as ma is going to Philadelphia and sent me with a message to Madam Imbert, asking her to go too. She said she would, and is coming down to the house, so I must hurry home."

"What a fool I am," thought De Forest, "I would rather have her go with me."

So he went to Cox's with Flora to offer his services. Mrs. Maroney appeared troubled and excited. He knew that he never made progress with her when she was in a moody state, so he timidly said that he was going to Philadelphia and asked her to go along. She said, "No!" very harshly, and he immediately vanished.

She started out and met Madam Imbert on the way down.

"Come back with me, I want to hire Stemples's team,' she said.

Stemples soon had his team ready for them, and they started.

"I didn't want any one with me but you, Madam Imbert, as I am much troubled and need your advice. I want to consult a lawyer, but don't know how to go about it. There is a lawyer in Philadelphia, a good man, in fact the same one my husband had at New York for consultation, and I think I shall ask his advice."

" I would not do it, if I were in your place," advised Madam Imbert. " If a lawyer once gets hold of the facts, he is much more likely to get all the money than White."

" That is the trouble. Last night after you left, Josh. came in and we talked the matter over. You know Josh. and the opinion I have of him, but with all his faults he is shrewd. His wife and he held the same opinion : that it would never do to trust White with the money, and Josh. was in favor of changing its hiding place. I did not tell them that I had told you all, but I intend to do so. I informed them that I was going to the city to consult a lawyer, but they were both against me, and now you are opposed to me and I don't know what to do, or what I am doing. I am almost crazy ! "

They drove up to a tavern on the way and she took some brandy, which seemed to give her more courage.

When they reached the city Madam Imbert wished to report to Bangs, but found it almost impossible to get away from Mrs. Maroney, who had concluded not to ask the advice of a lawyer. They went into Mitchell's and Madam Imbert managed to get away a few moments and reported to Bangs.

She had not been with him ten minutes before Rivers, who was shadowing Mrs. Maroney, came in and reported that she seemed very uneasy and had been out on the street several times, glancing anxiously around. Madam Imbert at once hurried back to Mitchell's.

"Where were you?" demanded Mrs. Maroney. "I am suspicious of you all!"

Madam Imbert drew herself up with an air of offended dignity which spoke more than words.

"I am sorry I have offended you!" said Mrs. Maroney quickly. "Please forgive me! I am so nervous that for a time I mistrusted even you and thought you had gone for a policeman or a detective; let's have dinner and go."

When they were on the return journey, Mrs. Maroney said:

"I feel much better on the road with you alone than when in the city. I want to talk continually, and you are the only one to whom I dare talk. However excited or miserable I may feel, companionship with you always makes me feel happy and contented."

At the various taverns they passed on the road Mrs. Maroney always stopped and invoked the aid of stimulants to cheer her up. She suddenly turned to Madam Imbert and asked:

"Would you be willing to run away with me? We could go down into Louisiana, where we are not known, buy a small place in some out of the way town and live secluded for four or five years, until our existence was forgotten, and then make our appearance once more in the fashionable world, with plenty of money to maintain our position; or we might go to New York and from there to England and the continent."

"Yes, we could do all that if we had the money," said the Madam; "but you forget that at this time we cannot use it."

"You have plenty of money of your own and you

might let me stop with you for three or four years, as by that time we could use the express' money without any risk."

"Yes, I would gladly keep you for years if that is all you want."

"When do you expect the man who exchanges your money? Could you not get him here at once? Then we could go."

"I could write to him," replied the Madam, "and he would come at once, provided my letter reached him, but sometimes I have to wait two or three months after writing for him before he makes his appearance. He travels a good deal, and comes to the place where he has his letters directed only once in a while. He is a strange man, but very honest. I will write to him to-night, if you say so, so that we can soon hear from him and get him here."

They arrived in Jenkintown without arranging any decided plan. After tea they again met. Mrs. Maroney said that she was so fatigued that even her brain was so weary that she felt completely broken down, and must retire early. Rivers arrived from Philadelphia on the cars long before the women, and went down to see Josh. Josh. had remained at home all day with his wife, and was glad of the excuse Rivers's coming gave him to go down to Stemples's. He was moody and would not talk much. Even Barclay could not get a word out of him. He was willing to drink, but spoke only in monosylables. At nine o'clock he went home. Rivers got into Cox's yard and watched the house for about two hours, when finding all quiet, he returned home and went to bed.

CHAPTER XXVIII.

TIME rolled on, and the third day after the trip to Philadelphia, Madam Imbert was with Mrs. Maroney, who talked incessantly about giving up the money. She alluded to Cox's idea of the question. He said that he would never give White the money; that he did not know the man, and that he would trust no one with forty thousand dollars. He declared that he had now got the money, and that he was going to keep it. She insisted that they should let her arrange the matter to suit herself. Mrs. Cox was, like her husband, bound that White should not get the money. Every thing appeared against White's chances of getting the money. At this time they were seated in a secluded part of the garden. Mrs. Maroney glanced around, saw that no one was near, and then said: "Madam Imbert, you are accustomed to attend to affairs like mine; won't you take the money, claim it as your own, and go with me to the West? You could then find your friend, and he would be willing to exchange the money for two or three thousand dollars — wouldn't he? I want to get away from here; my sister is against me, and Josh. treats me as if he was my equal, or superior."

Madam Imbert saw she must act very prudently. Mrs. Maroney must be quietly dealt with. She wished her to give the money to White, as if she took the money she would have to be a witness in the case. She wished to avoid this, but if she could not succeed in making her turn the money over to White, as a last resort she would take possession of it herself. She therefore replied:

"No, I don't like to take it; I have enough of my own to look after. If my poor husband were only out of jail he would get it changed for you in short order. I don't want any more money about me at present; it would go hard with me if I were discovered with the money on my person."

"There is little danger of that," said Mrs. Maroney. "I carried it all the way from Montgomery and was not much inconvenienced by it; you must help me."

"Mrs. Maroney, if I were in your place, I would do exactly as my husband wished."

"Yes, yes," said she, "but who knows White? I never saw him."

"We will let the matter drop for the present. I will do all I can to assist you. I wrote to my friend last night, and he will send an answer directed to you in my care."

Mrs. Maroney was greatly pleased and went home in high spirits. On the following day she got a letter from Maroney; he had seen White, and he would be in Jenkintown in a day or two. He said White was opposed to dealing with women, and if he did not get the money on his first visit, he would never come back. He finished by entreating her to give up all cheerfully, remembering that it was for the good of both. This letter arrived in the evening, and Mrs. Maroney, after perusing it, told Madam Imbert that she had made up her mind never to give up the money. "I will burn it before I will give it to White," said she. Madam Imbert was rather startled at this avowal, but on a second consideration was convinced that it was a bit of braggadocio, and that there was not the slightest fear of her carrying such a threat into execution. She found Mrs. Maroney in too unreasonable a state of mind to accomplish any thing with her that day, and she therefore returned to Stemples's.

The next day was decidedly a breezy day for all. Early in the morning Mrs. Maroney sent for Madam Imbert, who at once joined her at Cox's. Mrs. Maroney met her at the door.

"O, Madam Imbert, I am so glad you have come! Josh. has been acting in a most independent manner. I almost believe he is right, in protesting that he will not allow the money to go."

Madam Imbert appealed to Mrs. Maroney's sense of duty. She depicted in glowing terms the happiness of the wife who looks only to her husband's interests, and makes sacrifices in his behalf. She drew a touching picture of Maroney's sufferings in jail, and tried to impress upon her the conviction that it was more than probable that he had taken the money so as to be able to place her in a situation where she could command any luxury. What did Cox know about suffering, or of the steps her husband found it necessary to take in order to effect his release? When Maroney took the forty thousand dollars, he had to ship it at once down the Alabama river, and now they could see how wise he was in so doing. He had displayed consummate ability in every movement he had so far made, and was it at all likely that he had lost his cunning? "He loves you," said she, "and would do any thing for you.

Your duty as a wife is plain and simple; do as your husband wishes you to do."

Madam Imbert's reasoning was unanswerable, but to Mrs. Maroney it was a bitter pill. Without saying a word, she led the way into the house, where they met Cox, just coming up from the cellar. She had informed both Josh. and his wife that she had made a confidante of Madam Imbert, and they thought she had done wisely.

"Josh., have you been moving the money?" demanded she.

"No!" he replied, in rather a surly tone. Then turning to Madam Imbert, he said: "You must have the same opinion of this matter as I! I think it folly to give the money up to White. No one knows about this would-be book peddler, and I will not give up the money to such a man. Let him come to me and I will talk to him." Josh. strutted about the room with the air of a six-footer. "I'll have it out of him in short order. I'll show him he can't pull the wool over my eyes, as he seems to have done over Nat.'s. I'll be d—d if I can understand it."

Cox was ably seconded in his opinion by his wife.

Mrs. Maroney had very little to say.

Madam Imbert said that, in her opinion, Josh. was entirely wrong. Maroney knew better than they what was for his interest. As for her, if her husband was to tell her to give up all she had, she would cheerfully do so, as she knew he was best able to judge what was for the benefit of them both.

The day passed in a continual wrangle. Madam Imbert could hardly get away from Mrs. Maroney long enough to eat her meals. Mrs. Maroney and Josh. dealt exclusively in brandy. Toward evening Josh. proclaimed his intention of "raising" the money, and starting with it that night for the West. He would hide himself until Maroney got out of jail, when he would return and deliver the money over to him. Josh. was sublime in the purity and philanthropy of his motives. He did not want a cent of the money; not he! but he could not consent to see his brother-in-law swindled while he stood by and calmly looked on, without making an effort in his behalf. No! this he could not do. To his own serious inconvenience, he would voluntarily tear himself from his family, impose upon himself the task of becoming the watch-dog of Nat.'s treasure, and for a time lose himself in the wilderness of the West. Madam Imbert thought *his* would be a clear case of "Though lost to sight, to memory *dear*," but did not say so.

Mrs. Maroney rather took the wind out of his sails by saying: "Don't you dare to 'raise' the money until I tell you to! I am in no hurry to have it moved; the cellar has proved a safe hiding place so far, and I see no reason why it should not so remain. You will please remember that it belongs to Nat. and me. I am able to take care of it, so you may just let it alone."

Josh. said no more, but mentally washing his hands of the whole transaction, started for Stemples's. He found Rivers and Barclay there, but said nothing about what had happened, further than that he was having trouble at home.

In the evening Mrs. Maroney received a letter from her

husband, stating that the book-peddler would call the next day.

The next day was to be an eventful one for me. By noon I should know the fate of my enterprise. I had no doubts about what the results would be, but I should then have the proofs in hand to show my employers that the confidence they had bestowed upon me had not been misplaced; that the theory I had advanced and worked upon was the correct one; that my profession, which had been dragged down by unprincipled adventurers until the term "detective" was synonymous with rogue, was, when properly attended to and honestly conducted, one of the most useful and indispensible adjuncts to the preservation of the lives and property of the people. The Divine administers consolation to the soul; the physician strives to relieve the pains of the body; while the detective cleanses society from its impurities, makes crime hideous by dragging it to light, when it would otherwise thrive in darkness, and generally improves mankind by proving that wrong acts, no matter how skilfully covered up, are sure to be found out, and their perpetrators punished. The great preventive of crime, is the fear of detection.

There are quacks in other professions as well as in mine, and people should lay the blame where it belongs, upon the quacks, and not upon the profession.

In the evening I received a letter from Madam Imbert, telling me of the difficulties in the way of White's receiving the money. She was full of hope, and said she thought she could manage to make Mrs. Maroney give up the money; but if all else failed she would take the money herself. It was often offered to her by Mrs. Maroney, and Josh. had said he had no objections to her receiving it. She would make arrangements so that if White did not get the money, she would. The money would be in Philadelphia the next evening if she had to walk in with it herself.

The recovery of forty or fifty thousand dollars, to-day, is considered a small operation; but in 1859, before the war, the amount was looked upon as perfectly enormous.

I showed Madam Imbert's letter to the Vice-President. He was greatly pleased to find success so near at hand, and agreed to make a little trip with me in the morning.

White was with me, in Philadelphia, and I made all my arrangements for the following day's work. I was up bright and early the next morning. The sun rose in a cloudless sky, and the weather promised to be fine. It would most likely be excessively hot by noon, but the morning was fresh and balmy. White, in his character of a book-peddler, was to go into Jenkintown on foot, so as to give the impression that he had walked out from the city. Shanks was to drive him to within about two miles of Jenkintown, where White was to get out and walk in, while Shanks would drive back and wait for him at the Rising Sun, a tavern on the road. The Vice-President and I drove over from Chestnut Hill, put up our team at the Rising Sun, and took up our position as near the probable scene of action as was prudent.

Early in the morning, just as day began to dawn, Rivers came in and reported the condition of affairs. He had watched Cox's through the night, but aside from high words there had been no demonstration. I sent a note

to Madam Imbert by him, with instructions to deliver it
to her as soon as she was up. I told her to be sure and
do as she said she would — get the money to-day at all
hazards — by storm, if necessary, as I did not like to
trust Cox another day.

CHAPTER XXIX.

AT Jenkintown there was no lull in the fight. The battle was going on gloriously. Breakfast at Cox's was a meagre meal, even the children were neglected, as all the grown portion of the household were on the look-out for the book-peddler.

"Sister Ann! Sister Ann! do you see any one coming?" was the cry.

Every once in a while one of them would go to the gate and look anxiously down the road, in the direction of Philadelphia. Mrs. Maroney was impatiently awaiting the arrival of Madam Imbert. She did not have to wait long, as the Madam came down immediately after breakfast. Her commanding figure and decided expression made her appear like a general giving orders. She was perfectly calm, while all the rest were so excited that they did not know what to do or say. She controlled the position.

Mrs. Maroney had not slept any and was still unable to decide upon her action. She strolled out with the Madam a short distance, thinking to find relief in a quiet chat. She said she was filled with doubts and fears. She was afraid to trust Josh., and he might go off at any moment with the packages. Madam Imbert told her that there was only one thing to be done, and that was to give up the packages to White as her husband ordered.

"Are you sure," said she, "that the letter is in your husband's handwriting?"

Mrs. Maroney looked at her in a startled manner and pulled the letter from its hiding place in the bosom of her dress. She scanned it over carefully and said:

"Yes, it is Nat.'s writing."

"Then there is nothing to do but to give it up. If my husband ordered me I would gladly give up all I have in this world to please him."

They remained away from the house for some time, and when they returned it was nearly noon. On looking down the street they discovered a book-peddler slowly toiling along from the direction of Philadelphia and evidently bending his steps towards Cox's. As Mrs. Maroney saw him coming along sweltering in the sun and bending under the weight of his load of books, she gave an involuntary start, and Madam Imbert, on whose arm she leaned, felt that she was trembling with excitement. Cox stood beside his wife in the door-way with his teeth clinched. His wife looked unutterable things, but neither uttered a word.

Madam Imbert and Mrs. Maroney went into the yard and stood leaning over the gate, watching the peddler, who was rapidly drawing near. He arrived at the gate at the appointed time.

"Do you wish to buy any books?" asked he, at the same time handing Mrs. Maroney a novel to look at, which he opened so as to disclose a note. He spoke to her in a low tone and said:

"I am from prison," then glancing at the note, "I think that is for you."

She took the novel, and, holding it open as if reading it, scanned the contents of the note:

"MY DEAREST WIFE: This is the book-peddler. You will want to buy books from him. Buy what you want. Give him the packages for me. He is honest.

"All is well.   NAT."

When she had read the note she stood looking at it, apparently unable to speak. Madam Imbert looked at her, and as she began to fear that some of the neighbors might notice the long stay of the peddler, said:

"Have you no message for the man? Time is precious!"

"Yes," she answered, looking up as from a trance.

Madam Imbert spoke in a low tone:

"Tell him to meet you down the lane."

"Yes," said she, "I will meet you down the lane at two o'clock and take some books from you."

The peddler left a few novels and walked off. Mrs. Maroney and Madam Imbert walked into the house. Now was the time for Madam Imbert to show her power.

"Come, Mrs. Maroney, be quick! You must act at once! Get the money for the book-peddler, quick!"

Mrs. Maroney seemed to act mechanically. Madam Imbert's strong will had asserted a power over her that she could not resist. They went into the cellar accompanied by Josh. and his wife.

"Dig the money up," commanded Mrs. Maroney still in the same mechanical tone.

Josh. hesitated.

"Give me the spade!" said Madam Imbert. Show me where the money is secreted!"

Then, turning to Josh. and his wife, she said:

"*You are fools!* You would not only ruin Mrs. Maroney, but yourselves. Maroney knows best what is for his interest."

Mrs. Maroney pointed out the spot where the money was buried. The Madam struck the spade into the ground.

"Stop, I'll do it!" said Josh.; "if you are bound to make a beggar of yourself it is no fault of mine."

The money was about eighteen inches under the level of the cellar floor, wrapped up in a piece of oil skin. It was soon unearthed and taken up stairs. Mrs. Maroney said:

"I will go and get the buggy, or — no! Josh.! you go to Stemples's and get his team; tell him it is for me."

Josh., without waiting to fill up the hole, started off. Madam Imbert wrapped the money in two newspapers, and when Josh. came with the team, which he soon did, put it into the front part of the buggy and covered it with the apron, and, getting in with Mrs. Maroney, drove down the lane.

White, when he received the message from Mrs. Maroney, returned to the Rising Sun and reported to me. We (the Vice-President and I) secreted ourselves under some magnolias growing close by the lane, and near where the meeting would take place. At the appointed time the book-peddler was seen by us coming up the lane, and at almost the same moment a buggy came in sight going down. It was a moment of breathless interest to both of us.

They met almost directly opposite to where we were concealed. Madam Imbert said: "Let us have some books!" The peddler lifted his satchel into the buggy; the Madam hurriedly emptied it of its contents, and holding it open jammed the bundle of money into it and handed it back to the peddler. Not a word more was said. Madam Imbert turned the team around and started the horses on a fast trot toward Jenkintown, while the peddler sweltered along under the broiling sun in the direction of the tavern.

Madam Imbert drove up to Stemples's, took the books, which were wrapped in papers, to her room, and invited Mrs. Maroney up to take some brandy.

Mrs. Maroney was in a passive state, and did everything Madam Imbert told her to do, as if powerless to resist. She remained for some time with Madam Imbert, but finally said, in a pitiful tone: "Well, I believe I am sick. This excitement has nearly killed me."

Madam Imbert advised her to lie down, and accompanied her to Cox's. Josh. had gone out with Rivers, and Mrs. Cox refused to be seen. Madam Imbert administered an opiate to Mrs. Maroney, and then returned to the tavern. Toward evening she hired Stemples's team and drove into Philadelphia.

The Vice-President and I remained concealed until the two women were well out of sight, when we overtook White, who was slowly toiling down the road. I received the satchel containing the money from him. From the time he received the money until he handed it over

"The pedler lifted his satchel into the buggy; the Madam hurriedly emptied it of its contents, and holding it open, jammed the bundle of money into it, and handed it back to the pedler."—Page 268.

to me, I had had my eye on him — not exactly because I did not trust him, but I thought it wrong to lead the poor fellow into temptation.

We went to the Rising Sun, where we took dinner, but did not mention the subject which was uppermost in our minds. After dinner we drove into the city and placed the money in the vaults of the Express Company.

The Vice-President at once telegraphed to the President of the company to come from New York, as he did not wish to count the money until he was present.

In the evening Madam Imbert arrived at the hotel, and finding I was in consultation with the Vice-President, sent word in that she would like to see me. When I came to her she eagerly asked : "Is the money all right?"

"All right," I answered. When she heard this her strength seemed suddenly to leave her, and she nearly fainted. The victory was complete, but her faculties had been strained to the utmost in accomplishing it, and she felt completely exhausted. She had the proud satisfaction of knowing that to a woman belonged the honors of the day.

The President arrived on the third of August, and we met at the Lapier House, where we counted the money. The package proved to contain thirty-nine thousand five hundred and fifteen dollars — within four hundred and eighty-five dollars of the amount last stolen.

The officers of the Adams Express Company were much pleased at my success, and perfectly satisfied with everything. The money had been recovered, and the case had come to a stand-still.

I held a consultation with the President and Vice-President, and asked them if they had any further orders for me. The President said I had better finish the operation, and not give up until Maroney had been convicted and placed in the Penitentiary. I had done them invaluable service so far, but it still remained to "cap the climax" by bringing the guilty party to justice. This I assured him would soon be accomplished, and I left to give the necessary orders to my detectives.

I told Madam Imbert to return to Jenkintown, and ordered Rivers and Miss Johnson also to remain as before.

The Vice-President also told De Forest to remain in Jenkintown for the present. Green was to continue in Philadelphia. Roch, who had been sent back to Montgomery, was to await orders there, as was also Porter. White was to attend to Maroney, while Bangs was to continue in Philadelphia in charge of all.

CHAPTER XXX.

ON the fifteenth of August, White called on Maroney in Eldridge street jail. He detailed what had transpired at Jenkintown, and told Maroney that he had the money hid in a safe place in Philadelphia. This was undoubtedly the truth, as the money was safe in the vaults of the Adams Express. I deemed it best to curtail expenses as soon as possible, and instructed White to impress upon Maroney that Jenkintown was not a safe place for his wife, and that she had better leave there. He was to endeavor to get Maroney to send her to the west, and to Chicago, if possible. He told Maroney that he was afraid some of the express men were watching his wife, and if he did not look out she might be induced to "blow" on him and tell all. He dwelt on his repugnance to being mixed up with women with such effect that Maroney was convinced that she had better go to some other part of the country, and so wrote to her at once. He told her she had better go west. She was so near the headquarters of the company that he feared they might find her out, and make trouble for her. He hinted that he was not entirely satisfied with De Forest, and wished her to go as soon as possible. White said he was having the key to the pouch made, and would be able to show it to him in a day or two. He did not wish any one in the jail to see him with the key, and wished Maroney to be careful that no prisoners were in their neighborhood when he disclosed it. When he did bring the key Maroney examined it closely and expressed himself well pleased with it.

The day set for the trial of the suit in New York was near at hand, and Maroney would have to prove that he had not taken the fifty thousand dollars. He did not much care how the suit went, as he was confident he would be acquitted at his criminal trial in Montgomery. When the suit came off, we managed to get a judgment against him for the fifty thousand dollars in such a manner that it was not necessary to let him know that the money had been recovered, or that White was working against him. He was of course the principal witness in his own behalf, and if wholesale perjury could have saved him he would have been acquitted beyond a doubt.

The day after the trial White called on him and he laughed heartily at the judgment which had been obtained against him.

"Wait till I get to Montgomery," he said, "and then they will find that their judgment does not amount to shucks. White, I wish you would settle up my matters as soon as possible."

"I am going to Charleston this evening to see if I can't pass some of the money, and must hurry off and pack my satchel, as the train leaves at four. Good-by for a time; I will write and let you know how I succeed," said White, as he prepared to leave.

"I know you will succeed," remarked Maroney, and White hurriedly walked out of jail. This was all done to blind Maroney as to White's real character. There was no necessity of White's leaving the city to accomplish his purpose. All he had to do was to write letters and send them to the agents of the Adams Express at the different points where Maroney supposed him to be, and they would mail them to Maroney. He pretended that he was having great trouble in trying to exchange the money, and wrote that he would be in New York in a few days. At the end of a week he walked down to the jail. He met Maroney with a troubled look on his face, and said that he had been frightened away from Charleston after he had exchanged about five hundred dollars. He was doing very well when he found the detectives were close after him, and he had to leave without his carpet bag.

"It is up-hill work, Maroney, trying to exchange this money. The Adams Express are keeping a sharp look-out every where, and I have had a number of detectives on my track. I have no money of my own and need all of yours. So far I have exchanged only enough to get me to Montgomery, and to pay the girl for stuffing the Express money into Chase's pocket."

Maroney gave White what money he had, and told him to go on and fix Chase as soon as possible. Mrs. Maroney had all the money, so that we had to foot all White's bills. The company had already been at heavy expense, and I was desirous of stopping all unavoidable expenditures. White remained in Philadelphia or New York, as the case might be, performing on paper a journey through the South. Maroney received letters from him from Augusta, Ga., New Orleans, Mobile and Montgomery. He seemed to meet with many adventures

18

and reverses, but was slowly and surely accomplishing his mission. He had the girl in Montgomery, and she was rapidly winning her way to the innermost recesses of Chase's heart. In a couple of days came another letter. Chase was captivated, and had so far worked on the confiding, innocent nature of the girl as to prevail on her to consent to let him into her room that night. She had the money to put into Chase's pocket, and all was going well. Maroney could not sleep, so anxiously did he look forward for the coming of the next letter; he paced his cell all night. What would have been his feelings if he could have looked through about a mile of brick and mortar to where White was snoring in bed?

The next day no letter came. He grew almost frantic, and was so irritable and excited that his fellow prisoners wondered what had come over him. The following day the anxiously expected letter arrived. He hastily broke it open and found that the faithful White had been true to his trust. Chase had gone into the girl's room, McGibony had seized him as he came out, a search was instituted and the stolen money and a pouch key had been discovered in his pocket.

"Hurrah!" said Maroney, "I am all right now! Boys, here is five dollars, the last cent I have! We will make a jolly day of it."

We will now return to our friends in Jenkintown. It took some time for Maroney to impress upon his wife the necessity of her going West. She had little money, for though she had pocketed the proceeds of the sale of her husband's livery stable, and other effects, in Montgomery, her expenses had been heavy, and the money had dwindled away until she was nearly penniless.

One day Mrs. Maroney said to Madam Imbert: "Wouldn't you like to go out west somewhere and settle down for a while?"

"It makes no difference to me where I go," she replied. "I have to see the gentleman who exchanges my money for me, once in a while; but no matter where I go, he is sure to come to me when I send for him. Why would it not be a good plan to go to some place in the South? Swansboro, N. C., is a good place."

"Yes," remarked Mrs. Maroney, "but it is so dull!"

"What do you say to Jackson, Mississippi? It is a beautiful place."

"No, we don't want to go South now, it is altogether too warm. Were you ever in Chicago, Madam Imbert?"

"No; but it is a good place to summer in, I understand."

"Well, let's go there; will you?"

"Yes, certainly, if you wish," said Madam Imbert; and they at once began to arrange for their departure. It was decided that Madam Imbert should go ahead to Chicago, and see if she could rent a furnished house for them. She started off, and, as a matter of course, easily accomplished her purpose.

I had a house in Chicago, where I lodged my female detectives, and as I had only two in the city at the time, I easily found them a boarding-house, and turned the house over to Madam Imbert. The servants were well trained, and understood their business thoroughly. Everything being arranged, Madam Imbert wrote to Mrs. Maroney and Miss Johnson, telling them to come on.

Two weeks after, Mrs. Maroney, Miss Johnson, and Flora arrived in Chicago, and took up their quarters with Madam Imbert.

It was necessary to have a young man to run their errands, and Shanks was promptly furnished them. White did not need his services any longer, as he was able to run his own errands.

Business was crowding fast, and the time set for Maroney's trial at Montgomery was drawing near. The Governor of Alabama requested the Governor of New York to deliver Maroney for trial in Montgomery, which request was immediately acceded to.

I sent Maroney South in charge of an officer from Philadelphia, of course " shadowed " by my own men.

This was the last time that Roch was on duty in this case. He had done good service already in its early stages, and might be of service again.

The Vice-President accompanied the parties.

When they arrived in Montgomery, Maroney was not met and escorted to the Exchange by a bevy of admiring friends. On the contrary, he was led to jail. Hope never forsook him. He received letters from White, who said all was going well, and he expected to get the funds exchanged soon. Maroney wrote in reply that he hoped he would hurry up, as he wished to give a part of the money to his lawyer in New York. The lawyer was evidently expecting to reap a rich harvest at the company's expense. Little more need be said.

The Circuit Court was in session, His Honor John Gill Shorter, presiding, and Maroney would soon be tried before him. He was confident that he would be acquitted and had all his plans made as to what he would do when he was liberated. Not the shadow of a doubt had crossed his mind as to the fealty of White.

He heard that he was in Montgomery and received a note from him, saying that all was well; that the Adams Express had compelled him to come — an unwilling witness — to see if they could not force the secret from him, but they would find that they had "collared" the wrong man this time. Maroney was braced up by this note. He knew that White would not give up; he felt confident of that!

It was the morning of the trial, and before nightfall he would be a free man. It was a lovely day and the court-room was packed with spectators, among whom were many of Maroney's former friends.

He walked proudly into the court-room, between two deputies, with an air that plainly said, " I am bound to win !"

His friends clustered around him and vied with each other as to who could show him the most attention. Foremost among them was Porter, to whom he gave an extra shake of the hand. I will not dwell upon the trial. The witnesses for the prosecution were called one by one. They were the employés of the company who were in any way connected with the shipment or the discovery of the loss of the money, which ought to have been sent to Atlanta, when, in reality, it had gone down the Alabama in Maroney's old trunk.

The witnesses proved that the money had disappeared in some mysterious way; but they did not in the slightest degree fasten the guilt upon Maroney. His spirits rose as the trial progressed, and his counsel could not but smile as he heard the weak testimony he had to break down. He had expected a toughly contested case, but the prosecutors had presented no case at all.

At length, the crier of the court called "John R. White."

As John R. White did not immediately appear in answer to the call, Maroney seemed, during the brief period of silence, to suddenly realize how critical was his position. His cheek blanched with fear. He seemed striving to speak, but not a word could he articulate. As White deliberately walked up to the witness-stand, Maroney seemed at once to realize that White would never perjure himself for the sake of befriending him. His eyes were filled with horror and he gasped for breath.

A glass of water was handed to him. He gulped it down, and, vainly endeavoring to force back the tears from his eyes, in a hoarse, shaky voice, he exclaimed:

"Oh, God!" Then, turning to his counsel, he said: "Tell the court I plead guilty. He," pointing to White, "knows the whole. I am guilty!! I am gone!!!"

This ended the matter. The counsel entered a plea of guilty and the Judge sentenced Maroney to pass ten years in the Alabama Penitentiary, at *hard labor.*

THE END.

CPSIA information can be obtained at www.ICGtesting.com
Printed in the USA
BVOW08s1808011115

425156BV00001B/54/P